A Devilish Vacation

By

J S Austin

One

"We do believe."

"We will succeed."

The words were spoken by a lone figure in the centre of a dimly lit circle of hooded individuals.

"Chant the forbidden chant."

The lone figure spoke powerfully in a voice that demanded attention and to be obeyed. A chant, not of words but of sounds, spoken clearer than any word ever could. The tense air throbbed with a power and a meaning, rooted in the history of time.

The hoods echoed his chant. A euphoric, vibrating noise bounced around the ancient stone walls, shaping the sound into almost visible form. Starting softly, then growing louder – like a wave – the swell would peak before smashing at full volume against the cliff's rock face (or stone wall, as it were), with the whites of the water fading away before the voices started yet another wave. An unstoppable tide of chanting.

The room hummed with power. Then, without any sign or signal, all stopped.

"The Leader is the truth."

"He will lead us to the promised land."

They chanted each sentence hypnotically.

"Aktone."

The ancient word vibrated around the cold room. A word forgotten and the meaning no longer known. Aktone was a symbolic word, awakened now to represent the purity of truth.

The room fell dark and all was silent.

Two

Clothes lay everywhere. Suitcases were filled to the brim. An array of sun cream products, tanning oils and sunglasses was lined up, poised, ready to be packed, and the Devil sat, head in hands, on his inordinately sized bed, groaning a quiet moan. His bed, hand carved from human bones, topped with a water mattress filled with blood was covered by a blanket woven from human hair. The pillows were stuffed with feathers plucked from the most malign winged creatures ever to fly on planet Earth (baby snatching magpies, turtle-dropping eagles and the diabolical impaling shrike to name a few). To soften the tone, a scattering of cuddly toy bears tempered the demonic look.

"Simon!" the Devil bellowed.

Simon could make any situation better, he thought.

A few moments later and in glided Simon. The glide might have been considered a run by others but for him, the motion looked effortless. It was paramount he responded promptly, always striving to please his master.

"You called, sir?"

"I did!"

"Indeed?" Simon waited for a moment and then felt it was best to help the conversation along. "You called. Perhaps to ask me something?"

The Devil might appear as a rather intimidating sort of chap, if you were not prepared for the sight of him rising from his bed. Saying he was large would be to do him an injustice. He was a gargantuan figure. Not in a *fee fi fo* giant sort of way, just gargantuan relative to a human. His skin glistened deep red, sharpened gloss-white teeth were framed by thin leathery lips, and two black horns poked out from his bald head. These features might shock or scare an unsuspecting person, but it was the intense night-black eyes that really intimidated his victims and drew you into their oblivion. His huge muscles (which over the years had become more and more hidden by his growing pot belly) could rip a head from its spinal cord without breaking into sweat – a task that they had performed on numerous occasions.

Standing up, the Devil replied, "Of course, I'm so sorry Simon. All this packing. It's made me peculiarly...," he thought for the best word and settled for, "well, just peculiar. How do the humans do this? I was told a holiday would do me some good and help me to de-stress. Yet I've been packing for three weeks and still cannot decide on whether to take the dark tanned or the black, wingtip Oxford shoes."

"You have not been on a holiday before, sir?" Simon enquired with some shock.

With a sigh, the Devil answered, "There was no time for holidays."

"You are the Dark Lord, sir. Surely you can take a holiday whenever you desire?"

"I know, I know. But with all the work I put into torturing souls and making sure the business runs smoothly, I never seemed to find the time. And now in a few minutes, I should be relaxing on this damned holiday, but I'm tearing my hair out in frustration over luggage." This was not altogether true. Being a gentleman, whose head possessed less hair than a waxed bowling ball one might wonder how he could rip it out. Satan's barber, for one, wondered such things every time he came in for his trim.

"How many suitcases can you carry, Simon?"

"Just the two, sir. One in each hand is the normal technique. I could possibly manage a rucksack as well."

"Then that means I have only two suitcases and one large rucksack to fit all my holiday clothes in."

Simon raised an eyebrow and gave his master an inquisitive look.

"And why would that be, sir."

"Because you're coming to Heaven with me."

Three

Saint Peter was having a busy year. The earthlings were at it again. Wars. Why did they enjoy them so much? With all their wars came death and an influx of souls making their way to his famed garden gates (aka the Pearly Gates of Heaven).

All the work with these extra souls was stretching his wafer-thin patience to breaking point and then breaking the already broken points even further.

"No! No! Definitely not. Forget it! You're not coming in wearing those clothes. Hop it. Move on."

Gesturing for them to move, Peter refused entry to soul after soul and herded them to an area which was rapidly becoming congested. A few hundred people – with some in a mild panic – were now milling around wondering what was going to happen. Rejected at the gates, were they doomed to the eternal, flaming land of horrors and pain? Was this a cruel joke – first sent to Heaven only to be refused entry for failing to comply with a dress code?

Their thoughts were interrupted by an overly confident religious lady who – and she was quite adamant about this – knew her rights.

Marching back from where Peter instructed her to wait, she approached him again. "Listen here, Saint Peter, I have followed all the rules and regulations that God set down and paid my 'taxes' each week at church. So do not go telling me, a high priest in His Church, that I cannot enter. A contract is a contract, and I signed mine with God at birth."

Peter stared down at this human do-gooder and in his own polite way responded, "Does it look like I give a damn? You ain't coming in."

Shocked and taken aback the lady persisted but Peter didn't vary from his original position as she continued to argue her case: "I followed the ten commandments…. Forgiveness…. Prayed…."

Slowly, a volcanic eruption was building inside Peter's saintly head. The lava started to flow from his brain, burning the back of his eyes. Steam bellowed from his ears as he gripped Heaven's gate in anger, tightening his grip with every moment the human refused to leave. At last, the brain volcano erupted, and he ripped the wooden gate clean off its hinges and screamed, "Just get in the lot of you. If I see any of you still lingering here after 5 minutes, then… well… something bad will happen!" And with that feeble threat he stormed home.

Curled on top of his unmade bed, Peter pondered ways to reject the insensitive souls. But the fact was that once they arrived, they would be let in. Peter felt like a bouncer without the power to refuse entry. Perhaps if he wore a bomber jacket and shaved his head, he would look more intimidating. His skinny body, clothed in a casual, sleeveless vest with baggy shorts and a warm face framed by a huge afro, did nothing to enhance his authority. Peter's looks radiated a friendly vibe. But despite knowing his efforts to vet the human tide was pointless, it did not stop him trying. Oh, how he tried! He could tease, make them beg and promise all sorts of ridiculous stuff but, in the end, he had to let them in to Heaven.

A sharp pain went through his head when he thought of what they would be doing now. Without a gate and without Peter, the humans had no reason to wait. There would be hundreds of people stampeding through the great gates (or stepping over the broken un-hinged barrier). Thousands might flow across within hours. Heaven had not seen such an influx since the Great War.

Back at Heaven's entrance, just beyond the gates and unseen by most, was a short, hooded character who slipped slowly into the shadows whenever someone came close. The figure observed silently the great human herd making its way into Heaven.

He was watching in a manner that would unsettle the most trusting angel and perhaps even God, Himself.

Four

The hooded man, who we briefly observed loitering outside Peter's gate, moved swiftly down the dark and dangerous alleyways of Heaven. Or at least he would have, if any dark and dangerous alleyways existed. Instead, he darted from bush to tree, unsuccessfully trying to remain unseen. Humans watched him with mild curiosity but, being near the entrance, most were now inside Heaven and had more pressing thoughts to worry about.

It was getting late, and the light was fading. A chill in the air made the hooded figure shiver as he waited patiently by the last tree, checking that no one was watching. Ducking, he ran to the safe house. You might assume a 'safe house' would blend in and divert unwanted attention. But this was not a text-book safe dwelling. Constructed to resemble a castle, it could not have been more conspicuous if it had tried. Either side stood medium-sized cottages, designed in a way that made them look very un-castle like. Silently, he darted to one of the turrets of this decidedly noticeable house and banged thrice, paused, and then knocked twice more on the solid wooden door.

The door creaked open and spoke, "It is a fine day, sir."

"A fine day, indeed," replied the hood.

"What does the sun do on such a fine day?" asked the door.

"It, ummmm, it… I can't remember," the hood replied.

The door responded in a way doors love to respond most and slammed shut with a satisfying thud.

"Oh, for God's sake!" He'd come up with the secret password himself earlier that day and now, when the time came to say it, he'd fluffed his lines.

Banging thrice and then twice again the door opened an inch.

"It's me!" hissed the hood.

"A fine day it is indeed," started the door again.

"It's me. Just let me in. I have important news," demanded the increasingly angry hood.

"A fine day..."

"Let me in, you nincompoop. I have urgent information to relay."

"You know the rules. No entrance without the password. What's the point of a password, if I let anyone in?" Doors can be very stubborn.

"But you know it's me. Without me, there is no point to you being here," the hood tried logic on the door.

"You could be anyone pretending to be you."

"Just let me in!"

"It is a fine day…. owww."

The hooded figure, not the most patient at the best of times, acted. Forcing the door open, he proceeded into the castle leaving the door-opener and the owner of the voice flattened between a damp, stone wall and a mute, wooden door.

The entrance to this building led to a large, round room with a double height ceiling. Paintings of great age hung from the curved walls, collecting dust. The floor was mostly hidden by a heavily stained rug.

Forty hooded figures fell silent as the password-forgetting, hooded figure entered.

"All be silent!" the figure commanded, rather pointlessly.

Five

Simon had been dead for a few years now. Before accepting his death, he had received the shock of his life – or death. For one thing, the temperature was much higher than expected. The view was certainly dramatic. More fires burned than he had imagined, and the sea (now Simon didn't normally like to moan) appeared redder than he would have liked.

In life, Simon had been a butler to one of the most dishonourable, corrupt businessmen in the world. But Simon's route to Hell was more through joint enterprise than having committed any atrocities himself.

A tall, slender chap, he kept his face free of stubble and combed his hair with a side parting so exact that you might suspect he used a protractor. Usually, you would find him wearing a dark-coloured suit – the type favoured by many a traditional butler – and starched white shirt. Highly polished shoes made no sound as he glided effortlessly from one task to another. If ever a book was written on buttling perfection, it would have his picture on the cover.

He hadn't always been a butler to evil tyrants. His vocation started in his early twenties with service to a pleasant family whose money was old and values traditional. Unfortunately, their tastes were expensive and, when the last of the family's silverware was sold, Simon was an expense they could no longer afford.

In that two years of employment, Simon learnt all the skills he needed to perfect his craft. A colleague recommended him to another family who had recently lost their butler through ill health. Simon, delighted by this spot of luck, filled the position after the formality of a brief interview.

For many years he served his new employer, and the family boasted of his loyalty to all who would listen. It was at a social gathering of the hobs and nobs that Simon was noticed by someone who was to radically change his career and future life.

'She looks like a witch' is an over-used and cruel insult but to the woman watching Simon, it was an accurate and fair description. She was disgustingly rich in the filthiest of sense. Barging her way across the packed floor, she cursed at anyone who dared to complain, and targeted her prey – Simon. Money was offered but quickly turned down. More money was offered and again turned down. A heap of cash was added to the money that was offered plus the money that was previously offered, and a deal was struck.

Simon had not yet sold his soul to the Devil but accepting this position would lead him along the path to Hell. You cannot wait on a nasty piece of work without some of your own work turning nasty too.

When worthy souls reach Heaven, they adapt quickly and accept they are dead. Happiness floods through their body as they enter eternal paradise. But when a human drops into Hell, the brain is not so accepting. It protests and scrambles for answers, insisting it lived a relatively good life and in no way deserves this fate, before springing into action. Complain! That is what it should do. Marching up to the person in charge, it makes the mistake of accosting the nearest demon, a strategy with many possible outcomes, none of which would be described as positive. Perhaps a forced swim in the boiling sea of fire. Or being butchered into seven equal parts and fed to the seven-headed beast of Revelation.

Simon was different. Realising the predicament he now found himself in, he wasted no time protesting or forming arguments. Instead, he did what he had always done since becoming a butler and looked to serve. Simon assumed his best butler stance and, with a slight preceding cough, politely enquired, "Would sir like a cup of tea?" The cabbage-coloured demon he was addressing had no immediate answer. He was used to screams of fear and begging cries for mercy. Never had any human asked if he wanted a tea.

"Would you like sugar, sir? I do apologise but I have not been pre-advised on how you take your tea."

Confused, the demon decided he would like a tea and some sugar. What a 'tea' was he had no idea, but he was now certain he needed one.

Off Simon went. A few demons attempted to stop him; all realised, within minutes of meeting him, that they also wanted tea and directed Simon to where he might find the required apparatus. Like all great butlers, going to premises they have not frequented before, he instinctively found his way around.

Half an hour later, ten demons were sipping hot tea, some with sugar, some without and not one wishing to inflict harm on Simon.

Commandeered by the most senior demon – by chance, the first one he had met – Simon proceeded to fetch him biscuits, book dinner at one of Hell's many fine restaurants and carry out the various other tasks of a butler, while his newly acquired master went out.

Demons are naturally jealous. When word got around that the cabbage-coloured demon had this wonderful new 'thing' that served tea at regular intervals and made life more comfortable, they all wanted one. Without understanding the need for interviews or qualifications, the demons selected other humans who most closely resembled Simon, to become their servants. None were as good. Many were unable to make tea successfully and even put the tea bag into the water at the wrong temperature (the ideal brewing temperature became an issue of heated debate at demonic gatherings).

Other demons despaired that their own choice of butler was a hopeless, inadequate substitute. The cabbage-coloured demon soon had Simon 'acquired/stolen' by a more powerful, higher ranking, sprout-tinted demon, and the sprout-tinted demon lost Simon within a week to serve the parsley, creamy brown high duke demon. His fame spread quickly through satanic society until, one day, the Devil found out.

"Where is he?" the Devil demanded.

"Who, my Lord?" quivered the demon, feeling rather less high and mighty than a minute earlier.

"The human of course! I'm going to snap his neck, rip his heart out and throw him to the hounds."

"My Lord, please forgive me. I have succumbed to temptation and…"

"Shut your stupid gob. It's the last time you'll ever have lips to speak from." Flinging the demon through the ceiling, the Devil spun round in a rage. Standing behind him, holding a tray, was Simon.

"Tea, sir?"

Six

If you entered Heaven through the Pearly Gates, wandered along the red carpeted path, lit with neon lights, that led onto the great market square, then pushed your way through the throng of activity until you found yourself at the Bull Inn and there – having located the side alley that logically should be at the side and surprisingly (for things are not logical in Heaven) is at the side – felt your way along the tight, dark alley, climbed the stairs that led to a front door, you would finally reach a flat – of no distinct features – above the inn.

This is the residence of Hector. Not Hector the Great, or Sir Hector of Heavenshire, not even Dr. Hector. No, just plain Hector. It had been his home for as long as the place existed.

Hector shared many features in common with humans (legs and hair being just two obvious examples), but Hector was not human – he was an angel. Along his back he harboured two, large wings. Impressive ones at that. In a way it was a damn shame the rest of Hector did not live up to their impressiveness. His hair, which once flowed in curly locks, now looked uncombed in a mop of no particular style. He stood at the average height for an angel, which is about the average for a human male. (Angels, unlike humans are similar in height whether female or male.) The trained eyes of a detective might detect a slight bend in Hector's back resulting from years of hard work. Hector's body showed age, but his eyes radiated love through a worn face, etched by years of eternal boredom. His body was covered by a grey, woollen, hooded robe, held together by a leather, buckled belt. He wore the traditional dress of an angel. Many assume Jesus's biggest contribution to fashion was his sandals, but angels wore them first, and Hector followed this tradition by choosing an oak-coloured pair for his weathered feet.

Every morning, Hector rose early, opened his back door (which we now know is actually a side door masquerading as a front door), exited his home, locking and double locking the door behind him – a task seemingly without purpose as Heaven is crime free. Yet recently, Hector who never even considered the need for locks before, started worrying about theft. These days you can't trust anyone, he thought. Not like the old days when you could leave everything unlocked without fear, and you knew the name of everyone who 'lived' on your street.

"Good morning, Hector", boomed a friendly voice from the Bull.

"Hello, Zed," replied Hector to the landlord of the inn. "Hope your parents are keeping well."

Leaving Zed to his tasks, he followed the path which led onto the market square. The sun beamed down (without being there) and everyone around smiled with joy.

The occasional passer-by who offered a friendly 'hi', or 'splendid day', received an equally warm reply. Being elderly – something an angel could never be for they are eternal, yet age somehow invades everything – he walked slowly with a stoop.

On he went until he reached a drinking fountain where the likes of Elvis, JFK and a lady named Peggy had taken their first drink in Heaven. Many others wisely chose the Bull establishment for their celebratory tipple. Stooping down further than his standard stoop, he drank a mouthful from the fountain, just as he had done every day before.

After walking for nearly a mile and returning greeting smiles from familiar faces, Hector arrived at the same destination that he had reached for the past forever years. It was here, just off the main square, that he pulled the cover from a wooden, market stall and gave it all a quick wipe in preparation for the day ahead.

Vegetables of varying sizes and colours were selected from under his counter and meticulously washed, peeled and chopped. Lighting the gas stove, he poured them all into a large, battered saucepan and added water ready to create the traditional angel soup or stew, depending on the thickness of the finished product. He had stood 'selling' broth since anyone could remember. In the good old days, trade was brisk with angels too busy to prepare their own breakfast, preferring to stop off for an early energy boost. Eager angels were often seen, ready to fill their rumbling stomachs with wholesome food. But today there was no queue. No one queued yesterday, and no one would tomorrow.

Trade had been so bad that Hector had shrewdly invested in a comfortable chair. He now manoeuvred his behind carefully into this seat and sighed — as he did every day — and took a quick, hopeful glance down the street to see if a stampede of customers was on its way.

Seven

Simon, having effortlessly packed two suitcases and one large rucksack with exactly what the Devil didn't know he needed, was currently looking at the glorious sky of Hell through the large skylight in the Devil's grand bedroom. Thunderclouds, blacker than a black hole, threw fire-tipped lightning bolts. Winged beasts soared and swooped down out of sight until returning with a screaming soul clutched at the end of their talons.

Simon was viewing this scene of damnation – but not from a position of choice. Flat on his back, he felt much like an upturned turtle or a toppled snail. Having hoisted the heavy rucksack onto his back and lifted with great effort both suitcases, he'd become momentarily distracted by a scream in the air. Inadvertently raising his head upwards to observe the source of the scream, he found the rest of his body following its lead. With too much weight from the rucksack and with no arms free, he fell onto his back.

The Devil meanwhile was now dressed in what this month's 'Holidaying the Gentleman's Way' magazine reliably informed him was the contemporary holiday attire for the modern gentleman. He had selected the timeless elegance of a three-piece Windsor suit of pure wool fabric. The top three buttons of his crisp, white shirt were left unbuttoned, and he wore no tie. This, he felt, made the suit suitably casual for a holiday. To accompany such style, he wore his newly purchased and prized possessions from his extensive shoe collection. 'The epitome of timeless luxury' declared the magazine's review, and so the Devil had ordered a pair of crocodile skin shoes.

Seeing his luggage packed, and knowing the holiday was about to commence, he felt the stress, accumulated over millennia, pour from him. Stress that lived and breathed in every part of his body was flushed away. He knew that this break was needed. He was going on holiday. No Demons asking idiotic questions, no humans begging forgiveness and no meetings. God, how he hated meetings.

Without so much as a hint of effort, he hoisted Simon back to his feet. "Come on Simon. Stop slouching. We have a 'train' to catch."

Eight

Three hours, forty-four minutes and eleven seconds since he had planted his behind into the comfy chair, Hector slowly rose. Holding his bent back, a pain shot through to his brain which fired back that it was his own fault for sitting on his fat butt for so long. He waited another forty-seven seconds to steady himself, then made the four steps across to where the soup remained lukewarm. Filling a disposable, cardboard bowl with a large ladle and spilling half the contents over the side, he turned to where the alley joined the main square and waited a further seven seconds.

From the mouth of the alleyway, came a much younger looking angel, dressed in traditional clothing.

"Ah Hector, my good man. You always have it waiting. Such superb soup can be found nowhere else."

"Thank you, such kind words," Hector replied, almost bowing as he handed over the soup.

"Why I never have to wait for such great food, I will never know."

"Once there was a time . . .," Hector's eyes glazed over as he started to tell a story of time gone past.

The young angel, who had heard this story more times than was necessary, interrupted.

"Apologies, but I must be off," he said, placing a hand on Hector's shoulder to make sure he unglazed his eyes.

With that, the young angel fled like the wind and Hector meticulously cleaned the ladle and wiped up the spillage. He gave the soup a good stir and returned to his buttock-comforting chair.

Some forty-nine minutes and forty-three seconds later (and thirty-eight milliseconds, if you feel like being pernickety), Hector went through the same motions and served another angel. She was again younger and wore traditional garments. Assuring him business would pick up soon, she left.

Throughout the day Hector was up and down, serving several more angels, knowing exactly when each would arrive.

Nine

To travel from Hell to Heaven requires great knowledge, patience and, most importantly, a gullible demon to do the work. Gurmakian was one such demon. Soaked in acidic sweat, he was close to opening the path to Heaven. This, he knew, would give him the edge for the promotion that was well overdue. He had worked harder than he'd ever worked before to get this pathway open – and Gurmakian was not a fan of work. Knowing that the Devil encouraged self-improvement, he had sat through hours upon brain-numbing hours of management, soft skills and motivational training courses. He had perfected the use of PowerPoint, laser pointing and had showcased his presentation skills in many meetings. But today's work had placed the cherry on top of his quest for promotion to High Duke Demon.

The final chants and hand movements necessary to open the passage between Hell and Heaven were completed. With the complex operation now over, he collapsed and sat down exhausted but content.

There, in the middle of the floor, appeared a raging, circular blur of colours – a vortex between worlds. No sound escaped – yet the noise of a thousand hurricanes was trapped within.

On cue, in strode the Devil. Without acknowledging Gurmakian, he jumped straight down the hole. Wobbling side to side from the weight of suitcases and rucksack and leaning forward to balance, Simon followed close behind. His departure from Hell seemed more of a stumble and trip than the Devil's smooth leap.

The Master and butler had successfully passed through, and Gurmakian started work again. Chanting and dancing, he closed the path to Heaven and gleefully rubbed his hands together in the knowledge that the promotion was just around the corner. However, if his ears had been more alert, he may just have heard the Devil asking Simon for the name of the demon who had opened the passage?

"Gurmakian, sir. Earmarked for a promotion."

"Demote him!"

"Sorry, sir, I do not understand."

"Demote that lazy demon. Sitting down on the job. How dare he!"

Ten

Cecil was an angry man or, more precisely, he was an angry angel. If you smiled at Cecil, a growl was returned. If you complimented him, he felt insulted. In fact, if you entered his peripheral vision, you risked becoming his sworn enemy. Many people experience occasional anger but most enjoy periods of happiness. Not Cecil. He was always angry, and his rage intensified as the millennia rushed past. As if to prove the point, he was ranting at his bemused neighbours. With cheeks puffing and ears steaming, he was not a happy angel.

"A grey, tarmac driveway! No grass! No flowers! In Heaven, where you can have whatever you so desire. What's wrong with you?" he shouted.

Cecil's neighbours, Patrick and Pippa, who up until now logically thought angels would be angelic, politely answered, "We quite like the idea. It reminds us of our own home."

"It's bloody disgusting. Damn ignorant humans."

With his balding head, small, weasel-like eyes and pointed, bent nose, Cecil was not easy on the eye. If you met Cecil in a dark alley, you would not feel threatened, but you would feel unsettled by the encounter. So, although Cecil raised his voice angrily, Pippa and Patrick were not overly intimidated by him.

Pippa calmly explained, "You see it's for our cars. We do love our cars, so we need plenty of room on the drive to park them."

Eyes wide open, mouth foaming, Cecil stared at them for a moment in utter bemusement.

"Cars? Cars?! Cars are bloody banned you ignoramuses."

"We know dear. But I'm sure God will change his mind once we've had a chat," Pippa confidently replied.

Staring in sheer disbelief, Cecil spun round, waved his hand in the air and shouted just before he slammed his front door, "God does not speak to lowlife, blood-sucking humans."

Pippa and Patrick, who had only just arrived in Heaven were confused. They stood and looked at each other for a while. "Nice man that," Pippa finally said.

"Yes, lovely neighbour," Patrick agreed half-heartily.

"Maybe we could ask about moving the house?"

Patrick answered more positively. "Excellent idea, my love. Let's go and enquire now."

Cecil sat brooding inside his home and thought about the good old days in an attempt to reduce his anger from DEFCON 1to just plain mad. Wiping the sweat from his bald head and slapping both his cheeks on his bony face, he attempted to calm himself. Eventually peace prevailed, and his thoughts returned to more pressing matters. He picked up the well-read note on the table beside him and tried to think positively. Cecil knew his rage could be channelled into action. He had an important mission to complete, and the emotion would drive him on no matter how tired he became or how difficult the task ahead was. Earlier that day, he had received momentous news. It was unfortunate that the means of communication did not reflect the importance of its message. It was instead scribbled on a soggy piece of paper. He attempted to wipe a few mud stains away as he double checked its contents one last time. Now was as good a time as any; he stood up (having only just sat down) and determinedly set off to carry out his mission.

The secret instructions had been delivered via a carrier pigeon earlier in the day. Cecil had been preoccupied, eating what looked and tasted like porridge made with water instead of milk, when the pigeon arrived. With his spoon balanced halfway inside his mouth, Cecil sat motionless, watching the bird's activities. She had spent far too long perched on his freshly cleaned mailbox. The pigeon was having a bad day. She was simply trying to work out how to securely post the top-secret message entrusted to her.

Normally this was a simple task for a highly trained carrier pigeon, but alas, today she was finding it difficult to concentrate. Having flown for several hours without rest, she now felt an unstoppable urge building within. But she was very polite and would never dream of relieving herself on private property. However, it was getting very close to the point where anywhere would do.

Cecil could no longer watch motionless. He was angry and needed to apprehend the target, who he suspected was only there to defecate on his property. Creeping to the front door, he attempted to release the lock as quickly as possible to reach the offending bird. His brain knew how to open a locked door and his hands did too, yet the more he tried, the less the door opened. With the stress and anger levels rising, a co-ordination failure had resulted. Communication between brain and hands works best when the message is delivered as a clear, precise message. An irate brain sends a message which is indecipherable by the hands. The hands rightly claim they cannot be blamed for not following orders. With the brain's message becoming increasingly uninterpretable the hands took fighting action. Cecil punched the door. He needed to stop the pigeon defacing his property. Pigeons were always dropping their digested food onto his overly polished mailbox and this time he would stop it.

With one last attempt to open the door, before realising the door was not actually locked, he charged out with a war cry of: "Be off you vile, revolting, flying pest." The shocked pigeon reacted instinctively by flying into the air but, without a planned trajectory, almost collided with a tree before veering off at the last second to avoid disaster. It was too much. Her bowels opened, and the package hurtled towards the ground. Oh, the embarrassment! She had to get out of there. What if anyone had seen? Dropping her message, she flew away at high speed.

Without looking back, she failed to notice the note slowly float down and land by Cecil's feet. He gesticulated angrily whilst wiping a white, runny mess from his smooth, bald head. "If I ever see your filthy, grey feathers near my house again I'll... well I'd best not!".

Still incandescent with rage, Cecil instinctively picked up the folded message and stormed inside. After washing his head several times, he returned to the kitchen and, for the first time, became conscious of the note. It excited him. His heart skipped a beat. Unfolding the paper carefully he wondered, could this be it? Nervously holding the paper at arm's length to allow his eyes to focus, he read its contents. He re-read it several times. Each time Cecil became more excited, and a warm wave of joy enveloped him as the message became clear. Cecil felt proud. He had been chosen by the Leader to receive and deliver the great parcel of hope.

Eleven

Saint Peter felt calmer now. The influx of humans still troubled him, but he reminded himself that it was God's will after all. Now back at his gate (or the post with the unhinged gate leant against it) to welcome – in his own special way – the earthly souls into Heaven. God had obviously trusted him to perform such an important role.

"Then why does he not trust you to make the crucial decision?" said a voice.

Turning round, Peter saw it was the angel Slugart, a regular visitor in recent times. He had an unusual look for an angel, often adopting a military pose with one arm held behind his back. Being polite, you would say he was shorter than the average angel but to an honest observer, he looked short and chubby. Traditional woollen robes covered his well-formed belly. His hair was parted on one side with a floppy fringe left to grow longer than the sides and requiring an occasional flick from his eyes. On his chin he sported the most peculiar beard – a small square left neatly trimmed.

"There is no decision to make," replied Peter, "They are here, therefore they can enter".

Putting an arm around Peter's shoulder and pointing, Slugart asked, "So why is she allowed into the Kingdom?" Despite his strange demeanour, he spoke powerfully and with confidence.

The retired plumber, who Slugart had referred to, shuffled nervously from one foot to the other. Only five seconds earlier she had felt overjoyed at the prospect of eternal life. But now, just like an underage drinker stopped by the nightclub bouncer at the entrance, she panicked. Just as that young drinker had frantically rehearsed her fake age and date of birth responses, she was now reviewing her worthiness for Heaven with similar trepidation. How many toilets had she fixed for the needy?

"It's no use, Slugart. She's here now. She'll get in." Peter's demeanour was that of a down-trodden worker – he was not his usual brash self.

"Let's see, shall we, Saint Peter." Addressing the plumber, Slugart demanded, "Come hither. Why, frail human, should you bask in the glory of God's kindness?"

The plumber was prepared. In anticipation, she had quickly completed the review of her life and arguments were lined up ready to be fired out like rounds from an automatic rifle. The first bullet from the brain to the mouth, almost saw daylight as the mouth started to speak. But seeing Peter and this other intimidating angel waiting for a response, the argument paused, lost confidence and fled in fright. Panic prevailed, and all her other carefully constructed lines of defence evaporated leaving lesser, more unstructured evidence to emerge: "I have never murdered an innocent man!"

Peter looked at her in amazement. "You say what lady? You, asked by my bredwin over there to explain to us why I, Saint Peter, should let you into Heaven and the best crap you can tell us is about not murdering an innocent man?! Are you saying you murdered a woman? Or a guilty man? Your answer pisses me off." As he paused for breath the little mood destroyer on Peter's shoulder whispered to him, "You have to let her in."

Peter was deflated. "Just get in. All of you get in. You see, Slugart, it's futile. They all enter."

Slugart, who had been visiting Peter every day for the last two weeks replied, "Saint Peter, remember you are more than just a poster boy." And with that he left.

Peter sat down and thought.

Twelve

"What the hell am I going to do? Look at them! Bespoke, crocodile-skin shoes, ruined, all because that demon couldn't tell his arse from his horns." To describe the Devil as being mad would not do his anger justice. A man of lesser resolve would quiver in this situation but not Simon. He fought the temptation to simply offer a tea – for even Simon could not summon up a pot of Earl Grey in a swamp – and explained calmly how he would deal with this unfortunate state of affairs. The hapless Gurmakian had transported Simon and his Master into a stinking swamp, home to the crocodile but not to a pair of crocodile shoes.

"Firstly, sir, we will take note of this inexcusable error made by Gurmakian. Then I suggest, you mull over your punishment options." Punishment was something the Devil enjoyed.

"Unfortunately," Simon continued, "unless a crocodile is conveniently lurking in the swamp that we find ourselves in, we shall have to wait to replace your shoes for now. But I shall be making arrangements for a new pair to be delivered at the soonest possible moment. I have, however, packed your snakeskin shoes that you can change into once out of this mud."

"The ones with the diamond details?", the Devil looked up hopefully.

"Yes, sir".

"You do make things seem better, Simon."

"I try my hardest, sir. Now let's depart this swamp and locate where we are."

Normally, the Devil was more than happy to set cruise control and follow Simon's lead, but he was not going to pass up this opportunity. "Halt, Simon! I shall take charge from here. As you know, I've recently completed the 'Extreme Survival' course. This situation is ready-made for me to practise the knowledge and skills I now possess."

"Excellent, sir," Simon said, with as much confidence as he could muster.

"First, we need to find our bearings. Where is the sun?"

"There is no sun, sir."

"Oh, crap. I forgot. It's been so long since I've spent quality time up here. That damn trainer taught a heap of rubbish then. Always mentioning the sun."

Simon didn't want to spoil the Devil's fun but thought it would be wise to draw his attention to the sign. "Perhaps we should follow that signpost, sir? The one that says, 'Swamp Exit This Way'."

"Be quiet, Simon. Of course, we should follow that sign. Now, have we any empty bottles?"

"Yes, sir." Pausing to consider this request Simon enquired, "What, may I ask, do you want them for? I fear it would be inadvisable to drink the swamp water."

"Piss."

"Piss?"

"Yes, piss, Simon"

"Urine?"

"Stop being so slow, Simon. Piss, urine, wee, whatever you want to call it. We need to save it. We should bottle it all. It could be days before we find a source of fresh, clean water. In an emergency we will drink the wee."

"I feel that will not be necessary. The signpost suggests we will not have far to reach civilisation."

"For God's sake, Simon, fill the damn bottles with piss. Who is the survival expert here?! You won't be moaning when we haven't drunk for two days, and the bottles full of piss save us."

And so, they set off, ankle deep in mud, avoiding crocodiles and bottling wee.

Thirteen

It was getting late, and Hector was on his way home. He'd made the same journey at the same time the day before and the day before that and many, many more before that. Apart from the regulars, only four customers had 'bought' soup today. Three of them ordered a cup out of embarrassment, having mistaken Hector's counter for a baked potato stall. As he walked deep in thought through the busy crowd, he bumped into the evening revellers. He was sure what he was doing was right. He, the Great Leader, had said so, and he knew all. But somehow it also seemed wrong.

It was by chance that an encounter, many years ago, led him to the cult – or as they preferred to be known, the Brotherhood. Intending to visit a newly opened bingo hall, Hector had passed the neon sign and unintentionally entered the building next door. The room was lit by candles – a strange ambience for Bingo that Hector never stopped to question. He waited to be seated but was greeted by an angry voice bellowing from a stage. "Be gone, human!" the voice roared. Hector was wearing a casual tracksuit which put comfort very much over style and hid his magnificent wings.

"Are you talking to me? Am I too late to play?"

The angry voice was confused: "Play! This is not a game. We are discussing serious, angel business. Humans are not welcome."

"But I am an angel." Strange, he thought, that bingo was for angels only.

"You are?" the voice asked, taken aback. Hector's appearance suggested otherwise. "Prove it!" he demanded.

So, Hector did. Unfurling his elegant wings, he made sure to point the tips of each wing, emphasising their sheer grandeur. He proved beyond doubt that he was indeed an angel. Hector was a sight to behold. Despite his slightly bent back, messy hair and shabby tracksuit he looked magnificent, framed by those glorious wings.

"Brother, I am the Great Leader. You are amongst friends. Please stay. It is fate that has brought you here tonight."

Wanting to clarify that it was a leaflet someone had handed him and not fate, he agreed to stay and wished they would hurry up starting the bingo.

Hector sat and listened. Issues were discussed that resonated with his own thoughts. The way the speaker delivered these ideas caught him off guard, drawing him in. It only took this one meeting and he was addicted, craving to hear more from the Leader. Bingo's loss was the Brotherhood's gain.

Having completed his journey home, he took out a small book from his bedside drawer and switched on the table lamp. He found the section he wanted to read. It was only one small paragraph that worried him as he read it over and over again, seeking reassurance that the Leader spoke the truth. Had he misunderstood the meaning of the words?

It had taken a year for doubts to sneak into his mind. But that night the spell the Great Leader cast over him began to weaken.

Fourteen

"I still say we did the right thing, bottling our piss."

Simon returned a look of 'really' and raised one eyebrow.

"You dare question me?" roared the Devil, who noticed Simon's look.

"Of course not, sir."

"Well make sure you don't! I could skin you alive with merely one breath, if I so wished."

Without the slightest inkling of worry in his face, Simon answered, "Very good, sir. Most impressive."

"Now, which way to the beach?" asked the Devil, with his calm fully restored. Simon could always pacify the Devil. It was part of the job.

"As I'm sure you are already aware, and you're just testing me, over there is one of those handy signposts pointing to the beach." Simon gestured towards the sign.

"Errr, of course! You passed my little test, be quicker next time. For now, we should find the Mustang."

Simon mulled the word over in his brain for a moment and decided the Devil didn't mean a horse. "By Mustang, do you mean a car, sir?"

"Yes, that great oaf, Dantalion, parked one somewhere near here. That gullible demon thinks I will reward him for letting me use it. Punish him is what I'll do. How dare he keep unregistered property offshore in Heaven? He'll pay dearly, mark my word."

"I was only checking, sir, as are not all cars banned in Heaven?" A fact that Simon knew to be correct.

"I'm the bloody Devil. You cannot ban me from anything!" he raged as the rising anger began to transform his appearance. His red skin deepened in colour, his horns sharpened, and his whole figure grew in stature. The fury quite literally filled and expanded the Devil's body, emphasising his fearful features. "Soon, you will see no one dares tell me, Satan, what to do."

Simon had been waiting for a chance to bring up 'the elephant in the room' and he felt now was as good an opportunity as he was likely to get.

"Sir, do you think it is wise to show your true form? Should we not travel incognito to avoid unwanted attention?"

Initially ready to dismiss Simon with tales of angels running in fear, he conceded that, in the interest of a relaxing holiday, disguise of some description would perhaps be wise.

"I have taken the liberty to pack a false moustache and a cap. These should be sufficient to prevent your identity being exposed."

Snatching the moustache from Simon's hands, the Devil fingered it thoughtfully before sticking it to his face.

With a polite cough, Simon suggested, "It is more common for a moustache to be worn above the top lip rather than below it."

"Of course, I knew that. Don't make me angry. Do you need me to remind you of the skinning?" The Devil always grew angry when embarrassed. "The cap goes on my head of course," he said, placing it cautiously where he suspected it should go.

"Yes, sir." Simon felt it wise not to comment further about cap protocol and the direction it should sit.

Fifteen

Inconsiderate! That summed up the whole situation with humans. Peter was entering the ninetieth millennia of being pissed off with them. It began when his pearly gates had mysteriously disappeared. In their place, a brown wooden garden gate that lacked any of the grandness of the great entrance of old had been erected. How could new souls ever accept his authority if they failed to respect the physical boundary that controlled access into Heaven? In the past, Peter stood proudly at his pearly gates, then a tall (made even taller by his well-tended afro), muscular man, who invariably dressed with style. But now his hair had mostly greyed, and his muscles were no longer there. Of late, his stature projected a downbeat mood, and the respect he once commanded had vanished. As the line of souls approached Peter and his less than pearly gate, their negative comments would start:

"Is that it?"

"I thought they said it was made of gold."

"I've seen more impressive gates in a skip." And so the banter would continue.

Whenever he heard a derogatory remark, he vowed that person would pay. He'd make them sweat and force them to wait for a week before being allowed in. On one occasion, he hired a costume and, dressed as the Devil, scared the life out of a particularly rude 'gate insulter.

Nothing in Heaven was straightforward. But one thing was annoyingly straight and forward. Once a human boarded their first-class flight with the pilot named Mr. Reaper and landed at Heaven's Terminal Nine, he or she had arrived for the guaranteed holiday of a lifetime. No border checks by Peter were going to stop their party starting.

Doubts had been chipping away for thousands of years at Peter's rock-solid confidence and he now knew that something was wrong. He had never been able to fully define exactly what bothered him until recently. It was conversations with Slugart that revealed the awful truth. The realisation that he – the great Saint Peter – had no real power or authority was a devastating blow. At first, he rebuffed the idea. It was ridiculous, preposterous. He was Saint Peter, the most powerful of all saints, the gatekeeper of Heaven and the guardian of the Kingdom. No one entered without his permission. But every morning Slugart returned, prepared with arguments that Peter could not refute.

"I decide who enters," Peter would insist while doubting it himself.

"No, you don't."

"Yes, I do."

"Stop him then."

"Well, obviously I can't," Peter would grudgingly admit.

Slugart had earlier handed Peter a leaflet (or at least one had mysteriously appeared in his pocket) advertising a meeting entitled, 'How to Become All You Were Meant to Be'. Everything was bothering Peter now as he sat reading the pamphlet. Looking deep into the roaring fire burning brightly in his sitting room, he scrunched it up and tossed it into the flames.

Sixteen

The Brotherhood gathered in the same grand, yet somehow incongruous, building used for the previous meeting. The room was full, barring two empty seats. There had been no confusion at the door this time and no forgotten passwords. Inside the main hall an open fire roared and the occasional ember crackled as it fell onto the soot blackened hearth. Large candles majestically lit the room, maintaining the suitably dramatic atmosphere. Despite the heat from the fire, there was a dark chill in the air. It was perhaps fortunate that the Brotherhood's dress of traditional angel robes with the mandatory hood kept the attendees warm.

The room fell silent. Without any sign or prompt, everyone in the room simultaneously started to chant.

"We do believe."

"We will succeed."

"Chant the forbidden chant."

Their voices reverberated around the room.

At the front, their leader stood with the aura of someone who knew he was in charge. He raised his hands and, with a click of his short, chubby fingers the candles burned brighter, their flames dancing, fighting with the chilly air and flooding the room with more light. He exerted a mystical power, and the group knew it.

The leader, filled with pride, surveyed his followers, loyal, obedient and dressed in customary robes – like proper angels, he thought. In the future, all angels would revere him as they did here. For now, no one knew the identity of anyone else in the cult and it was vital they kept it that way. But one day it would be revealed that he, Slugart, was the leader they followed and admired.

Another chant flowed round the room.

"He that knows the truth, shall be the truth."

"We follow the Great Leader."

"He will lead us home. To the before land."

Slugart lowered his hands, the flames dimmed, and all sat down.

A less senior member of the Brotherhood, nominated as the meeting organiser, rose and walked to the stage, stumbling and tripping on the way.

"Right lads," he began.

"And ladies," piped up a hooded figure, who was now very much suspected of being a lady.

"Yes, and ladies. Now, where was I?"

An attendee helpfully reminded him. "Right lads."

"Ah, yes so I was. Right lads."

"And Ladies. You forgot again," the suspected lady pointed out the mistake once more with extra oomph.

"Forgot what?"

The candles around the room flickered in rage as the leader ordered, "For God's sake, get on with it. How many times do we have to hear this? The agenda. Now. And be hasty."

"Right. First, we would all like to thank whoever it may be for providing this splendid spread of biscuits and tea." Everyone agreed full heartily (and full bellied) on this first point. "Secondly, we need a volunteer to provide some nibbles for our next meeting."

Angry flames flickered once more. "It's not a meeting, or a friendly get together or a bloody club. This is a highly secretive, immensely important …," Slugart paused for a moment struggling to find the correct word. After realising it was in fact at least two of the things he said it was not, he opted for, "Well, it's seriously important and will change our future forever."

"Sorry, yes, I must remember. Well, anyhow, who will provide the refreshments? Come on, don't all just look at your feet. I will pick someone myself if I have to."

The leader burnt a stare into the head of the follower he had selected. "I will happily do it," the angel reluctantly agreed.

A few more minor decisions were made, with 'willing' volunteers picking up tasks.

"Now we have that settled, we come to our main item on the agenda," the speaker mumbled through a mouthful of cake. "Our Great Leader wishes to give us all an update on the progress of our destiny. All hail our Great Leader." The cake did nothing to offer the statement the dramatic effect it deserved.

Each candle the leader passed instantly went out, leaving a line of smoke rising in his wake. The sound made by each step grew louder as he made his way to the stage until his final step echoed around the large room. Only a few remaining candles dimly lit the room.

"Brothers," he let the word resonate, "our power has grown." As if to prove the point, the extinguished candles burst back into flame. "We are on the crest of a new horizon. Our vision, one that adheres to the rights and glory of Heaven will put back what God intended. Our goal will be reached through a chain of events. The first link in the chain has been set free. You will remember I spoke of a hero that will be chosen from amongst you to perform a great task". Slugart pointed at two empty chairs. "Well, this seat is the one."

Blank faces stared in confusion at the chair. Slugart was always prepared for moments of stupidity from his cult and quickly ascertained why they all looked confused.

"Not the chair! The one that was chosen is already on his mission. The chair is a symbol of where he will sit on his return. A hero!" This was met by cheers from the angels and someone, who perhaps should not have joined such a serious and mysterious group, started whooping and whistling. "He will bring back the vital parcel of hope, the first of three keys to unlock the passage to our glorious future. The second link has yet to grasp the greatness of our goal." Pointing to the other empty chair he said, "I was hopeful that he would join us today, but, for now, we shall have to continue without him." Gasps and a sole shriek met the announcement. "But do not fear. I have made contingencies for this. We do not need him to know all and only require him at the climax of events. He can learn everything later." A few cheers greeted his words, but the response was altogether more muted. With a serious tone of voice, bringing silence to the room, the leader continued, "But we must not waver from our aim." Clapping his hands, the room darkened. The sound of thunder rumbled and again the candles ignited. "Soon, I will reveal all and enlighten you, my faithful followers. I shall leave you now. For the greater good!"

All chanted back, "For the greater good."

The angels looked around the room in amazement. The leader had disappeared, yet the words still echoed around them.

When, the followers first saw their leader they had dismissed him as being too small to be powerful, simply a short angel with a stupid beard and greasy hair. They would snigger at his manic style as he started speaking, throwing his arms around, shouting erratically and making strange salutes with an outstretched arm. But when he spoke, they found themselves fixated on him. To see the way Slugart could control a crowd with his use of language was to witness his true power. No longer did they see a weak, diminutive angel but one of power, the head honcho, a chief, commander, the numero uno. They saw their leader.

"Right lads, getting back to the agenda now our Great Leader has popped out," the organiser said as he stumbled and tripped again on his way to the front.

"Let's break for biscuits," interrupted another angel.

"And tea," added a second.

"Oh alright. But it's not on the agenda."

Seventeen

Back on Earth, unless you are affiliated to the mad or insane and postulate that the Earth is flat, you would know it is very much spherical and spins its merry spin on an axis all day long. This motion creates the illusion of a sun that rises each morning and sets each evening, with a schedule that depends on your location on Earth. This is in stark contrast to Heaven, where morning in the west starts at the same time as morning in the east, and a simple on-off switch controls day and night for the entire Kingdom.

The switch was turned on, and so a new day had started. It was morning for all – even for the night owl dozing off to sleep. In another zone of Heaven, far from where the owl snored, Hector had risen and, with no enthusiasm for the day ahead, started his daily routine. He had slept uneasily, troubled by the words, but awoke feeling reassured that the Leader was always right. Normally he would leave the book safely in his bed side drawer, but today, he tucked it carefully inside his cloak. Hector felt he should read it once more – just in case.

It was not only Hector who had a disturbed night.

It is said by the baboon – the wisest of all monkeys – that Heaven is a living thing. It reacts. Heaven can be defensive or welcoming, responding to events as they arise. One baboon elder was making various monkey noises to this effect as she warned her troop of impending doom.

None of the others took much notice. They never did. Who can take anyone seriously with a bum like that? With a well sculpted face, framed by tufts of luscious hair on either side, she boasted a large muscular body covered in soft brown fur and a long delicate tail; a spectacular creature thus far… and then the bum. A red hairless rump that did little to blend in and everything to look ridiculous.

Baboons had theorised on time and space, grasped particle physics and cured all diseases – but come on, with a bum like that they were always going to be ignored. Sulking that her peers dismissed her warnings so readily, she wandered off to investigate further.

Eighteen

"This, I think, sir, is an ideal opportunity."

It was, truth be told, the third ideal opportunity. Simon worried that a cap and false moustache may not, in fact, divert attention from the Devil's red shade of red skin, nor from his ginormous size. On Earth, his red skin might have been explained by an extreme case of sunburn. Yet, with Heaven's sunless sky, that idea had no credibility. What was needed, Simon thought, was a test. He wanted the Devil to mingle with some Heaveners to gauge their reaction. It was now the third opportunity to do this. On the first two occasions they had tried, the Devil made feeble excuses. He kept losing his nerve. This time, Simon took control.

They approached their target who wore a tie dye, brightly coloured vest, old shorts and sandals. His hair was either unwashed and matted or purposely dreadlocked. Simon initiated proceedings. "A fine day it is to be in Heaven, do you not think, sir?"

"Dude, this is not Heaven, man. It's all a trip."

Simon, who thought much more in black and white than luminous pink, searched for some clarification. "Perhaps I misunderstood you, sir, as this is very much Heaven?"

"Bro, I was like tripping and then saw this awesome eagle flying off the cliff, so I like chased it and with my wings..."

"Wings?" This was confusing territory for Simon. Clearly the man was a human and had no wings.

"Yeah, they just sort of grew, so I jumped and was flying over the sea with this eagle and then, wow, this old age pensioner guy, wearing all black, started flying next to me and I was like ... this is sketchy. The dude was flying with a gardening tool, and he gave me this pill, and then I suddenly felt like dead and found myself here."

"That was not a pensioner. It was the Grim Reaper, you fool. Can't you see you are dead, sir?"

"Hey, man, chill. The oldie must have slipped me some dodgy LSD. Longest trip ever, man."

Giving up, Simon reverted to his plan. "My friend and I," – leaving a pause, so the hippy could observe his master – "were just saying how great God is."

"God? Man, God doesn't exist."

"Ah well, the fact we are in Heaven suggest he does," Simon said, pointing to the flaw in the guy's argument.

"We're not in Heaven, dude."

The Devil looked sheepish and worried but was becoming annoyed – a sure-fire way to calm his nerves. He stood up and loomed over the hippy, their noses nostril to nostril. "Enough of this crap. You are in Heaven; God does exist. Do I look like the Devil?!"

Simon despaired. I go to all this trouble of casually introducing us and you barge in and even say the word Devil, he thought very, very quietly to himself.

"Whoa, this trip is intense. It's like I can smell your grotesque breath, yet you ain't even real."

"Do I look like the Devil?!" he repeated. Satan could get quite tetchy.

"Chill your boots, dude. You can't be the Devil. You have a moustache. Insane cap. Love the horns, dude."

"Enough. Come, Simon. We have successfully tested the disguise. Let's rid ourselves of this imbecile."

A minute later, having thought how best to approach the subject, Simon asked, "Are you certain, sir, that the human we chose was adequate for the test?"

"Of course! Now shut up and find this car. I'm fed up with walking."

Simon did not get this far in life and death without knowing when not to question his master further.

Nineteen

Hector had finished serving the first orders of the day and would normally sit waiting for the next anticipated customer or, on the rare occasion, an unexpected one. But today he was walking along the ragged, red carpet that led from the great market square towards the gates of Heaven. Once a rich, red colour with properties of both velvet and silk, now it was no more than a moth-infested, dirt-covered rag.

Walking slowly over its worn pile, he carefully carried a bowl of soup in his wrinkled hands. It was years since he last saw Peter. Hector had always found him rather rude, but who was he to judge. In the good old days, the saint used to buy soup each morning, without fail. Yet, like many others, his visits became less frequent. Hector often found himself thinking, it's been ages since so-and-so last came to my stall.

Not many people (or angels) approach the gates from Heaven's side as, once a soul has entered, there is no obvious reason to do so. Peter had a well-rehearsed script for whenever anyone approached and, seeing Hector, he wasted no time. A devout Catholic currently had the pleasure of Peter's attention. "I see my brother here has respected all the rules and regulations in the Big Man's book."

"Yes, your holiness."

"And your religion game was sick?"

"Yes. My religion game was sick. I'm sorry, did you say sick?"

"Means good, bro. So, in you go."

Opening the gate, Peter let the Catholic fella through. Then, as Hector approached, Peter screamed, "Holy crap! He has returned. Run, bredrin, run. That bro approaching you is Judas Iscariot. He has returned to kill us all." Quite the actor, Peter's face was a picture of fear. Everyone screamed and ran in no particular direction, most not even knowing who Judas was. Others joined in the screaming and running, unsure why but damn sure they should be.

Peter smiled, while he watched them stampede in panic. This was entertainment.

"That was mightily mean, Peter." Hector, a kind and gentle angel himself, was now more convinced of Peter's less than perfect character.

"What brings you here, Hector? I don't often see you down in my manor."

"A gesture from an old friend. He asked me to bring you a soup to remind you of the good old days."

"Cor, I forgot about these soups. They were sick back in the day. Leave it there. I best sort this lot out first and then I'll have it."

It took a while but eventually calm was restored amongst the out-of-control, stampeding herd of humans. Hector was gone, souls were patiently queuing, and Peter was quietly finishing his soup. This, he felt, was better. It was good to taste a traditional homemade soup once more. It made him feel warm, just like old times. Scraping the bowl to extract the last spoonful, he was surprised to see a ball of something wrapped in tinfoil. Unravelling the foil, he found a note inside.

"The good old days. Simple life. How all should be," it read.

On returning to the stall, Hector was shocked to find no one waiting. Years of slow trade had failed to dint his belief that everyone craved his soup.

Carefully lowering his creaking old body into the comfy chair, he felt proud. Proud to be the angel delivering the secret message to Saint Peter. Yes, he was an irritable twerp, but in Hector's experience most saints were. Hector felt important; he was the one chosen by the Great Leader to conceal hidden messages in his famous soup and not just for Peter. He was the only one – apart from the Leader – who knew the members of the cult. Each day he received a new message – most only contained details of the next meeting – which he copied and distributed. Finding a technique to do this was a challenge. His first attempts at concealment did not fare well – messages soaked for hours in soup were a disaster. Earlier meetings were only attended by Hector and the Leader, due to dissolved or unreadable notes, until the wrapped method was perfected. Some objected to using tinfoil – a material not found naturally in Heaven – but the alternatives just didn't work. (Members of the cult were opposed to anything untraditional.)

Sat in his comfortable chair that was both firm and soft at just the right points, staring into space, he reflected on the Great Leader. He appeared so knowledgeable and powerful, wise and enlightened. Yet still he was not sure.

With Hector gone, Peter also felt the urge to think. Having temporarily implemented an open door (or gate) policy for the arriving souls, he sat on a graffitied park bench, installed some years ago. A gold plaque declared: 'For Peter. Here he sat watching humans argue. Creation – Elimination.' Reading how 'Sarah luvs Kyle', he wondered why the humans defaced his bench. Just because he had attached a plaque did not mean others were welcome to add their own words. Peter found himself fingering the note delivered earlier. Removing it from his pocket he read it again. He was not one to get excited by predictions in a fortune cookie but something in this message struck a chord. Unconsciously turning it over, his eyes noticed there was more on the back.

"You CAN decide," is all it read.

Twenty

Carrying two large suitcases and a full rucksack through a muddy swamp was something Simon had little experience of, but he accomplished it without moaning or incident. A butler must adapt to perform unexpected tasks for one's master under all circumstances. Simon lived by this code and had no complaints. After escaping the swamp, he and the Devil circled round and round the same streets, looking as lost as an octopus dropped on top of Mount Everest.

Walking with his head down and centre of gravity firmly forward, Simon found the bags were manageable. The tricky part was stopping. He would forget about the extra load strapped to his back. Each time his forward motion ceased he relaxed and stood upright, which caused him to topple backwards. Initially the Devil found it hilarious, but even he was becoming bored with lifting his butler every five minutes. It is Simon who should be helping me, he thought, not me exerting effort to help him.

"We've been here before. How the hell did you get us lost?!" the Devil cursed.

Simon, although annoyed at the false accusation, showed no outward emotion. He felt it wise not to mention that it was the Devil who had ignored the simple directions and instead answered, "Perhaps if you let me lead, we might find an alternative route."

"Have you recently completed an orienteering course?" the Devil snapped back.

"I regret not, sir."

"Have you twice won the demons' annual orienteering competition?"

"Not being a demon, I have not done that either, sir."

"A simple 'no' in future, Simon, will do. And stop looking at the floor when talking to me!"

"My apologies, sir, but if I look up, I suspect I shall fall again."

"Enough excuses, first you get us lost, and now you have the audacity to disobey me when I ask you to look at me." The Devil was annoyed. Normally he could vent his anger on a passing demon or a doomed soul, but without either being available, it was Simon who received the brunt of his rage. "Look me in the face. Now!"

"That, sir, I cannot."

"Do it now before I rip your head off and fix it to a pole, so you permanently look me in the face." Some would say the Devil had lost his temper, others would say he had lost the false, polite calm he so desperately wanted to portray.

Not wishing to risk losing his head, Simon briefly looked the Devil in the face, then the horizon, before toppling over backwards once more to finally peer at the sky.

Admitting to himself that he may have been harsh, he helped Simon back onto his feet. "On this occasion, you can take the lead," he conceded, remembering Simon always knew best.

With Simon taking charge, the car was located swiftly. The keys were in the ignition, the tank was full, and the bodywork glistened. This did not prevent the Devil roaring with anger. A roar that could shear a flock of sheep in one.

"Who has done this?"

On the car's gleaming windscreen were fixed a number of yellow notes. "It appears that Heaven's vehicle police department have, sir." Simon replied, as he read the first one.

"And why have they done this?"

"For parking on double yellow lines." To Simon, the rule that had been breached was quite clearly stated on the parking tickets, yet the Devil was not quite so quick on the uptake.

"Why can't a crappy car park on yellow lines? Does it hurt the lines?"

"Well, no..."

"Can I park on pink lines?"

"I do not think there are pink lines..."

"Course there are you ignoramus. Why can't a line be pink? Don't say dumb things like that again."

"You misunderstand, sir. Traditionally on a road, double yellow lines indicate that one cannot park. People do not draw pink..."

The Devil interrupted again. "You're talking drivel, man. Lines can be any colour. And it's the scum that go around drawing lines on roads that should be punished. Not the car. Who goes around drawing lines anyway?!"

It was clear that the Devil would never grasp the concept of yellow lines, so Simon moved the conversation on to a more pressing concern. "It does not look like we can use the car, sir."

"We bloody well will." They were both looking at the clamps placed securely on every wheel. "I'll rip them off." And without an ounce of effort, the Devil grasped the first clamp with both hands and tore it apart.

"And what do you think you are doing?" The words came from neither Simon nor his master and gave both quite a shock. Two rather odd-looking men suddenly appeared from behind a bush and were observing Simon and the Devil in an aggressive, yet strangely timid, manner. The speaker was a well-built man who clearly enjoyed a pie far too often for his health. The other resembled Popeye in build – though very much before he'd got his hands on any spinach. Slight of build with a receding hairline and knobbly knees that would show through even the baggiest of trousers, he was a sight to behold.

"If you do not have a very good reason, why you have damaged police property, I will ask my good partner here to arrest you." It was the skinny one who spoke this time.

"We are police officers," the larger man added, as he thrust a shiny badge in Simon's face, "Unit one of the Heaven District

Police Force, sir," he spoke, or rather shouted in a loud, aggressive manner.

"Oh, that's strange I thought Heaven would have no need for a police force," challenged Simon.

"It bloody well does. We once arrested a demon and..." He stopped swiftly after his colleague kicked him quickly in the leg. "Yes, we need one, sir."

"No demons or other beasts here," Simon hastily added.

"So, I repeat," the officer gave them both a look of disgust, "why have you damaged police property?"

Simon thought quickly. One of the worst ways to stay incognito is to get arrested.

"Clamp testers."

The words took time to process, as they were not one of the many potential replies the police officers had expected. "I'm sorry, did you say clamp tasters?" asked the puzzled, skinny officer.

"Not tasters, testers."

"Ah, in that case... Hang on, clamp testers? There is no such thing." The larger of the two was still getting his head around these people being clamp tasters, so it fell to the smaller one to talk.

Simon was prepared for this. "Heaven Protocol 2.6.5. All clamps used within Heaven must have valid documentation or else they will be destroyed. That is what my friend here was doing. No documentation, so it was destroyed."

In a flap, the officer protested, "But you have not asked for any documentation."

Simon was in the driving seat now. The Devil stood watching, confused, and wished he was in the driving seat of the Mustang – but this would do for now. "Papers then, please," demanded Simon.

The now up-to-speed larger officer eloquently responded. "Ermm, we don't have any."

"Well, we had better destroy the rest." Turning to the Devil, Simon instructed, "Destroy the illegal clamps."

The larger officer, who was always keen for action, stepped forward. "I wouldn't be doing that, sir." For an instant the devil hesitated.

This brief pause gave the other officer time to think. "Hold on. Where are your papers?"

"Our what?" replied Simon.

"Your papers, declaring you have the power to destroy these clamps."

Patting his pockets, Simon confessed, "I appear to have left them in the office."

"Yes, we can see that." The smaller officer took charge again. "But as you have no papers, we will require you to present them at the station within two working days, else we will have to take further action."

"Of course. And no doubt you will be able to show us yours?" replied Simon.

A moment of foot shuffling and general awkwardness followed, with neither the officers nor Simon knowing who should walk away first. As the Devil looked on, bemused, the impasse was broken. "Before we go, can I have drink from your bottle, please?" the larger officer asked politely, looking at the Devil hopefully. Having staked out the car in Heaven's midday heat, he had built up quite a thirst. With a mouth so dry it felt similar to sandpaper baked in the Sahara, and absolutely gagging for a drink, he had uncharacteristically resorted to politeness.

The Devil by now had lost interest and wasn't listening. "What did you say?"

"I noticed you have plenty of water bottles, so could I have a drink? Thirsty work, policing." With the prospect of a refreshing drink staring him in the face, he could have been compared to a dog drooling and begging for a scrap of food.

"We don't have any." The Devil was still not interested.

"You both have three bottles tied to your waist." He gestured to make the point.

"Oh these, these aren't…" and then he became interested. These interfering pests were going to get punished – and punishment was the Devil's one love in life. "I'm so sorry, of course you can. Warm, I'm afraid, but a drink all the same. Take a bottle each." Simon looked in worried disbelief as the Devil handed a bottle to each officer and saw them gulp it down, and down and down.

"Here you go." Wiping his mouth, the larger of the policemen handed back the empty bottle.

"That's fine with us, they were just our emergency drinks in case we ran out." Smiling, the Devil was loving this.

The small officer wiped his finger round his mouth and asked, "What was that drink. I didn't recognise the taste?"

"Wee." The Devil beamed in sheer pleasure.

"Wee?" spat out both officers.

"Yes, I think you had mine and you had Simon's."

"You mean urine?" Already the smaller officer was making gagging noises.

"Yes, as I told Simon, it's imperative in a survival situation to save all fluids for emergencies. Luckily for you two, we had no such emergency, and our plight is no longer considered to be in a survival mode. Now, we must be off. Goodbye." Simon and the Devil quickly scurried round the next corner and ran.

For the next two minutes, all that could be heard beside the clamped Mustang was a lot of coughing and spitting, leaving the two officers feeling understandably angry.

"Who pisses into a bottle and stores it?" the smaller one raged.

"A classic survival technique. I've often thought about doing it myself," the larger policeman replied without thinking.

"Oh, shut up!"

Both officers were deep in thought as they left the scene of the clamp crime and headed for the nearest shop to 'purchase' a drink. The 'suspicion' hairs on the back of their necks were standing to attention. There was something strange about the clamp inspectors but for now they couldn't quite figure out what.

"We should follow them two, Roger," the larger one suggested.

"Yes Guy. Yes, we should."

Twenty-One

Now rumour has it that, in his youth, Cecil got into a spot of bother with the authorities. Not like a teenager, brought home by the local Bobby to be given a stern telling off for stealing a chocolate bar. No, when an angel gets in trouble with authority, it means he has felt the wrath of God's 'wooden spoon'. Only one has ever received the full lashing from God's tongue and no prizes for guessing who that was. Lucifer's fall from grace and into his land of fire should have put any misbehaving angel off being put on the naughty step.

No one knows what Cecil did to annoy God. Some say he tempted Jesus with wine, others that he sent Adam and Eve their first leaves. But everyone agreed, Cecil had been angry ever since, with few angels calling him a friend and many avoiding his company all together.

At present, he was very much alone, laying concealed in overgrown pampas grass, waiting to receive further news about the parcel of hope. He could sit there forever – but not in comfort. Unfortunately, he had chosen a plant with razor sharp leaves, but the constant pain from their cuts would not deter him from his mission. Cecil's resolve grew in the knowledge that the Great Leader's plan would return Heaven (and him) to the glorious days of the past. The words filled him with pride: "A hero will be chosen," and the Leader had chosen him to deliver the package; nothing would stop him becoming that hero.

Only a few moments in Cecil's existence could ever be considered happy. There was the time he witnessed Gabriel slip on ice, causing him to fall down the stairs and topple several other angels on the way. On another occasion he was almost crowned champion of Heaven in a game similar to poker – until he was caught cheating. But nothing came close to the happiness he felt at being selected to collect and deliver this mysterious parcel. Now he was the chosen one – the one to be revered and spoken of forever.

It made him happy – still angry – but very happy. All he could do now was wait. Wait and be angry.

Eventually the message arrived, delivered by the same carrier pigeon that accidentally defecated on Cecil earlier. Seeing Cecil hidden in the pampas grass, she hesitated. Would Cecil recognise her? She could not face that embarrassment, but she had to respect the carrier pigeon code. Pigeons must deliver, no matter what, where and to whom. There was only one way out of this mess – and that was disguise! With few options for a pigeon in this department, she reluctantly adopted the parrot look to hand (or beak) deliver the message. Disappointingly for Cecil, it didn't contain the heroic task that he had imagined – just directions to a safe house where he was to wait until further instructions arrived.

Leaving the grass patch behind, he thought to himself, what a funny looking pigeon.

Twenty-Two

Meticulously planning his holiday months in advance, the Devil knew the 'what, where and when' of his scheduled activities. At their base camp – a luxurious hotel – Simon was attempting to resolve the only thing the Devil had neglected to plan.

"Smith," Simon replied to the hotel receptionist.

"I'm sorry, there are no reservations for a Mr. Smith tonight, nor for any of the other names you tried. Taylor, Rogers, Clarke, Sampson – I forget the rest."

"We must have booked it under my name instead. "

"And your name is?"

Leaning over the desk as far as he could, without being obvious, Simon desperately tried to read the reservations. "Cooper."

"Ah yes, we have a Mr. Cooper for tonight. A deluxe suite."

"Yes, that is the one we booked," a relieved Simon confirmed.

"There is just one problem."

"Yes?"

"Mr. and Mrs. Cooper checked in an hour ago." The receptionist smiled an unfriendly smile.

Simon thought quickly. Swanky hotels are never keen on upsetting important guests, so he went on the attack. "This is an incredibly sad state of affairs. The hotel has gone downhill ever since the old receptionist left. He never made mistakes like this."

"Mistakes! Mistakes! The only mistake made here is that you keep getting his name wrong." He pointed rudely at the Devil.

"I would keep your voice down If I were you. You wouldn't want the paps hearing you talk to him like that. Not with how famous he is at the moment. His fans," Simon gestured at the Devil, "would ransack the place if they found out."

The receptionist felt aggrieved at being compared unfavourably to his predecessor, and he particularly disliked the idea of possibly being blamed for angry fans destroying the hotel.

"Famous you say?"

"Yes, very."

"These fans, they wouldn't really do that would they?"

"On more than one occasion they have left buildings with only rubble for walls."

Weighing up the risks compared to the ego-crushing, apologetic alternative, the receptionist replied. "I do apologise. In my haste, I failed to recognise him." The receptionist was not one to follow popular culture in glossy magazines, so it did not surprise him that he had no idea who the celebrity was. "I can assure you I do not usually make mistakes. Let me check the list once more. Ah yes, here we are. Another booking for Mr. Cooper. A suite with complementary full body massage. Let me just get your keys and the porter will take your bags to the room."

While the receptionist looked for the key, the Devil quietly asked Simon what all the fuss was about. "This is nonsense. In Hell I don't have to book a room". Simon lacked the energy to explain.

Twenty-Three

Hector enjoyed the thrill of belonging to a secret organisation for the first time in his long, dull life. He had lived a mainly mundane existence so was damn well determined to feel part of this movement and share the same experiences felt by all the other members. That day, as he sat down for dinner, he dipped his spoon into the soup – which for some strange reason (at least to him) had failed to sell – and picked out the object lying at the bottom of the bowl. He tried his best to look surprised before washing the ball under the tap and carefully unfolding the foil wrapper. The note inside revealed the time of tonight's meeting and the secret pass phrase to gain entry. Of course, all this was pointless. He could have read the note when he received the original, but he now felt connected having experienced the excitement of being a Brother. Without going into full details, there was one time that Hector came to the end of the soup and found nothing. That evening was passed uncomfortably.

Preparing for the meeting, Hector ran a bath to wash away the day's grime and unintentional sins. What sins needed cleansing he wasn't sure, but the Great Leader insisted they bathed before every meeting. He dried and put on the brown robes that all would wear that night and headed for the secret location.

Outside the air felt cold as he hurried along the dark streets. Heaven always used to seem warm, even at night, yet over the years, the temperature appeared to have fallen. The human scientists living out their eternity in Heaven theorised that the lack of CO_2 in the atmosphere caused this global cooling and suggested bringing excess CO_2 from Earth with each new soul. Two parts of this theory irritated the angel scientists. Firstly, they hadn't thought of it and, secondly, they didn't know what CO_2 was. But they were not going to admit that to the humans.

As he rounded the last bend, Hector was surprised by an owl hooting loudly overhead, and in an involuntary reflex action, he threw himself against a crumbling brick wall. This was not a movement that came naturally to an angel who walked slowly with a crooked back. Why was he so scared, he wondered? Hector had been inexplicably jumpy the past few weeks. Regaining his breath and bravery, he continued the journey. He felt safe in the Brotherhood, it was the true. Yet why all this secrecy? The Great Leader insisted it was necessary, but why?

Arriving at the stated time, he knocked on the door twice, waited and then made the sound of an injured toad through the letterbox. For some reason Hector knew how to impersonate an injured toad but others before him had struggled and were lucky to be let in.

The door edged open and two eyes, lit by a neighbouring security light, stared and asked, "If a witch knows which witch is which, how does a wizard know?"

"A wizard can never know which witch is which, for which witch would a wizard pick?" Hector whispered back.

"You may enter, Brother," the two eyes answered.

The door closed softly behind Hector. This annoyed the door as it preferred to be slammed. Slamming was respected by other doors.

The Leader had certainly made an effort. The customary candles had doubled in number and registered twice their normal intensity. A fire glowed white in the middle of the room as its flames flickered and crackled. Large mirrors hung on every wall reflecting the light, giving the impression that the room was engulfed by fire, which surrounded those gathered in the middle. There were no vacant seats, so Hector sat on the floor and waited for the late comers. His old, aching back hoped they wouldn't be too late.

After ten minutes, all the attendees had arrived. Quiet chitchat stopped abruptly as a cold wind swept through the room. Everyone fell silent. Angels looked around in excited anticipation. A loud bang rattled the room as the door slammed shut (giving the door some respect at last). Another louder bang drew their attention back to the stage and there stood their Leader with arm outstretched in his customary pose. Pausing to allow the Brothers enough time to acknowledge his greatness, then with a click of his fingers, all the candles were extinguished. Only the fire burned, with the occasional crackle sending embers flying towards the closest angels.

The fire, now the sole remaining light in the room, captured everyone's attention. They found themselves mesmerised by the dancing flames changing from whites to yellows, then to oranges and reds. The flames entranced the crowd, while they watched hypnotically. As they stared, an image began to form in front of their eyes. It slowly morphed from one shape into another until it assumed the profile of an angel they recognised – it was him, their great, all-knowing leader. He moved closer and closer to the fire and then, accompanied by an intake of breath, walked straight through the flames emerging on the other side completely ablaze. He clapped his hands, and all went dark but, seconds later with another clap, the candles were alight, and the fire blazed once more. The Leader stood before them, unharmed – and considerably less on fire.

"The power is ours. Every day I grow stronger, and through my strength we grow powerful together. Can I hear an amen?"

"Amen," they all chanted in unison.

He waited and then continued. "They come here in droves without any respect for our culture. No respect for God or angels. Humans! Who here has to live next to them?" Most raised their hands.

"Inferior things. They should keep to their own areas. Why should we live with these dirty, smelly creatures? Who has to listen to their music all day, inhale the stench of their disgusting food, see them touch lips with their kissing?"

"We do," came the robotic response.

"Trousers! I have seen angels wearing these human clothes. They are forcing their unwanted alien culture upon us without our consent. It should not be allowed. And more and more flood in each day – no one can stop them!"

"What can we do?" shouted a particularly enraged angel.

"First, we stem the flow and then drain the swamp. How? I cannot say today, but we can!" Slugart spoke with such passion and energy, even the walls were starting to hate humans. "Search your homes for trousers, check your larders for chips, noodles, cereals – anything that these humans have brought to God's land. I want you to gather them all together and burn them. Burn them until they are ash." He spoke at speed, yet using language that everyone could understand, lingering on certain words for emphasis. Commanding the stage, marching with one arm behind his back and flicking his fringe, the sweat noticeably dripped from his forehead. "If you see angels wearing human clothes then we must enlighten them. They will one day destroy the clothes themselves." He recited a chant that his followers eagerly repeated.

Slugart stopped to observe the crowd. Dialling down his rhetoric a few notches, he continued, "Is it fair that we are made to queue?"

"No!" came a passionate response.

"Before they came, we never queued. We managed perfectly well without queues. Yet again, their queuing culture was forced upon us."

The audience muttered angry comments in total agreement.

"Is it right that we are compelled to say 'please' and 'thank you'? We had no need to use these dirty human words until they made us! Why should we? What was wrong with not using these words? It has only become impolite to not say them, since they were brought here from their world. I say throw those words back where they came from, burn their clothes, compost their food and rid our Heaven of their culture."

"For too long we have talked of the problems. You have listened, eager to hear the final plan and now the time for action is edging closer. Not today but soon. Our Great Hero is poised and ready to bring us the first key."

A spontaneous amen followed by a cheer that lifted the roof and, for a worrying moment, plunged the room into darkness. When the light returned the Leader had miraculously vanished.

With Slugart gone, a hooded figure from the crowd took to the stage. "Right. Now our Leader has left for today and has asked me to carry on with the meeting – after a short break for tea and biscuits. He wants me to assure everyone that his plan is on track and the details will be revealed soon."

Eventually the meeting ended, and the angels drifted off into the night.

Back home, a weary Hector collapsed into bed. All the excitement of the meeting had zapped his energy. Clutching the book, he turned to the page that troubled him. "Why did it still worry him so?"

Twenty-Four

Light filtered softly through the net curtains hanging from a large window. Outside the bird song annoyed those still trying to sleep as they hit their snooze buttons repeatedly. It was morning in Heaven, and Simon started to lay out the day's clothes for his Master. The Devil finished a double portion of full English breakfast and felt in good spirits. Even though the first day had not gone to plan, he could already feel the benefits of being 'out of office'. In half an hour, he'd normally be at the weekly catch-up meeting with Hell's most senior demons. Scheduled to last for an hour, the meeting always overran as though oblivious to the importance of his time. Most of the demons kept their reports brief and to the point, yet some (and always the same 'some') felt it necessary to wander off topic and blabber on about some unrelated crap that no one else gave a monkey's about. They seemed to have a talent for going over and over the same topic, often repeating what others had said in slightly different ways. Just thinking about it made his stress levels rise. So, he stopped, and concentrated instead on the clothes Simon had laid out – a sleeveless, blue and white vest with matching knee-length cream shorts and Jesus sandals. Along with his cap and moustache disguise of course.

Most of Simon's former employers had required some help to dress (tying their bow ties, adjusting their dinner jackets) but only the Devil required a head-to-toe service. The Devil stood stark naked, while Simon dressed him, like a mother dressing their spoilt ten-year-old child. Although now a veteran in seeing Satan in the buff, Simon had not once lowered his eyes – and this morning would be no exception.

"Ah, I feel good today, Simon. We should visit some of these tourist sites I have read so much about." Retrieving a book from his bedside table, 'Travel Guide for Demons,' he opened it to a selected page. "This art gallery, 'Musee moderne du Louvre'," he read slowly, "We shall visit it today."

In truth, the book he referred to (which the Devil had confiscated from a demon) had thoroughly confused him. The attractions were clearly more boring than watching a snail run the London marathon and then watching the replay with extended highlights. The art gallery seemed the best of a bad bunch and even that confused him. Why would people go to look at very badly painted pictures? As far as he was concerned, since the invention of photography, paintings had become obsolete. Simon, though, could not know this.

"I shall particularly enjoy viewing the Picasso, 'Le Pigeon aux Petit Pois'," the Devil continued, with great difficulty. He always craved to be cultured and if he had to visit an art gallery, as culture dictates, then he would make every effort to act the part.

"It's a masterful painting, sir."

Not certain if Simon was taking him seriously, he threatened in an uncultured way. "You'd better not be patronising me, Simon! I know my art and I shall show you so today."

"Yes sir, very good, sir." And Simon backed out of the room to ready their bags.

They arrived at the gallery in good time without getting lost, mainly due to Simon guiding them, on the unspoken understanding that the Devil was leading – but from behind.

The spectacular building was beautiful and extravagant but also a hideous mismatch of architectural styles. This unfortunate feature, common in Heaven, was caused by a clash of egos and expertise. Specialists in their field, arriving from different eras, would argue that their designs or ideas were superior. Where once they were regarded as the best of the best while alive, they now found themselves working in teams with others who thought they were a cut above the rest. After days of arguing and much drinking by great architects (ranging from cave dwellers to post modernists), plans for new buildings would emerge, displaying the inevitable compromise and amalgamation of styles.

The art gallery before them possessed some of these interesting contrasts, from the glass pyramid roof, to the imposing cast-concrete walls and the impressive marble columns surrounding the gunmetal-grey steel door.

Simon struggled his way up the granite steps, which led to the main entrance, keeping his bags balanced to prevent tumbling back down. A corridor, with its captivating ceiling mural displaying unbelievably detailed depictions of angels in flight and its floor of polished concrete, channelled all visitors into the first exhibition. This enormous space was brimming with art: statues, paintings, sculptures, modern and pre-historic art, and artefacts not quite modern or ancient. The place reeked of culture. Each piece dazzled with perfection.

Simon recognised and enjoyed accomplished art when he saw it. He'd acquired a sound education whilst working for wealthy employers, but the Devil, on the other hand, possessed little artistic knowledge. He stood confused, wondering where the exhibits were. A tricky situation. Not wanting to appear the idiot, unable to see any art in a room full of art, and craving to be considered cultured, he cast a line hoping Simon would take the bait.

"Would you say the art displayed here is as good as that on Earth, Simon?"

"No, sir. Every piece here is majestic. Infinitely better than anything on Earth."

Scanning the room, the Devil still failed to see an example. He kicked an empty, crushed can – inexplicably guarded by a red rope around its perimeter – and continued with his fishing expedition. "Which piece would you judge was the best?"

Gesturing with his hand, Simon answered. "That oil painting on the wall, sir. The one depicting Jesus painting the Mona Lisa."

"That one?"

"Yes, sir."

"But it doesn't even look like Jesus! It's all blurry."

"I believe, sir, that is the style of the artist. Much admired for capturing the atmosphere," and, with a quiet cough that always meant something important would follow, Simon continued, "May I make a suggestion, sir?"

"What is it, Simon? Don't tell me you like that stone statue? The guy doesn't even have clothes."

"Considered, sir, to be the finest statue ever created. But my suggestion is we should hastily move to the next room. You accidentally kicked and potentially destroyed the newest installation in the exhibition, named 'Can'."

Confused, the Devil returned a blank stare.

"What I am trying to say, sir, is that you kicked that can, which is in fact a priceless piece of art. And now everyone is staring at us. While normally not a concern for yourself, but being incognito, it is not wise to stay where everyone stares." And indeed, the whole room had their eyes fixed on the Devil.

"For once, Simon, I completely agree." And they darted into the next hall.

Again, the paintings oozed class and the statues were still missing their clothes.

"Another suggestion if I might, sir."

"Don't push your luck!" The Devil knew a suggestion was effectively the way Simon told him what to do.

"Perhaps, no matter how lacking in merit your well-trained art eye perceives the art in this room, you could possibly not touch it?"

Rather embarrassed, the Devil held back his anger and agreed without answering.

They wandered through room after room. Satan occasionally took a quick glance at his 'Art Guide for the Demonic Novice' – while Simon pretended not to notice – and made a comment on a piece. After visiting five rooms, they were nearing the end of their tour.

"Simon," said the Devil eying up a sizeable painting.

"Yes, sir," Simon waited for the Devil's critique.

"That painting. The large one with the two people in it."

"A wonderful description, sir. Your knowledge of art is second to none."

The Devil lost his train of thought. "A nun or all nuns?"

"I beg your pardon, sir?"

"This nun you dare suggest has better knowledge than me. Who is she?"

"Sir, you misunderstand me. I mean none not nun."

"Stop saying nun. A nun is a bloody nun. Forget about it!" he gestured in a frustrated manner. "Anyway, Simon, before you interrupt me again," and the stare made sure Simon stayed quiet, "I was talking about this picture. It has, I believe, been in every room. How, Simon, do they make the eyes follow you around?"

"A skill many an artist wished they could master, sir. Only the most talented can perfect the illusion."

"I see. Well, we have many more places to visit, so let's keep moving."

"Would you like a tea first, sir, in the gift shop?"

"Yes, and don't wait in one of those pointless queues. Just make it yourself!"

"Very good, sir."

Once the Devil and Simon had left, the large painting became eyeless. There were now four holes where once four eyes had been.

"I don't like it one bit," said Guy.

"Why would two clamp inspectors be visiting an art gallery?"

"It smells fishy. Let's arrest them," Guy suggested hopefully.

"No. Something tells me we must follow them." Roger, as always, erred on the side of caution "If this is what we think it might be, then we could prevent the crime of the century. We will be heroes!".

"I always wanted to be a hero," muttered Guy.

Twenty-Five

A chirpy, red-breasted robin flew overhead. Many a worm would object to the notion that a worm-murdering bugger can enter Heaven, but the bird was not thinking about this. He was on his way out of the human zone of Heaven while thinking they were bird-eating buggers. Down below, if he had bothered to look, he may have seen Peter enjoying his soup whilst Slugart approached in the distance.

"I see you appreciate the good soup of old, Peter," Slugart commented, as he went to embrace his old friend.

Avoiding the contact, Peter replied, "Tastes good when my man Hector brings it. You'd know nothing about that, would you?" Peter was sure as hell that it was Slugart who was behind the secret messages being delivered.

"A fine angel, Hector. He keeps serving the traditional food even when those God-hating humans try to drive him out of business."

"Calm down there, bredrin. I agree. Some of those humans are nobs but most are alright. God-hating is taking it too far."

"Is it? Ask them."

They were talking openly at the gate, ignoring the noise coming from hundreds of souls waiting impatiently to enter the Kingdom.

"Oi, listen up," shouted one of the crowd. "I've been here for hours and when I finally get to the front you call us nobs. How dare you? I demand to see the manager!"

"Who?" asked Peter absentmindedly, "You mean God?"

"Yes. Whichever one it is that owns this place."

"Which one did you believe in?" asked Slugart, with a tone of contempt in his voice.

"None. Never believed in any till I got here. Not that it's any of your business."

"That's where you're wrong, fam." Peter hated the disrespect. "I'm Saint Peter, and if you don't believe in our God, you'll be sent to Hell." That'll get him sweating, Peter thought.

"No, I won't. I just saw you let in five people who all believed in different gods, and one was a border line Devil worshipper."

"I am Saint fecking Peter, and you will beg to be let in." Peter, when roused, could be an intimidating figure but for once it had no effect.

"Just let me in, Pete." And the arrogant man walked calmly around the saint and jumped over the gates.

Peter felt his energy drain away. That was it. Even the humans had stopped respecting him. At least, before giving them the green light to enter, he could tease and play with them. But this! This was humiliating. Unlatching the gate (which fell off in his hands) he walked back to his house without saying goodbye to a smiling Slugart.

The humans all waited, not sure what to do. Then one brave (or perhaps stupid) woman walked very slowly into Heaven as though, at any moment, the ground would swallow her up. The human herd followed swiftly behind.

Slugart followed the dejected saint and caught up with him at his front door.

"Peter, I can fix this. Let us meet tomorrow for dinner. I have a proposal to help you regain your respect."

"Yeah, sure whatever." And Peter closed the door and went straight to bed.

Pleased with the events he had witnessed, Slugart headed home. He was determined to dine alone with Peter. It was the only way to convince him that the authority of 'Saint Peter' could be restored. And then there was the other concern that occupied his mind. He had resisted acting because the risks were high. If he moved too soon, he could potentially lose everything.

Twenty-Six

The dark of night had drawn in quickly. In an ancient wood, you may have seen the moon shining and heard owls hooting but outside all that could be heard was the sound of the 'not-so-lesser-spotted' humans enjoying a late BBQ by the light of a garden lamp.

Simon and the Devil had retired to their hotel having visited the art gallery, followed by an afternoon of sightseeing. Spread-eagled in bed and exhausted, the Devil slept soundly.

The downside of being a butler is that you can't relax until your master is asleep, and even then, there are tasks to complete. Simon despised butlers who took the opportunity, whenever they met, to complain about their employers. But this evening even he had a niggling moan forming in his mind. He could not understand why he had to carry both suitcases and the rucksack around all day when they had a secure hotel room in which to leave them. Dismissing the thought from his consciousness – as the Devil is aware of all, even when sleeping – he dressed for bed and fell into a deep sleep.

He awoke the next morning, not to the sound of a cockerel crowing but to the Devil calling. Simon made himself presentable and went to investigate.

"Simon, today we shall attend this," the Devil proclaimed as he handed Simon a leaflet, pointing to the key headline: '**Anger Issues? Learn to control them the easy way**', it shouted in bold, angry type.

"Very good, sir. Would you like to wear casual or smart today?"

"You understand though, Simon, I can control my anger?"

"Yes, sir. Would it be casual..."

"It is just to learn new techniques that will inspire the demons to focus their anger."

"Of course, sir casual or..."

"My emotions are completely under control. But the demons need this."

"I completely agree, sir. But if you could just let me know if you want to wear smart..."

"Smart! I want to wear smart! Just shut up about it!" roared the Devil, venom flying from his mouth.

Not flinching or showing any sign of shock, Simon silently retreated to find suitable smart clothes for the day.

Once they were both ready, Simon led the way from their hotel room carrying the suitcases and rucksack. The Devil followed, looking dapper in his Italian suit and shiny shoes. Suddenly he stopped, touched his head and rushed back to his room. He had remembered the great disguise. The moustache was stuck permanently in place, but he'd forgotten the cap. Simon followed the Devil at a leisurely pace and found him in front of the mirror adjusting his headwear. Again, Simon faced a dilemma. How to raise a subject that had possible repercussions of death (for the second time) if the Devil took it the wrong way. He considered a variety of tactful approaches to raise the issue of mismatched styles, but every angle he considered presented the same problem. Even if he told the Devil, there was nothing that could be done now. The agenda for the day was too tight to allow returning for a change of clothes. He had to wear the disguise.

"Simon, what is the first activity today?"

"The fairground, sir." The planned seminar was an evening event.

"Ah yes, the fairground. A place where people scream in fear and happiness at the same time. A bit like my kingdom then."

Raising an inquisitive eyebrow, Simon asked: "Including the happiness, sir?"

"Ok, Simon. Without the happiness."

As they walked along the hotel corridor, two Spanish gentlemen gave a less than energetic hello in response to the Devil's booming 'morning' as he passed by. He always tried to be polite.

"Mucho gusto," the larger Spaniard said to the smaller one.

"Enough of that, Guy. We don't need to stay in character when the suspects are not around."

"Sorry, Roger. I heard actors stay in character all day to make the performance more believable."

"And when I said to find us a Spanish disguise, I didn't mean sombreros and blow-up donkeys," Roger huffed.

"You're certain there's nothing in the law-book we can nick them on? I could catch up and arrest them now. Did you notice his head before he put his cap on?"

"Patience, Guy. This will, I guarantee, be the crime of the millennium. I can smell it."

The 'law-book' they were referring to, detailed all crimes that the Heaven Police Force (which consisted of Guy and Roger) decided should be outlawed. They had taken it upon themselves to document these laws. Well, mainly Roger had – Guy was more interested in the arresting rather than the rules. However, they had never actually got as far as charging anyone to test if the laws were legally recognised in Heaven. If they had thought further, they would also worry about the absence of courts required to obtain a conviction. Watching Simon and the Devil wander off, they wistfully imagined themselves as heroes.

"Simon, please explain how the ground in this place is fair? Is this a human thing again?"

Simon gave this some thought. "I do not believe I know, sir. I have heard the word countless times in my life yet never questioned the meaning."

"Typical human."

"Indeed, sir."

"Now in the travel guide it insists we should ride the roller coaster, drive around in the bumper cars, throw balls at a coconut, eat candy floss and enjoy the thrill of the big wheel. These are the things I wish to do. I shall leave it up to you to choose the order."

"Yes, sir," Simon replied, already formulating answers to the inevitable questions that he knew would arise.

And just within earshot, the two 'Spaniards' watched as the 'bulls' they were destined to fight left for the fairground 'ring'.

Twenty-Seven

The wooden table had felt his anger. Stab marks ruined its once glossy finish. And then there was the wall. A poor innocent structure, always doing its job, occasionally getting in someone's way – but that's what the door was for (and we will come to the door in a minute). Why, the wall wondered, did it now have cracked plaster and a knife protruding from its surface? The door felt little sympathy for its comrade's injuries and thought these minor as it lay on the floor, helpless. These three objects had suffered the effect of Cecil's mounting frustration.

Cecil assumed all would be over by now, but he was still sitting in that grey, monotonous room, waiting (and waiting some more) for news. No one had dared to mention that the plan required patience – probably nobody had been brave enough. And then the letter had arrived. Cecil instantly assumed this was 'it', details about the package, bringing the waiting to an end. Hands shaking, he opened the letter and read. This was not the 'it' he had expected. The letter merely explained that for now Cecil should lay low. He had already waited enough!

The table had felt the pain first. Sitting in its accompanying chair, Cecil had tried to relax by whittling away at a piece of wood, but the stick still looked like a piece of wood and not the intended sculpture of the Leader he had gone for. Frustrated, angry and bored, he spread his fingers flat on the table and proceeded to stab in-between each digit, slowly increasing the speed of the game. Outside a dog barked, stealing his attention for a fraction too long. "Arghhh," he screamed as the knife stabbed his finger. In frustration, he dug the knife into the table – it was only fair that something else should share his pain. But still he failed to calm himself. Next, he aimed his knife at the wall, which expertly deflected it towards Cecil, once more piercing his hand. With increasing rage, he impaled the blade deep into the wall. In that moment, the knife performed as only a good stress ball could, by relaxing him slightly. Feeling his focus return, he decided to check outside for any sign of the package. This required passing through the soon-to-be damaged door. Turning the handle, the door failed to open. It would not make that mistake again – and probably couldn't as it now lay broken on the floor.

Not knowing what the package contained, where it would be or what to do with it once it arrived, rattled his cage. Cecil had his suspicions, but for now, he decided to inspect the perimeter of the building. The trees looked on worriedly as he wandered past. All this stress would be worth it eventually, he thought, when the Leader recognised his efforts.

Twenty-Eight

"Are you sure?" quizzed the Devil.

"Quite sure, sir."

"But they are cars?" The Devil wanted to be certain.

"I am not certain, that if they were scrutinised, they could technically be classed as cars, sir."

A horn sounded loudly, and they were both jerked backwards by the acceleration of the car (that was not actually a car).

"If they call them bumper cars, then I am bloody well going to bump them!"

"If you insist, sir." Simon had tried to explain the 'no bumping rules' on the badly named 'bumper cars' ride. To be fair, the Devil did obey the rules for the first few laps, even driving in the correct clockwise direction. It was never going to last.

"This is boring, Simon. No one tells me what to do!"

"Very good, sir." Simon reluctantly agreed.

The Devil scanned the circuit looking for a victim. He drove a purple car with a snake motif painted around the sides. Keeping his head tucked close to the steering wheel to create an aerodynamic profile, he identified a target. A blue car, sporting a tiger along its length, zoomed past, almost hitting them. That would be their target the Devil decided. He stalked the tiger for two laps, obeying the clockwise rule, but halfway round the next lap the Devil turned sharply, forcing Simon's body against his. A warning grunt informed him not to do that again. Heading along the straight, they took a sharp left near the barrier, bringing them head-to-head with the tiger. The occupant of the tiger car was, at that moment, thinking how he remembered bumper cars being a lot more fun on Earth, when he saw the snake car heading for a direct head on collision. That reminded him why – bumping! Lowering himself into position, he peered over the top of the steering wheel and prepared for impact. Bang went the cars as they collided.

"Oi! no bumping. That's a warning!" the woman in charge shouted over the noise of sparking electrics and music.

Some of the seven remaining cars, still driving clockwise, saw the collision and others heard the woman's plea. Bumping! they all thought excitedly. Within thirty seconds there was chaos, cars rotating any way they pleased, bumping galore and cries of excitement.

This was more like it, thought the Devil. "Simon, I told you it was called bumper cars for a reason, didn't I."

"Yes, sir." Simon gripped the car in fear of his soul. The Devil was getting more aggressive by the second, bumping and bashing everyone. But there was one car, the tiger, that always seemed to dodge the Devil's aim, yet it never missed hitting the Devil.

"Why does that car always evade my attacks?" It was a concept unknown to the Devil.

"He appears, sir, to be rather good at this game."

"Are you suggesting, Simon, that he is better than me?" A look, that lasted rather too long for comfort, was aimed at Simon. "I could bump this idiot anytime I want. Hold on tight, Simon!"

They had come to a stop at the far end of the track. The tiger saw the snake. The tiger stopped. Eyes met, locked in a challenge. Two men (well one man and the Devil) revved their electric engines. Sparks flew from the roof. Like two great rhinos they charged each other, neither swaying from their line. A head on collision was certain. This was reckless behaviour. They knew it; the operator knew it and issued one last warning before losing her voice. Speeds reached three maybe four mph. Collision in five, four, three, two, one.

It has been said before – but worth a reminder – that magic doesn't actually exist but occasionally things happen in Heaven that, if studied closely, could potentially be deemed as magic. But since it has been categorically stated that there is no magic, other explanations are required. The cars collided. Everyone looked on in astonishment. In one car sat Simon (who wished he wasn't) and the grinning Devil. This car was behaving normally and most definitely, still attached to the ground. The other car, however, was doing something a tiger could never do – flying. It flew backwards before landing, quite elegantly – for a bumper car – in a tree.

All the remaining drivers, in a sudden unspoken joint decision, resumed their clockwise circuit, carefully avoiding each other.

"Sir, it would perhaps be a good idea not to use your powers in front of others, while we are in disguise. It could attract questions we would struggle to answer."

"Yes, Simon," the Devil sulked. "It was fun, though. All that bumping on the bumper cars, which you aren't allowed to bump." He looked at Simon in a manner suggesting he was looking for praise.

"Yes, sir. And you showed them who was boss." The Devil pulled an expression of happiness. Not a smile, for when the Devil smiles it is triggered by evil, not happiness.

The ride finished and everyone departed, keeping a good distance away from the Devil and Simon. Only the operator made eye contact and gave the Devil a look that made even him wince.

"Where next, Simon?"

Simon surveyed the map of the theme park and looked for the closest attraction on their 'to do' list. The large park boasted all the classic rides: a pirate ship (which legend claimed contained wood from Noah's ark and to which Noah would respond "you think I could fit eighteen million animals in that?"), a log flume, roller coasters of varying sizes, carousels and much, much more.

'Heaven's Tallest Roller Coaster', the Devil had noticed the sign, while Simon was still looking at the map. "Never mind Simon, we shall try this."

The blood rushed from Simon's face. He'd planned to avoid this one. Not only was he terrified of heights but more so of roller coasters.

"But, sir, it is not on today's itinerary. It could have serious detrimental effects on the timing."

"I said, Simon, we are going on this one."

"But sir...." The ever-calm voice of Simon had a quiver and a hint of pleading.

"You wouldn't be trying to avoid this ride, eh Simon?"

"No, sir," he said, while almost looking at the ground.

"You wouldn't be scared, Simon?" Now the Devil started to enjoy himself. Never had he found a weakness in his butler before, and that irritated him. "Not scared like those small children over there?"

Straightening up, Simon regained his butler-toned voice. "Me, sir? Of course not."

"Good. Then we shall sit in the front. I read that roller coasters are more fun at the front, and to increase the thrill, we should raise our hands in the air and not hold on."

"Excellent idea, sir," said Simon, spoken with the enthusiasm of a teenager getting out of bed.

"Good man." And the Devil smacked Simon on his rump to guide him towards the entrance for this popular ride.

A good forty minutes later and they were approaching the front. Not one to hold back when having fun, the Devil had devised over fifty ways the roller coaster could end in tragedy. Each one made Simon's stomach churn. Not an ideal start – feeling sick before boarding. "Sir, I really must visit the men's room. I will meet you at the exit of the ride."

Placing his large, red hand on Simon's shoulder to deter any thoughts of escape, he issued his response: "If you have to, then piss in this bottle. You are going on this ride with me. Understood?"

"Yes, sir."

Children often experience peer pressure, cajoling them to do things they would otherwise avoid. Such pressure might help overcome a fear, while in other cases it might have a negative influence leading eventually along a path towards addiction and early death. Today, Simon recalled a similar scene from his youth, queueing with friends for his first roller coaster ride. It took half the waiting time to realise he was terrified and the remainder deciding whether to go on or be called a wimp by his mates. Looking scared in front of the Devil was no longer an issue, he just wanted to avoid the ride. But that option had been unilaterally withdrawn.

Loud, rattling wheels zoomed past accompanied by excited screams, the noise failing to improve Simon's current mood. They were nearing their turn, and he could see and hear the full horrors awaiting him. The carriages stopped, and the adrenaline-pumped thrill seekers departed. This was it. Simon had felt no fear when he first arrived in Hell, yet now he experienced the horror most sinners suffer when they enter the land of doom.

As they approached the front, the Devil pulled Simon back by his collar. "Wait here, Simon."

For a brief moment Simon felt he had been granted a reprieve. Perhaps the Devil had changed his mind, and they would escape this terrifying monster. But no! "We will wait for the next one so we can sit at the very front," the devil stated, dispelling all hope.

"Of course, sir." His bubble of optimism had been inflated and popped. No chance now, this was it, Simon thought. I'm going to die in Heaven.

Another ride screeched to a halt, and this time they boarded. Simon sat anxiously, praying for the nightmare to be over. Three times Simon asked the assistant to check he was securely fastened before the ride finally started. Up and up it went, slowly clinking and clanking all the way to the top. From the highest point the view was astonishing, but Simon's view was black, dark black with images of his impending death. He scrunched his eyes so tightly shut, they hurt.

In that instant his belly had a brief chat with his brain regarding the type of food that might be coming its way, while the ride shot downwards like a rocket in reverse. Down it went breaking speed barriers and ignoring any notion of terminal velocity. Then up and down again, looping several times causing immense g-forces on the riders before finally, with a screech of the brakes, it was over.

Everyone departed and the Devil was happy. He had enjoyed the roller coaster. "Come on, Simon, get on out."

With his eyes still closed Simon replied. "I'm sorry, sir but I do not think I can. "

"What do you mean? Come on, we have much to do."

"I'm sorry, sir, but my legs appear to have frozen." Indeed, they had. Fear had left him legless.

Impatiently, the Devil hoisted Simon out of the carriage and onto his back in an impromptu fireman's lift.

"Thank you, sir."

Upside down, Simon caught a glimpse of two familiar Spanish looking gentleman running from the ride, hands clasped over their mouths.

Twenty-Nine

Time declined to budge. It refused to go any faster for Slugart, who felt on edge about his dinner date with Saint Peter. The plan hinged on Peter agreeing to help, and Slugart knew the saint would not co-operate without some delicate persuasion.

Then there was the parcel. Another pressing issue on Slugart's mind. He had sent the details to Cecil, outlining where and when the parcel was to be delivered and had asked for an update on progress. With none yet received, he grew increasingly frustrated.

Cecil had indeed received the message. It had taken an unfortunate amount of time to understand its content due to the complex code devised to deliver it. Owing to various misunderstandings of owl hoots, crow cries, and pigeon calls, the message was eventually delivered in person without any code. Both the messenger and Cecil agreed that the lack of encryption should be brushed under the carpet and not mentioned in the next meeting.

The message had been direct: a place, a time and what to do. It even suppressed Cecil's anger. That was until an owl hooted, leading to half an hour trying to decipher a code that was in fact not a code, since there was no code to decipher. If Slugart had happened to see Cecil's bumbling efforts, he would almost certainly have regretted his choice.

Trying to relax in his leather recliner, Slugart's brain whizzed from one worry to the next. The parcel, Cecil, Saint Peter and of course, the final key. This last worry fought for his attention, but Slugart's brain tried hard to ignore it, convinced that even thinking about it could wreck his plans. Who, though, would know what it meant? There was no one trying to stop him as far as he knew. For he was doing good he thought, returning things back to how they once were. However much he tried to convince himself that no threat existed, he always failed to fully relax. And soon it would be actions not thoughts that were required. He knew the time was approaching to collect it but what if it was not there? What if it did not contain the details he had been promised?

A reliable indicator that a person has lost all hope and self-belief is when they appear publicly, dressed in their pyjamas and dressing gown. Today, the newly deceased souls stood in a long line at Heaven's gates, trying to figure out if the robes Peter wore were ceremonial or, indeed, his nightwear. Unlatching the gate – that again toppled onto the ground – Peter paid little attention as the humans streamed through but instead mused about Slugart. Maybe he should listen to Slugart's suggestions over dinner. He hadn't actually agreed to meet, yet he sort of knew they would.

Thirty

His head vibrated as though a ringing ball was bouncing around inside his skull; blurred vision and the loss of feeling in the legs added to his woes. A cocktail of tea, made with two tea bags and sugar, helped Simon back from the abyss. "Sir, if we could return to the schedule. We need to ensure there is time for everything, so let us locate the log flume."

Still enjoying Simon's suffering, the Devil considered making him ride the roller coaster again – but even Satan was occasionally sympathetic.

"Which way, Simon?"

"I would hazard a guess it will be in the direction of the rather wet looking people over there."

And sure enough, after passing groups with varying degrees of dampness, they found the log flume. 'Sit in the logs from the Garden of Eden,' it claimed. 'Ride on the water from the Red Sea'. Both were ridiculous claims and blatant lies but who would sue a fairground operator in Heaven?

Unlike the roller coaster, the drops were quite tame and the speed sensible as far as Simon was concerned.

"Everyone does seem a tad wet." The Devil had his doubts. Having dressed smartly, he was not in favour of ruining his suit.

"Yes, sir. They would be the people who sat in the front. Everyone behind is protected and will receive only a few splashes of water."

They were nearing the front, and Simon was looking forward to this. Being one of his favourite attractions as a youth, he was overjoyed to be able to ride one again.

"Yes, well that seems logical. You shall sit in the front to protect me," the Devil commanded

"Of course, sir."

It was their turn. A bored teenager, attempting to manage the queue whilst listening to music on his headphones, summoned up the energy to rise from his seat and – as if he were doing them a favour – unclipped the rope and let the Devil and Simon board their Adam and Eve log.

Off they went, ascending the flume with Simon assuming the defensive position at the front while his brave general hid behind. At the top, the ride meandered around like most log flumes, with only occasional small descents creating minor sprays of water, gradually building suspense before the inevitable fall towards the big splash.

"This is boring, Simon."

"I rather enjoy it, sir. There will be one fast drop at the end where, regretfully I will be drenched."

"Oh yes, I forgot about that." Thinking of Simon, drenched, compensated for the boring ride.

"Here it comes, sir." And sure enough, the angle of the log took on a steep downwards trajectory before plummeting them down the final drop. The log crashed into the water causing a deafening roar as a mini tidal wave arched over the ride, seeking out riders to soak. Waves jumped over the sides in a pincer movement of water. Fantastic fun, thought Simon, smiling.

"Simon!" bellowed the Devil. The air from the Devil's mouth rushed out at such speed it would have instantly dried Simon. That is, if he had been wet. "Simon!" Satan roared again.

"Yes, sir?" Simon replied meekly.

"I'm soaked! You said I'd remain dry, you lying son of a demon!"

Simon felt the insult to his mother was unfair but decided to not bring this up. "Are you sure, sir?"

Not the best question to ask the most evil creature ever to live. The Devil sat raging, two levels over the extreme rage threshold and soaked to the skin. "I'm half sea. I've got more water on me than a flood in flood season. Fish could happily swim on me.

And you said the person at the front would get wet. You're as dry as that desert I got stuck in with Jesus."

Checking himself and feeling rather pleased, Simon had to admit he was rather dry.

"Look at my suit. My brand new Italian tailored suit. And worse – look at my shoes. Ruined. Ruined!"

Simon had made the mistake that many had made before. Yes, if you apply basic physics, the person at the front will take the greatest impact. But these laws cannot be applied to log flumes. Their rules are simple: whoever tries to stay the driest, ends up the wettest. Einstein formalised this in his theory of relative positions, but it had been long forgotten following his less useful publications on general relativity.

They reached the end of their ride. The assistant started helping the two out but backed away once she saw the drenched Devil, steaming in all his anger. With water pouring from his suit, he stepped clear of the ride. Without giving Simon a chance to follow, he turned and hoisted the log and Simon into the air. "I'm going to make you wet."

"Sir." Simon looked anxious.

"I'm going to throw you and this stupid log into the dirtiest, deepest water I can find."

"Sir, you must not attract attention."

"You dared to intentionally lie to me, ruining my suit."

"Sir, I assure you, it was a mistake." Simon stayed seated and calm. "We must, however, remain incognito."

"After I throw you, I'll destroy the whole ride. Just watch me!"

"An excellent idea, sir, but unfortunately, with the schedule we are trying to maintain, you would miss your anger management seminar, which of course you have no need for. You control your anger perfectly well already."

"Be quiet!" It took the Devil a second or two to register Simon's comment. "Anger management? Yes, I certainly don't require that. I hardly ever get angry." He fought to calm himself.

"Excellent, sir. Now if you could just put me down. We should, perhaps, quickly move on as we are getting quite a few suspicious looks."

Sure enough, anyone within earshot was staring at them.

The Devil looked and felt the glare of too many eyes studying his disguise. "Er, yes. Perhaps you are right." And carefully he replaced the log, helped Simon out and hurried away from the scene.

Thirty-One

The good old days. Does this have any meaning in Heaven? All time should be 'good' and, in a place with no beginning or end, can anything really be 'old'?

Hector failed to consider the strength of this logic as he thought about the good old days. It was lunchtime, and the queue for soup – in times gone past – would have stretched beyond the horizon. It should be mentioned that Hector's memory had a tendency to exaggerate, but it was a long queue, to be fair.

Daydreaming while stirring the soup, he recalled times before the humans arrived. Angels enjoyed simple pleasures then. Or at least that is what the Leader kept reminding them, but Hector seemed to remember angels arguing a lot and generally grumbling about God. According to the Leader, everything changed with the influx of the humans. Happiness turned to discontent when they imposed their modern ways, he told them. Hector, however, remembered making new friends and learning about the interesting new ideas they introduced. But it was true, they had ruined his business.

Lost in a world of thoughts, he straightened up slightly, leaving him stirring thin air. His waiting customer watched on. "Cough, cough," she mouthed quietly to attract his attention.

Startled, he dropped his spoon onto the floor. "I'm sorry, I was miles away. Let me fetch your lunch." The angel was a regular customer who knew a message would be hidden in her soup. "Here you go. Enjoy your day," he said as he passed her the bowl. He tended not to talk for too long with the regulars in case it attracted attention.

"Thank you," the customer said hesitantly, aware that her the soup had been served using the spoon that moments earlier had dropped to the floor. She didn't complain. She wasn't going to eat the soup anyway; it was always thrown in the bin. Hector's stall only provided cover to receive her secret message, and today she fancied a Greek kebab to eat while reading the information.

As the angel left, Hector returned to his thoughts. In the last meeting the Leader had promised great news, but for some reason, Hector's initial excitement had waned. He tapped his right pocket to check the book was still there and continued to stir his soup.

Thirty-Two

A soggy Devil put the flume experience behind him and tucked into his cheese and tomato sandwich. Simon had packed their lunch earlier and now poured piping hot tea into a fine china cup from a pot he had conjured from somewhere.

"Ruined," the Devil mumbled, through his mouth full of sandwich.

"Once home, sir, I will ensure the suit and shoes are returned to their former pristine state. In this heat the suit will soon dry, and we can enjoy the remaining day's activities."

The day was hot. (Surprisingly, it is hot in most parts of Heaven. Of course, there are certain zones that need to be kept colder for animals such as polar bears and snow foxes. Not penguins though. They hate the cold. No longer required to huddle behind another penguin's backside is a luxury that penguins only experience in Heaven's hot afterlife.) The Devil, however, was not prepared to wait for his suit to dry slowly. Instead, he merely let his blood boil, heating the suit from the inside. Steam escaped from him like that from a boiling kettle, ensuring his clothes were dried in minutes.

"We have one more short activity left to do, sir."

"Really." The Devil raised his eyes to give Simon a penetrating look. "Will it involve water?"

"Er yes, but we will not touch any, sir."

"You promise, Simon? I don't want anything unfortunate to happen to you if we do." He gave Simon a heart sinking smile.

"I am confident, sir, you will not get wet."

"I trust you, Simon. For now." This of course was not a confirmation of trust, more a threat of pain and suffering. "What is this activity then?"

"A selection of games that are found at all good amusement parks, sir. There is coconut throwing."

"Sounds pointless."

"Fishing for a duck."

"You mean fish, Simon, not duck."

Deciding to ignore the comment, Simon continued, "and horse racing."

"Ah, that sounds more fun. Saddling a great steed and racing …"

"No, sir, not real horses. We will try to roll small balls into holes which cause a wooden horse to move forward. There are several horses, and we will race to see whose finishes first."

"Ah, that sounds crap. But I'm dry now, so let's get on with it." His suit was indeed dry but badly stained from the water damage and looking far from suave.

Two gentlemen, both also soaked, followed at a distance.

"We've got enough to charge them with now. That business on the dodgems alone could send them down."

"No, Guy. Not yet. Have you not noticed something odd about the larger one? And while we are on the subject, why would two, wheel-clamping inspectors be at the theme park? I would add impersonating a clamping official to our final list of charges, but it's not mentioned in the law book."

"Bloody law book ruins everything," Guy mumbled under his breath.

"Sorry?" Roger asked, who was rather overprotective towards the book.

"Nothing. Yes, I've noticed strange things. Like his extreme strength, steam rising from his body, his size and how badly sunburnt he is."

"Sunburnt?" enquired Roger.

Guy gave him a stare saying *are you blind?* "Yes, he is more sunburnt than I've ever seen anyone. Amazing considering the lack of a sun in Heaven."

"Yes," replied Roger, deep in thought, "he is rather red. How strange." Roger's career may have progressed further back on Earth if he had developed his observational skills. "Hummm, interesting, red you say..."

Thirty-Three

Like two cowboys in a Western movie, the Devil and his sidekick strolled up to their horses, ready for the game. They mounted their steeds – or more precisely, their stools.

The Devil's anger grew (not that he needed anger management) as Simon struggled to 'mount'. In Simon's defence, he did have two suitcases and a rucksack to unload first. Losing his struggle with the straps, he gave up and left the bag on his back and mounted the 'steed' in a manner comparable to a drunken octopus climbing onto an oiled fishmonger's slab.

"Come up, come up. In it to win it," the fairground stall holder called, as he fired out his usual patter. "Roll the ball, don't let your horse fall."

In an uncharacteristically subtle way, the Devil whispered to Simon, "What is this idiot on about?"

"It's just how they speak at the fairground, sir. They are born into this life and learn the lingo from a young age."

"Well, I wish he'd hurry up. One thing, Simon, just so that you are clear, how do we play this game?" The Devil hated not knowing something and always tried his best to appear knowledgeable.

"See the holes in front of you, sir? Each has a number, and you aim to throw the ball into the ones with the highest numbers. The greater the number, the further your horse moves."

"Ridiculous game. I'm blaming you, Simon, for this." But secretly he had two balls already aimed and was eager to start. You cannot be the Devil without a competitive streak within.

"Ladies and gentlemen, the horses are under starters orders. Three, two, one, go!"

The Devil's hands became a blur of speed, rolling the balls as quickly as they came back. But his horse did not move. "Damn this game. Simon why is my horse not running? I've been given a three-legged worm! He's slower than Sad Ken."

"Although I'm sure you already know, sir, perhaps slowing down and aiming carefully would prove more fruitful than rapid fire."

"Of course, I know that, Simon. I was just testing out a new technique." Taking more time and aiming carefully, he began hitting high number after high number. His horse sprung forward as each ball fell into his targeted hole, and despite the hopeless start, his horse started catching the competitors.

Simon turned his attention to the race and noticed he was in the lead with the Devil still last. Simon was winning. Excitement shot through him. He was winning and winning always feels good. His throwing, or rather rolling, technique was not as precise as his master's, but he was building a steady, unassailable lead. Chancing another glance at his rivals revealed a horse flying through the field into third place. The competitor was gaining. Panic gripped him, and beads of sweat appeared on his brow. He wanted to win! All he needed was one more high score, and his horse would cross the finish line in first place, but his hands decided not to play ball. Communication between hand and brain was lost, and he froze, unable to roll. Angry that it would be deprived of the adrenaline shot from winning, the brain fired an electric pulse to the hands telling them, in no uncertain terms, to roll the last bloody ball.

The Devil and Simon were neck and neck. Unlike Simon, he knew who he was racing against. With one hand rolling his ball for victory, the Devil used his other to knock Simon's throwing arm as it went to aim. The Devil's ball headed straight for its target. Simon's bounced around aimlessly, hitting both sides as it went. The Devil's hit the hole, but with too much speed, and popped out like a golf ball following an over enthusiastic putt on the last green. It rolled past, hit the back wall and rebounded towards the Devil's despairing hand.

With his ball bouncing around, Simon watched, transfixed, waiting to see where it would land. It hit the number one and number three holes but bounced over before it rolled slowly towards the number five. A five would win the race. Time stopped as the ball circled the rim, but then sirens sounded and lights flashed. Simon flung his arms in the air to celebrate and tried to eject a celebratory cry. But it came out as, "oh crrrrap". His arms shot too far back. The extra weight of his rucksack threw him off balance, leaving him with feet in the air, reminiscent of an upturned turtle. Delighted by this misjudged celebration, the Devil decided to ignore the fact that Simon had beaten him. "My dear Simon, don't you know it's just a game?" And he once more effortlessly hoisted Simon back to his feet, with just one hand.

Simon's jubilation, cut short by the turtle episode, returned his brain to butler mode. "Thank you, sir. Apologies for getting over excited. I believe it was due to recalling similar occasions in my youth."

Without looking or saying anything, the Devil made it perfectly clear that his 'youth' had better never try to beat him in anything ever again.

"Of course, sir," Simon responded, acknowledging the unspoken message.

His prize for winning the race was twenty tokens, which they saved towards a potential souvenir gift.

Nearby, Guy and Roger looked on.

"That sunburnt guy's strength is unreal. Did you see him lift that fella up again?"

"Let's cuff him?"

"No. Be patient."

Smashed into smithereens by the Devil, the coconuts wished they had been overlooked by Simon's agenda. Years spent casting humans into the sea of fire had prepared the Devil well for this game. More tokens were added to their collection.

Have you ever seen anyone with such a powerful throw?" asked Roger.

"I've seen angels in the All-Heaven Baseball League throw hard but never like that. Look, the guy behind the coconut shy is petrified. His stand is ruined. Arrest him! Destruction of coconuts."

Without bothering to consult the trusty book of Heaven's laws, Roger replied, "You can't arrest someone for breaking coconuts when it's the aim of the game."

Sheepishly, Guy replied, "I suppose."

"But we are building a case. This surveillance mission is going as planned."

The last item on the agenda was 'hook a duck' and there was nothing special about Heaven's version. Just the standard setup. A pool full of plastic ducks swimming around in a circle, waiting to be hooked using a stick with, unsurprisingly, a hook at the end.

The Devil, after a quick overview, now knew for certain that humans were idiots. He grabbed the stick and caught his first duck without effort.

The duck keeper inspected the duck's bottom. "That's five hundred points," he called.

Another duck was caught.

"Seven hundred points."

Simon was frantically adding the scores. "Wait, sir, wait!"

"What now, Simon. Let me hook this duck and we'll be out of this place."

"But sir. We, I mean you, only require four hundred more points, and you can choose any of the cuddly toys over there."

"Simon, why would I want a stuffed toy?" Secretly of course he did. He'd seen people carrying large toys around all day and others regarding them in admiration. It must be a trophy of some sort, he concluded. One that commanded respect.

"I'm feeling tired, Simon. Hold this stick, while I yawn. And keep an eye on the ducks."

"Yes, sir," Simon smiled. Having worked with enough evil people, he recognised the signs of impending foul play.

The Devil yawned, propelling a wave of energy from his mouth. The ducks felt the full force and momentarily capsized, revealing their numbered bottoms to all, before quickly regaining their swimming position.

"Fishing rod, Simon," he clicked his red, dry fingers. "Which duck, Simon?"

Simon directed him to the duck with sufficient points and the duck keeper confirmed: "four hundred points but..." he started to protest at the blatant example of cheating but paused. You tend to stop when eyes of black fire glare menacingly at you.

"Right, yes, umm. Which animal would you fine gentlemen like?"

"The biggest one of course." What a ridiculous question, thought the Devil.

"Are you certain, geez, that you want the biggest?" the duck keeper queried, with a directional movement of his body towards the largest prize.

"Yes, the biggest one, just hurry up before I hook you!"

If the duck keeper had known the Devil was due to attend an anger management seminar in a few hours, he would have said it was about time.

"Sir, are you quite sure? Not perhaps the slightly smaller one there? The one that looks ferocious." Simon also had doubts about the largest toy.

"I'm going to say this once more. Give me that big one!"

Watching on at a distance, Guy and Roger were confused. "I think you were wrong, Guy. It can't be him."

"Maybe. Maybe. Or perhaps it is a cunning ploy to disguise himself."

"Yes, but surely he wouldn't choose that!"

They watched as Simon and the Devil exited the park. Satan holding, or even perhaps cuddling, the pinkest, cutest, cuddliest, tutu-wearing bear you ever did see.

Thirty-Four

Infinitesimally small quarks roam in, what appears to them, a cavernous, empty space of nothingness, meandering for years in search of others, unaware of their complex role as the building blocks of life. Electrons are much larger and humongous compared to a quark. Both patrol the same microscopic area of space. These electrons are locked in orbit, spinning around in a never-ending circle while constantly searching for energy to fire them into a higher orbit. Unable to see anything except colliding electrons, they lack understanding of their role beyond random movements in the darkness. Protons and neutrons share similar worlds, though protons did devise a basic religious concept – something about fission and big bangs. The atoms they inhabit have no brain or scientific understanding of this conglomerate of small particles. They would label you an outright liar if you claimed that they could create complex forms of life when combined in the right sequence. One example, composed of billions of atoms, built machines capable of toasting four slices of toast simultaneously.

Humans are know-it-alls. Scientists being the worst, always theorising, asserting definitive answers and, years later, proving them incorrect. Now imagine if humans and dogs, whales, bats, seas, trees, stars, planets and more, behaved like electrons, protons or neutrons and formed the equivalent of an atom on an infinite scale which, when combined with others, generated a life form of universal size. That of course is ridiculous and the ant, being one of the most intelligent of God's creations, would have told you so. One such ant wandered over the rock wedged under Peter's gate, leaving the entrance open to all-comers. Heaven means freedom to ants; they are released from their life of slavery. Heaven to a queen ant is non-existent as they will all burn in Hell.

Peter had left the gate open in an act of 'can't be arsedness'. His energy was ebbing away, and he resigned himself to the fact that humans could enter with or without him. Slugart had made it quite clear that he, Peter, was powerless to control their migration. Peter knew Slugart would make it even clearer during their meal together that evening. Slugart seemed annoyed about the lack of authority Peter exerted over the humans. He agreed, but why was Slugart annoyed? Maybe tonight he would shed some light on it.

In perhaps one last act of defiance, Peter pinned a note to the gate reading, 'Welcome to Hell'. A good hour or so passed before the bravest ventured through.

From his current horizontal position on the sofa, he viewed the mountain of dirty dishes piled up in his sink and similar scenes of chaos throughout the rest of his bachelor pad. Oh crap, I must get this place sorted, he thought to himself. The days of holding dinner parties with angels ended centuries ago, and these days no one visited his home. Peter's attitude to housework had become lax. 'What's unseen, doesn't need tidying', was his mantra. Searching through the cupboards, he gathered a selection of cleaning products, lined them up on the dust covered table and went outside.

"Free VIP tickets into Heaven for the first five lucky people," he shouted, hands cupped either side of his mouth to amplify his voice.

People came running, some attracted to the word 'free' and others to 'VIP'. Spoken together these words guaranteed a scrum of eager volunteers.

"You five were first so step this way. All you have to do is clean this house."

Well, you can't expect a saint to do it, can you?

Thirty-Five

They had arrived for the anger management seminar. There had been no time to change as they were running late. The Devil's suit – water stained and smelling of damp – gave the impression he was sleeping rough. It was far removed from the suave Italian outfit he had chosen to wear, and even his once shiny shoes still squelched. Simon was bored of being reminded that the seminar was, of course, not for the Devil himself, but for the demons. He was more than pretty sure it was for his master.

The Devil liked to think of himself as a modern-day leader. He recognised that angry bosses of old were deemed dinosaurs in the current business world, and he craved to be considered a progressive. He held away days, played golf, used Power Point and spoke the latest business lingo – waterfall project management, agile practices, lean distribution – he had tried them all. But in the end, when anything went wrong, the cards always came tumbling down, and his suppressed anger would erupt. Afterwards, the Devil would sit embarrassed, ashamed and disappointed in himself just like a relapsed addict following a weeklong binge. This seminar, he secretly hoped, would fix all that.

They arrived and entered a cramped conference room with twenty seats neatly arranged in rows. Just as night follows day, on a bus or in a classroom, the naughty kids will always head for the back row. So, it made sense that the naughtiest 'kid' of all time gravitated to a seat at the rear.

Up-tempo music played, while the room slowly filled with delegates until only one empty chair remained. Two ladies approached, and as one sat down, the other objected.

"Excuse me, you have taken my place."

"No, I have not," insisted the other.

The organiser had arranged the correct number of seats but unfortunately, had not foreseen the arrival of a tutu-wearing, giant bear. The one remaining chair sat watching as a simple misunderstanding quickly escalated into a full-blown argument. It despaired and wanted to say, "Try being an object, unable to move, bums sitting on you and then, at the end of the day, facing the indignity of being placed on a lesser life form – the table – just so the floor could be cleaned."

"Ladies and gentlemen and others," a voice boomed out from the speakers – with the echo effect turned up to the max – bringing an abrupt end to the chair fracas. "Please, all be seated and welcome your teacher, Dr. Angerrrrrr." The speaker rolled the final letter in a way that made your ears want to curl up and hide.

Everyone, ignoring the explicit seating instruction, stood and clapped enthusiastically as a surprisingly shiny looking man took centre stage. Before any brain was conscious of Dr. Anger's suspiciously relevant name, it would label him 'the shiny man'. A silver suit and overly polished shoes complemented his glowing orange tan and brylcreemed hair.

"Thank you, thank you," the shiny Dr. Anger shouted, while making 'please sit-down' gestures with both arms.

The music changed beat, gradually building in tempo as the Doctor spoke.

"Tonight, people, we will fight anger. We will defeat the demons within. Can I hear a 'Hell yeah'?"

A less than enthusiastic reply was returned – apart from one American who almost exploded with enthusiasm.

"You will learn the facts. The ancient secrets of anger management. Do you want to learn?"

"Hell yeah!"

The music was at full tempo, attempting to excite the crowd further. "Then I will teach you."

The music stopped. The crowd stopped and, for a second or two, Dr. Anger froze. Then, with a burst of energy, he flung out an arm and pointed directly at Simon. "You. Why are you angry? The finger was clearly aimed at Simon. Everyone could see it. Simon knew it and was struggling to respond – he wasn't angry and had no issues to report. For once the Devil's arrogance came to Simon's rescue.

"I am not actually angry myself," replied the Devil to a question that was not his to answer, "but I wish to understand your techniques, so I can pass them on to my employees." Normally the Doctor might have insisted on Simon replying, but the Devil's answer was one he liked.

"I see. And these 'employees' you mention, what line of business are you in?" He made quotation marks with his hands as he said 'employees'.

Coughing to give himself time to answer, the Devil replied, "Human Accommodation. That is to say, hotels."

"After I help you, perhaps I could stay in one of your hotels?" the Doctor joked. Simon laughed spontaneously but for different reasons to everyone else in the room.

"So, tell me Mister …?" The Doctor was angling for the delegate's name.

"Lucifer." Oh crap, the Devil thought after revealing his real name. "That is, I mean Lucy."

Everyone laughed.

"What makes you, I mean your 'employees', angry?"

"There are many situations that enrage my employees," the Devil replied and shot the lecturer a meaningful stare.

"Describe an example, Mr. Lucy."

Gritting his teeth in annoyance over choosing a girl's name, the Devil replied, "Meetings mainly. Meetings to discuss having other meetings, meetings that should last ten minutes but go on for days, meetings where there are no biscuits, meetings that…"

Placing a hand on the Devil's shoulder and quickly removing it due to the extreme heat radiating from his body, Dr. Anger cut him short. "Relax, you have made your point, sir. Now sit and listen." In an overly theatrical dance-like movement, he made his way back to the stage.

"Anger." The sound of a drum filled the room. "Anger!" Bang went the drum again. "Anger is in all of us. Anger is powerful. Now you can let this emotion control your life or you can focus that anger to succeed." Drumming again. "If you learn to master it, you can exchange that sense of rage for motivation. Motivation to succeed!" The sound of a louder drum and accompanying cymbals boomed out from the speakers.

He could have carried on like this for a while. This was a performance, practised and mastered over time. It would mesmerise his audience and get them cheering and energised. He wasn't expecting interruptions though. But then he wasn't used to the Devil.

"That's all very well and everything, but how do we control our anger?" the Devil asked forcibly. Interrupting was a technique he'd used successfully in meetings. Bored of hearing presentation after presentation, most lasting an hour or more and providing nothing of value to anyone, he found interrupting and returning to the point worked well. Every time a discussion went off topic, he would interject.

With their trance broken, the crowd agreed, and a few shouted, "Yeah, give us the techniques."

"Hurry up, Doctor!"

"If you can't solve my issues, I'm going to smack this chair round your meat ball head!"

"Not again," thought the chair.

"Everyone, calm down. I'm building towards the techniques," he continued.

"Don't give us this crap. You're just going to drone on, get us hyped up, and only when we get home will we realise you told us absolutely zilch," screamed an irate delegate.

"Give me one fact, now!" the Devil shouted, punching his fist into the other hand, causing steam to hiss from the gaps in his fingers.

Totally disoriented and losing his flow the Doctor stuttered, "Ummm."

"I'm waiting!" The Devil's eyes locked onto the Doctor. A feeling of dread would overwhelm anyone in this situation.

"A fact? Right, ummm, a fact?" Ruffled by the Devil's stare, beads of sweat formed on the Doctor's forehead and spidered their descent from head to toe. "Try breathing deeply perhaps?" was the best the Doctor could propose under the glare of Satan.

"I knew it! You're a phoney." The Devil stood up, clutching his pink bear in a protective manner. "You're just like the rest of them. Talk the talk, but when you analyse it, you find crap comes out of your mouth instead of your arse."

Dr. Anger could see the Devil's fury swelling inside him like a pressure cooker about to burst. "Take deep breaths, Mr. Lucy, and sit down. Let me show you how to control your rage."

"I'm not cross!" the Devil roared as he tore apart the pink bear, splitting it in half.

This, the Doctor thought, illustrated the point quite admirably. "I suspect you might have issues," he offered.

Chairs know that anger spreads quickly – they had witnessed it many times – and in this room furious people shouted, while chairs were thrown, and Dr. Anger made his hasty escape.

Looking at his once lovely pink bear, one half held in each hand, the Devil snorted, threw it down and set off. "Come on, Simon, we are leaving!"

Carrying the bags past the arguing crowd and broken chairs, Simon followed obediently, aware that now was the time to bring his buttling skills to the forefront. He must calm his boss down.

"If you come this way, sir, I shall bring you some tea."

Thirty-Six

Plans. Slugart formulated them constantly. Having literally lived forever, even for an angel of his considerable age, existing before time began, he'd managed to rack up an impressively large collection of schemes.

There were the early classics, such as the 'hierarchy of angels', where angels were granted a vote to elect representatives for various roles. His suggestion was enthusiastically backed with a high turnout at the first ballot. The idea worked well, and all were happy until many years later, after the fifth election, suspicions grew when the same candidates were always re-elected. The marginalised majority became unhappy with decisions that only benefited the few. This made no sense as the disgruntled angels far outnumbered those in power. A disillusioned angel took it upon herself to investigate and discovered that the rules had secretly been changed, giving added weight to the votes of the powerful. It was effectively impossible to remove an incumbent angel from their official position. Well, once the fraud was revealed, instead of protesting or complaining, angels just ignored their leaders. When the ruling classes have no one listening to them, they soon get bored and relinquish control.

Other proposals had suffered similar fates. It wasn't that his ideas were unrealistic or that he failed to push them through, but more that they always failed to survive. However, this latest idea was different. He had devoted an enormous amount of time, research and effort to get this far. It was a scheme born out of anger, jealousy and greed, and now he was so close to success. Touching the plan's third vital key, he felt his increased heart rate pump a wave of excitement around his body. Unexpectedly, a noise from the adjacent room caused him to jump back and pretend to admire a random book he located nearby. It was too dangerous for anyone to suspect anything now.

When the first humans appeared in Heaven, the angels were both surprised and amazed. These new 'creatures' were a novelty and treated as royalty. Angels loved meeting the initial hundred or so that arrived, each one different in appearance and personality. Then, like people who soon bored of moon landings, angels started paying less attention to their new guests. No longer would they comment on the latest taller human or 'the new arrival with only one leg'.

Of course, the migrants needed housing, and it was only natural that they would want to reside where others had already settled. It's human nature to do so, providing comfort in unfamiliar surroundings. The number of homes increased, and the angels referred to this settlement as 'Human Town' – not out of malice but simply because it was almost exclusively inhabited by humans. Thousands upon thousands of humans continued to arrive. Angels no longer considered them unusual and even took them as friends. Soon the more adventurous humans moved into the traditional, angel suburbs. Time drifted by, and the 'unusual' completed its metamorphosis into the 'normal'. Humans lived alongside angels as though it had been that way forever.

Slugart hated them, even in the early days when the first few trickled through. Perhaps it was not hate that he felt to start with but more the annoyance at the attention they received. Comments about how fascinating these humans were, or how God had created perfection were commonplace; little things like that gnawed at and tormented Slugart. A jealous angel by nature, he found these remarks diminished the grandeur of angels and, more importantly, his grandeur. Gradually, frustration turned to anger as more began their second life in Heaven, but when the angels became the minority, his fury turned to outright loathing.

'If you can't beat them, join them' is a well-known saying. Slugart twisted this when referring to the human infestation to menacingly 'joke': 'if you can't beat them, beat them with a stick'. Clearly, he required a better solution than that, yet an obvious, quick answer was not forthcoming. Over time, Slugart had started to voice his grievances with the human race. 'What have they ever done for Heaven?' he would regularly argue at the local pub while drinking that human import – beer. 'They can't be trusted!' he'd insist – yet unlike the angels, humans had been vetted before entering Heaven. Another of Slugart's senseless arguments proposed: 'They always talk in their own tongue; they should learn how to speak our language if they want to live here.' A point perhaps with some merit, if it had affected their integration into society. But, as all in Heaven hear conversations in their own language, irrespective of that spoken, it rapidly fails as a valid concern.

The burden of carrying such hatred was overwhelming. Seeing them around every corner sent shivers of rage through his body. Slugart struggled to sleep. He started ranting his hateful arguments in front of the mirror. As his mental well-being deteriorated, he became somewhat of a recluse, until one day he awoke to a wonderful epiphany. There could only be one solution – to rid Heaven of all humans. Whirring noises could have been heard streaming from his head. The gears and cogs that in recent days had ceased to work, were trying to turn once more. He now knew the plan's end goal but how could he achieve it? Thousands of new humans entered each day, and he couldn't figure out how to rid his neighbourhood of even one.

With a purpose to his life established once more, Slugart set about his task. Plan after plan was discarded and thrown into the bin. Years of scheming spilled out of his metaphorical bins, but he was never disheartened. He had faith that enlightenment would come.

It was in the Righteous Club, a favoured haunt amongst angels, where the light bulb moment sparked. Relaxing by a roaring fire where many a famed angel had once sat, Slugart was doing his best to be left alone to think. Of course, those wanting solitude automatically attract unwanted attention from the most annoying person in the vicinity, and it was over a drink with one such angel – considered on the limit of the eccentric scale – that a story was told which was to change everything. Not particularly concentrating for large parts, Slugart's attention was suddenly grabbed when the angel described Heaven's borders. He recalled how Heaven is split into zones and essentially has boundaries in a very loose sense. There was, however, one specific border that was vastly different to the others. After the angel repeated the account to allow Slugart to confirm his understanding, he swiftly finished his drink in one large gulp and left, thanking the angel for his time. What he had heard that night interested Slugart greatly, and he needed time alone to reflect.

Over subsequent years the complex plan was constructed. It consumed Slugart totally as it grew from an embryonic idea to a fully-fledged masterpiece. He had almost devised a way to control, or even stop, humans entering Heaven. The smallest details of the operation were carefully added, but the realisation dawned that he was missing two vital elements to guarantee success.

The first he couldn't just collect. For a start it was something Heaven did not control and, by all logic, never could. It's not that he didn't know where to find it, but he was unable and unwilling to risk contact. Sleepless nights and days of thinking produced no magic resolution.

When Slugart's exasperation with humans began, he always expressed his negative thoughts openly. Yet he found most of these angels 'tut tutted' and suggested his views were dated and old fashioned. Initial rejection only made him more vocal but the day his plan was conceived, he realised the need to adopt a lower profile. His views (he now understood) were not shared by others. This presented him with a conundrum, since for his plan to succeed he required the majority of the angels support him. Something this radical needed trust to be built quietly and in secret. Slugart required a way to re-educate (he did not like the term brain wash) the angel sceptics, so that his views became accepted, and the cult, or Brotherhood as he preferred it to be known, was formed.

Initially small in number, the membership grew quickly. Slugart's rhetoric pulled more in, making them truly believe in his cause. The speeches he delivered contained enough energy to split an atom. When he spoke, his body animated every word, leaving his robes drenched in sweat. On occasions, he could appear manic, but his passionate views became firmly planted in the subconscious of the Brothers.

Still holding the third key, Slugart heard someone approach. He let go and slipped quietly out, returning home without it. It was too risky to be seen with that many people about.

Time passed and still the humans arrived.

Thirty-Seven

The baboon had crossed into human country. She had previously studied them and concluded that as a species, they were gravely stupid. Yet occasionally their stupidity, when combined with hints of genius, made a life-form of such evil that even the much-maligned red ant feared them. Her observations had identified their obsession with appearance, which made the baboon more conscious than ever of her own red butt. As she pondered her rump, she effortlessly swung over a garden fence and grabbed a bed sheet conveniently hanging from a nearby clothesline. Jumping onto the roof of a neighbouring house, the baboon wrapped the sheet around, like a sarong, giving her the confidence to mingle amongst humans.

Guided by her nose, she climbed down to street level and bounded on all fours along the road. A strong smell of food drew her onwards while her stomach made it clear that sustenance was needed. On reaching a line of street vendors, she joined the queue and waited patiently. Occasionally, people looked inquisitively at her, but most had seen stranger things living in Heaven than a sarong-wearing baboon queuing for food.

"Can I help?" enquired the stall owner. Without waiting for a reply, he handed over a bunch of bananas. Well, the indignity, the baboon thought, stereotyping me as a banana obsessed creature. She hated such out-dated thinking and protested that she did not conform to his stereotypes. The vendor was most embarrassed and apologised as he passed her the ham and cheese crepe she had selected from his menu.

With the food stall far behind, she bounded up a large tree to regain her dignity and composure. Now alone, the baboon tentatively tasted the crepe. Yuck! Why would humans eat such rubbish, she wondered as she tucked into a large, ripe banana.

Thirty-Eight

Evening had made its long-awaited appearance. Heaven, having twenty-seven hours in each day, had really angered Evenings. Three extra hours and Heaven had granted an additional hour to Morning, Afternoon and Night. Why nothing more for Evening, it wanted to know? This injustice was unacceptable. One day, Evening would start a petition to campaign for an extra hour too.

Today, the evening could not arrive quickly enough for Slugart. Prevented from getting his hands on the item he so desired, his attention returned to Peter. Without him the plan failed – nothing could be achieved unless he co-operated. Had his gentle manipulation of Peter's ego been enough? Would he agree?

These thoughts played in Slugart's head, which bobbed up and down in time with each step he took on the short journey to Saint Peter's house. Checking that his robes were properly fastened in line with tradition, Slugart knocked on the door of the saint's pad.

"Bruv." Peter greeted Slugart with more excitement than he had intended. "Enter my crib," he added and Slugart followed him in. The ramshackle interior sparkled with a spotless sheen. Slugart's brain privately admitted it had expected to find the house more dust covered than dust free, while Peter's brain was still smiling as it remembered the cunning plot to get others to clean for him.

"Fancy a drink? Rum, beer, wine?"

"All such filthy, modern stuff, Peter. Have you no traditional angels' drink like Fallgron?"

"Sure, whatever." Peter found a bottle of Fallgron, which had been gathering dust quite happily after years of remaining untouched. Even the deep clean had failed to remove the last layer of grime.

Peter and Slugart settled into brown, cracked-leather armchairs and relaxed with their drinks, passing the time with small talk prior to the much-anticipated meal. Peter had carefully prepared a roast dinner, certain in the knowledge that he could cook a dish that everyone would savour. As they ate, Slugart predictably commented on the 'untraditional' roast and 'how meals were better in the past'.

After dinner, they retired to the armchairs, both swirling a Fallgron around in their brandy glasses. Peter, curious to know how a drink from a bottle last opened centuries ago would taste, found out in his first sip – and instantly regretted his choice.

"Now, Slugart. I ain't no fool. I know you've come round my manor as you want something from me."

"Peter, dear fellow, I merely came to catch up on old times and drink to the new."

"Bollocks you have. Now spit it out man."

"Well, there is a delicate subject I wouldn't mind discussing."

"Go on."

Preparing his words carefully, Slugart took a deep breath and went for it. "Peter, these humans you let in."

"We've been through this. I can't stop them, I know. No need to remind me!"

"Before I answer that, let me first explain why you do need to stop them. Have you wandered around Heaven recently?"

"I tend to stick to my patch. I know these streets, I've no business in other parts these days."

"If you did, Peter, you'd be shocked. Houses everywhere. Not the elegant traditional homes we used to build. Streets full of so-called modern buildings that these humans design. I even saw one with a grass roof. My neighbour has an eyesore in his back garden. A monstrosity –a trampoline they call it – a dirty, rusty metal frame with an annoying bouncy thing in the middle, I'd call it." Whenever Slugart started a rant, he became worked up and visibly agitated. "And all these extra people and their homes are causing overcrowding. It's unfair on us – the natives."

"I thought God had devised a special way of increasing the size of the land, so that building houses never changed the amount of free space in Heaven.

"A minor detail, Peter. Food though! It's even worse than the housing crisis. If you want fish and chips, a curry, Chinese takeaway..." (Peter's brain was desperately telling his mouth not to drool) "... any of those disgusting, stinking foods, then just take a walk and you'd trip over a multitude of takeaway restaurants peppering our streets. Look for a traditional soup vendor, and it's like looking for a beagle in a haystack."

"Needle."

"Sorry?"

"A needle, not a beagle."

A 'don't be stupid' stare was aimed at Peter as Slugart continued. "I'm not saying they are all horrible. I mean, I count some of them as friends, but they are ruining our traditional values and promoting their foreign ways." This was a blatant lie. Slugart did not regard any human as a friend or even a colleague, but he felt he had to tone down his natural rhetoric to engage Peter's interest.

"That's your take on it, Slugart, but what can I do?"

"I will come to that. Let us first discuss your gate. There are too many of them coming through. We need to control their numbers."

"Can't be done," Peter firmly retorted.

"It can and it will. But I want to make some suggestions first. How about a checklist to vet them? See if they hold our values. Did they follow a religion on Earth? We sent them countless versions of holy books with laws to guide them. We even let them choose which one to follow. Some up here said we should only send the one book to avoid confusion, but no, the liberals won, and we gave them a choice. And now God allows even the ones that don't believe in Him to wait at your gate."

"To be fair, mate, it was you angels that decided to send the books down, not the Big Man."

"We were just performing God's orders."

"Of course, you were, geez." Peter rolled his eyes.

"Anyhow," Slugart continued, "if we rejected the ones that failed to follow a holy book, it would exclude a large percentage of God's pets straight away."

"You can't call them that; you know it's offensive." 'God's pets' had become a derogatory term for humans in the last few years.

"Sorry, Peter, slip of the tongue. The rest should have to sign documents promising to abide by angel tradition. Any that refuse will eventually be sent to zones reserved for these foreign invaders." Slugart was not a stupid man and could sense Peter was not on his side, so he switched his attack to a line he knew would work.

"How much do you hate it, Peter?"

"Hate what?"

"What you have become. You were once the respected gatekeeper to Heaven, and now you are just a door stop, or 'gate stop' to be more accurate. These humans laugh at you. When you say 'no', they walk right past."

"They do not! They cower at my presence."

"Don't dribble rubbish, Peter. You know, and I know that God put you in charge of Heaven's gate. Somehow, the power God intended for you was never formalised, and so they stream into Heaven without any vetting – an uncontrollable flow of his pets."

Peter went to protest again but Slugart continued. "Peter, we can change that. Do you want to know how?"

Peter had to admit he was intrigued. "Go on."

And so, they continued their chat late into the night, emptying the bottle of Fallgron as they discussed many things.

Finally, they parted, both feeling pleased with the evening's conversation; both had much to consider.

Thirty-Nine

A beautiful evening drifted into darkness as night arrived once more. Evening was jealous of the extra hour gifted to Night, but Night was not happy with Heaven's arrangements either. On Earth, Night enjoyed watching the youth get up to all sorts. Whereas in Heaven, most people used darkness for what it was intended – to sleep. This meant Night had little to view for entertainment and never tired of moaning about the silence to any passing dream.

Night descended and Heaven slept. Peter and Slugart both dreamt of an exciting future. Hector's dreams, though, were full of worry and confusion. Cecil could not sleep, knowing the package had arrived and collection was imminent. Simon slept like a log, exhausted after his exertions. Guy dreamt of chasing dangerous criminals, while Roger tossed and turned, reciting the laws of Heaven. And the Devil? He dreamt of sandcastles.

Forty

Morning took over from Night and said, as it repeated each morning, "Let there be light".

Simon drew back the curtains in the Devil's room, and the light sprinted through.

"Close those curtains, close the god damn curtains!" the Devil screamed, his eyes not expecting such intense brightness so soon after waking.

Obliging the Devil, Simon switched on a small desk lamp and proceeded to lay out his master's clothes. There was only one choice suitable for the day: beach shorts, beach vest and beach sandals. The cap would at least match his outfit today. Simon though, still wore his suit despite the Devil's insistence that he should wear beach attire for their trip. Today they were off to the golden sands of Heaven. A must for any tourist.

"Has the morning paper arrived yet, Simon?" Keen to keep abreast of the latest news, Satan avidly read the paper in bed each morning. He always took advantage of the impressive range of journals available back home. (Many newspaper owners and editors have evil pumping through their veins and write their final editions in the fires of Hell.)

"I shall check if it has been left outside the door, sir."

He opened the door and neatly stepped aside with the intuition that only a butler has. "Good morning," he greeted the two Spanish gentlemen who had tumbled past him, one still holding a glass to his ear.

They recovered quickly and muttered something that sounded Spanish. If Simon had heard clearly, he would have wondered why they were mumbling the names of well-known Spanish foods. Unfortunately for Roger and Guy, their attempt to use Spanish as a cover had one major flaw. If you converse with a Frenchman in Heaven, you hear the conversation in your own language, and your reply is heard in French. But when an Englishman speaks in Spanish, then you only hear the Spanish.

"Excuse me, sir," queried Simon, "you appear to be speaking Spanish, yet I would normally expect to hear an English translation."

"Sorry, wrong room," they called, and ran off along the corridor.

Returning to the Devil, without his paper, Simon coughed.

"I wish you wouldn't do that, Simon. If you want to speak, just speak."

"Sorry, sir, it is my training as a butler. Unfortunately, there was no paper. I shall try to acquire one from reception. Just to report, sir, the two policemen who caught us destroying the clamps the other day were outside our room, dressed in disguise and spying on us. I thought I should warn you. They may be suspicious of who you are."

"Hmmm, yes Simon. Thank you. I shall think about this, while you fetch my paper." This was followed by a stare that clearly meant, why are you still here? I want my paper!

After running away in a most unprofessional manner, the two officers headed towards the hotel's dining room where Guy chose the full English breakfast, and Roger selected the lighter continental option.

Sitting down they digested their respective choices and proceeded to plan. "I heard the small one say they are off to the beach today. We should follow them," Roger proposed.

"Enough following. Let's cuff them pronto. There are too many escape routes from the beach. Here we have them contained." Always eager for action, Guy, energised by his full English, wanted results fast.

"A fair point. But we have no evidence to hold them in custody."

"No evidence?! What about the fact he is bright red, has superhuman strength, was seen attempting to drive a demon's vehicle and has horns! Who do we know that has horns, apart from him?"

"It would help if we had proof the horns are real. They could easily be attached to his cap to create an amusing look. He may be sunburnt."

"By what sun? You know there is no sun in Heaven."

"Perhaps someone has an illegal sunbed. Anyhow, today we need to gather proof that the horns are real. If they are, then we will arrest him on charges of 'crimes against Heaven'."

This pleased Guy. Arresting always pleased him.

Forty-One

Cecil awoke from his sleep-deprived night. His insomnia inflamed underlying feelings of anger and frustration, but this morning both were tempered by the exhilaration of knowing that today he would receive the parcel – a long-awaited key to the Leader's plan. God's pets would be finally banished from the land of angels. Yes, the Leader had accepted that some could stay, and possibly others may still arrive, but this was just the start. The dawn of his homeland being cleansed of all humans.

He fastidiously dressed himself in traditional robes and ate the breakfast soup of times gone by. After cleaning his bowl and putting everything neatly back in its place, he left the house that had been his home for the last few days and set off towards the delivery point.

Forty-Two

Without a moon or other celestial body to orbit the flat Heaven, there can be no daily ebb and flow of the tides. (Earth's moon, of course, denies all responsibility for the movement of the unimaginable tons of water back and forth, twice each day. For one thing, it points out, it has no means to touch or grab the seas, let alone create a tide. And why would it want to move the water in the first place?)

Although lacking tides, Heaven still has waves, perfectly sized at different depths. Some are for paddling, others for the amateur body boarder, and further out, huge, barrel-forming, surfing waves. The Devil was currently enjoying his first experience of body boarding, but his pleasure was hampered by the size (or lack of it) of the board. The initial thrill of catching a wave always ended with a mouth full of ocean-blue, un-salted water as he spluttered and sank, his board not built to handle such weight.

Simon occupied himself by constructing the traditional, British beach fortress that would protect them from any slight breeze (or minor hurricane). The absence of wind circulating through Heaven never stopped any former Brit erecting at least one wind break. It not only provided shelter but, more importantly, stood as a visible marker of claimed beach territory. While he struggled with the canvas, Simon realised his initial fear of the Devil being recognised, when stripped down to his beachwear speedos, had luckily been misplaced. He smiled as no one even batted an eyelid – proving the moustache and cap were working wonders.

The Devil returned from the sea, dragging his board behind, just as Simon hammered in the last pole. A three-hundred-and-sixty-degree ring of defence had been created to encircle their beach towels.

"Simon. Get me my towel and a drink. A cold drink this time, not a bloody tea."

"Yes, sir. At once." He quickly wrapped a towel around the Devil and handed him a cold juice. "Is everything alright, sir?"

"No, Simon, it's not. This sand keeps sticking to me. I can't wipe it away. Get it off." Discarding his towel before being fully dry, the Devil lowered his backside onto one of the beach towels laid out on the sand. His huge muscular legs were covered with sand, which the Devil was unable to remove despite all his attempts.

"I shall try my best, sir, but sand is notorious for sticking to one's body at the beach. A wet body acts like glue to dry sand. My advice would be to first let it dry and then brush it off."

Unwilling to wait, the Devil gave the stare that Simon knew meant 'just do it'.

Rubbing sand from your employer's legs could be seen as degrading to many, but Simon accepted it as part of his role. Working swiftly, he managed to eradicate the particles from the Devil's body and strategically placed more towels to create a physical barrier against the sand.

"Blurghhh," a sound of disgust came from the Devil's direction. "Simon, what have you put in my juice? It's full of gritty stuff now."

Simon spent the next twenty minutes explaining all the potential discomforts that sand can inflict while at the beach.

"So, why do you humans go to the beach? Why not concrete over the sand?"

It was a fair argument, Simon thought, and one that took a good few minutes to counter. But by imagining himself as a boy again, he remembered the joys of playing with the sand and explained to the Devil all the fun one can have with it. The one thing Simon talked about that intrigued the Devil was castles.

"So, you can make castles out of this stuff, eh Simon? Show me!"

Forty-Three

Cecil moved like a pumped-up fighting bull on steroids, yet he still had that skulking look about him. There was currently no need for stealth, no requirement to arch his back and crouch on all fours, creeping around like a house cat stalking a mouse through the garden undergrowth. The parcel was still some distance away; he would change tactics when he was closer. Stopping to scan the surrounding territory, he noticed a leaflet blowing in the wind advertising an anger management seminar. He briefly read it, screwed it up and discarded it. He had no anger issues, he angrily shouted towards the advert.

To a casual observer, Cecil's smooth head (more in the style of an elderly gentleman than football hooligan), skinny build and general sinister looks gave no hint that he was about to become an icon. With all the adrenaline (or whatever chemicals pump around an excited angel) urging him on, he certainly felt heroic. If he delivered the parcel successfully, he was sure to be recorded in history as a key player in the uprising. Cecil would achieve legendary status amongst the Brotherhood and be rewarded by their Leader, or so he told himself.

With his heart beating to the rhythm of 'drum and bass' (occasionally speeding up to 'happy hard core'), Cecil drew closer to the target. He stepped furtively into a small alley just off the main road and paused, blending into the shadows. Cecil knew the parcel was close but where – he couldn't see it yet.

Forty-Four

"The drawbridge will go there, Simon," said the Devil, gesturing towards the gap between the five-foot tall castles, with walls of sand joining them together to create a defensive square. The whole structure was surrounded by a ditch, soon to be filled with sea water to form a moat and, hence, the Devil's requirement for a drawbridge.

"I'm afraid, sir, it is impossible to build a drawbridge using sand."

Overexcited with the castle construction, the Devil vehemently disagreed. "Anything is possible, Simon!" Picking up a handful of sand as if to demonstrate the point, he watched as it trickled through his fingers. "Although perhaps you are right in this one case," he confessed – a rare event for the Devil. "Get me another drink, Simon. All this digging has worn me out."

The surrounding beachgoers had earlier stared in amazement. The Devil had quickly become bored watching Simon turning over a sand filled bucket, giving it something called the 'magic tap' and easing back the bucket to reveal a partially collapsed 'castle'. He impatiently grabbed the spade, dispensed with the pointless bucket and began digging. How the Devil could dig! The onlookers watched as the castle rapidly grew larger. Amazed observers offered to join in, but the Devil clearly had no need of assistance. With incredible speed, the fort was completed (barring the bridge) but it was becoming somewhat of a tourist spectacle and attracting unwanted attention.

"Are you certain you were doing it correctly, Simon? Seems bloody stupid to go to all that effort for your crappy, little pile of sand. Now the way I did it was fun."

"Yes, sir. I was always told by my father that the 'magic tap' was the key to success. Children enjoy building them, but they are much happier stamping on them afterwards."

A bemused stare was shot towards Simon. "Humans go to all that effort and then let those miniature versions destroy it? Madness."

He sat with his drink, staring at his grand castle, deep in thought. After finishing his refreshment, he handed the glass back to Simon, who appeared without notice to collect the glass. "Simon. I am going to destroy my castle. I think it will be fun."

Two familiar members of the crowd observed the Devil's construction techniques more suspiciously. With their cover blown and no longer posing as Spanish tourists, they waited for an ideal opportunity to make their arrest. Well at least Roger did. Guy, having watched the Devil, now stood waist deep in a hole and was pretty pleased with his efforts. Not many things compete with the satisfaction of digging a large hole on a beach.

"We'll wait until they are packed and ready to leave. Then we shall calmly apprehend and arrest suspect one, and if he comes quietly, we shall arrest his co-conspirator." Roger felt a well-planned arrest was imperative.

"You sure that's a good idea? What if he runs? I say we wait until he is facing away from us, I rugby tackle him from behind and you cuff him." Guy felt a flying tackle was almost always necessary in any arrest.

"An excellent idea," Roger replied.

Surprised and pleased that for once his colleague had listened, Guy smiled in childlike satisfaction.

"Unfortunately, though, regulation number eight, sub-section twenty-three states that: 'no rugby tackles shall be utilised to enforce an arrest, unless there is imminent danger to an officer or member of the public'."

The smile quickly evaporated.

"That is to say, it would have been an excellent idea if we planned to cause a stampede on this beach. Remember, we do not want to cause panic amongst the general public. Our aim is to keep this under the radar until we have confirmed his true identity."

Sulkily, Guy agreed that Roger's boring approach would be best in the circumstances. So, they carried on digging and watching, waiting for the Devil and Simon to pack their belongings and leave.

Forty-Five

Hector felt excited and invigorated, even anxious. For such a stolid character, these emotions were seldom experienced and certainly never shown. He knew there was a meeting tonight, although at what time he would only find out when he ate his soup. Their Leader had promised to unveil great news, news that would signal the start of the revolution and a return to traditional values. All his doubts, for now, were pushed aside, knowing that this momentous announcement could change Heaven for ever. Basking in this euphoric mood, Hector almost forgot, for the first time in years, that he was expecting one last customer. He hurriedly filled a cup and added the secret message.

The final customer was late arriving. His soup was becoming cold and no angel, even the most traditional, enjoys cold soup. Hector decided to retrieve the message and place it into another, warm serving. Inserting his fingers into the bowl, he tried to hook the foil ball. Mid-fishing, a cough interrupted him.

Slugart had arrived for his soup at last. Hector, like all the Brothers, was unaware that Slugart was the great, all-knowing, powerful Leader and treated him as a regular customer. Slugart knew that collecting his own message was illogical, yet it ensured no one suspected his identity. "Good afternoon, Hector. Is that my soup you have your finger in?"

"Yes, it is," Hector replied, with his brain running in slow motion shock.

"And why, may I ask, have you placed your fingers in my soup?"

Hector, with his fingers still wet, struggled for an answer. "Ummm, I am trying to fish the message out to place into a hot soup, as this one has turned cold."

"A message?" enquired Slugart in a manner that said 'we do not talk about the messages'.

"Er, no. I'll just get it out and pour you another one."

"Perfect." Taking his hot soup, he said good day and left.

As Slugart walked away, he was unable to concentrate. His mind was in a mild panic, wondering if the parcel had been collected. With the meticulously detailed plan slowly approaching its climax, Slugart was uneasy. He was concerned that all three keys were still far from his reach. Yes, it appeared Peter was, in principle, closer to making a decision, but there was still much to convince him of. Then there was this parcel, which was now late, or at least any confirmation of success was late. And lastly, there was the third key. The one he had tried to collect the previous evening. Time was running out, but in such a busy part of the day he could not risk being seen making another attempt.

Forty-Six

A postman generally collects parcels each day from a sorting office and waddles off on his round to deliver them, regardless of wind, rain or snow. They need not be stealthy – except when there is a postman-hating dog on the loose. Similarly, there is no need to hide or be wary when collecting that day's mail. But Cecil, unlike your 'run of the mill' postman, had hidden behind a wall, occasionally poking his bald head over the top, trying to glimpse the much-anticipated package. Not one to think ahead, Cecil had failed to plan how he might collect the parcel unseen. It was in the middle of a crowded area, and people would surely notice – especially being such a large parcel. Unable to resolve this puzzle, he was determined to remain calm and focus on his objective. Now was not the time for anger.

Forty-Seven

"Let's have an ice cream," families enjoying a trip to the beach often say on Earth. "It will cool us down on this summer's day." Off strolls Mum, across the beach and up the concrete steps to where the ice cream kiosks are found. Time goes by and the expectant group left on the sand start to ask: "Mum's been gone a long time. I wonder where she is?" She is, of course, in the ice cream queue, a long, meandering line, similar in length and speed of progress to a post office queue (a place where old folk meet to withdraw their weekly pension). However, the ice cream queue is one with no happy ending – only the mirage of exotic flavours beckons.

Approaching the front, Mum can see the options available. An ample selection to choose from; every colour of the rainbow and flavour in the known universe to drool over. In her mind, she chooses peanut butter, raspberry cheesecake, gooseberry with lime and chocolate fudge rum. A conservative range to sample, she thinks.

Meanwhile, Dad and the kids wait and consider sending out a search party but decide to give it more time. Perhaps an unplanned toilet trip has delayed her.

"…. And one scoop of chocolate fudge rum, please." The order is placed, and then the universal mantra of all beach ice cream sellers is heard: "I'm afraid we are sold out of those flavours. We only have strawberry or vanilla." Two strawberries and two vanillas are ordered, and money is exchanged.

Taking the baton of ice cream filled cones her race is now on. They need to be delivered before they melt to oblivion. Steadying herself, a tactical lick is applied as the ice cream attempts to revert to its liquid form. Haste is required. She has only just made it to the steps, and already drips trickled down the sides. Seagulls are circling as she reaches the sand, and her family see her approach. They wave encouragement and gesture to hurry. But like a raiding bandit, down swoops the first seagull for an incursionary foray. The mother flaps her arm at it as the bird returns for a second strike, and one strawberry scoop flies onto the sand.

Other seagulls join in the attack and dive towards the now abandoned ice cream. They leave the mother alone, happy to fight over the unprotected slush on the floor.

Finally, she makes it back to base and hands over the cones, but her effort goes unrewarded as her strawberry ice was surrendered on the battlefield. The three surviving cones are shadows of their former selves, and the two children whine in disappointment at the substituted flavours.

This, on Earth, is the reality of the seaside ice cream experience. But in Heaven, even when it's hot, ice cream never melts, and seagulls are confined to Hell.

The Devil was enjoying his quadruple scoop of champagne, coconut, chocolate and fudge. Time had been ticking, and they were nearing the end of their trip, one the Devil had fully enjoyed. Sadly, the beach was the last activity on the Devil's holiday itinerary, but before leaving, they planned to have a farewell lunch and then return to his Kingdom. (Inhabited by demons and the evillest spirits to ever live, it was unwise to leave your throne unoccupied for too long.) Upgrading from a towel to a deckchair, the Devil crunched on the last of his cone, while Simon busied himself with packing.

The policemen were busy too, planning their arrest.

"We cannot let them leave. There are too many escape routes."

"I thought you didn't want to make a scene by arresting him in public," Guy said in a huff. He was still annoyed about the ban on any form of rugby tackling.

"The beach has emptied significantly, so I think it prudent to arrest them here. Once they reach that wall by the steps, I'll confront them and read him his rights. Then you can calmly handcuff him."

"I'm always calm!" insisted Guy.

Simon, having slung the huge rucksack once more onto his back, lifted both suitcases and paused to regain his balance.

"Aha, I see you are ready at last, Simon."

"Yes, sir. I have made arrangements for an afternoon tea at a local café before our return home."

"Very good, Simon. I have read about the teas you have in the afternoon. They sound very much like sandwiches to me?"

"Indeed, sir". Simon just wanted to start moving and decided to explain when they arrived. The sand made balancing with the luggage even more difficult as they moved towards the steps.

The policemen followed.

Sixty-nine yards to the exit. Both policemen's hearts were pounding. This would be the arrest of the century – to apprehend Heaven's 'Most Wanted', masquerading as a tourist. They would be heroes.

Twenty-nine yards to go.

Simon's movement was laboured. He needed to get off the sand.

Twenty yards to go.

"Now. Let's do this," Roger whispered to Guy.

"Stop in the name of the law. Turn round slowly and make no sudden moves," Roger announced excitedly.

But Simon and the Devil carried on, unaware that the command was directed at them. They only half heard the request and assumed it was aimed at someone else.

Guy, resisting an animal urge to rugby tackle, shouted more directly: "You. The Devil and accomplice. Put your hands behind your head and stop. Now!"

This time he did get a reaction from the Devil and Simon. They looked at each other with a *what's this all about* sort of glance and turned around.

"Raise your hands slowly above your head," Guy demanded as they advanced toward their dangerous suspects.

"You heard him. Put them up. Now!" Roger shouted in the most aggressive manner he could muster.

"Good afternoon, officers," the Devil replied calmly.

"Now! Put them up or I will be forced to physically restrain you," Roger shouted in a high pitch squeal while letting Guy edge ahead of him.

Simon gasped. "I'm afraid I cannot with this heavy luggage, officers."

"Drop it and do what he says. I'm warning you!" Guy's instinct was screaming, *rugby tackle!*

They were now five yards from their suspects, and Roger started to read them their rights as Guy stepped forward to cuff the Devil. What the officers were not expecting was to be thrown onto the ground, mouths full of sand, with Simon and a ton of luggage on top of them.

Once they had managed to untangle themselves, the Devil was nowhere to be seen. This surprised Simon most of all.

Forty-Eight

It was worth all the effort and delay. After visiting five ice cream vendors along the beach, the baboon had finally found one with a banana flavour that had not sold out. Between licks, she told herself that on any other day a nice strawberry flavour would have taken her fancy, and it was just a coincidence that she craved banana today.

While sitting comfortably on a wall with her feet dangling below to avoid sand getting in her fur, she noticed an odd couple on the beach. Thinking that one had skin as red as her behind, she watched them briefly. And why the smaller chap was wearing a suit and carrying three bags on the beach, she could not understand. But humans were a mystery. Losing interest, she looked around for signs of the impending doom. But none was forthcoming today, so she bounded off in search of more banana ice cream. If only she had waited. Just thirty seconds later she would have witnessed the attempted arrest of the Devil. The course of impending doom never did run smooth.

Forty-Nine

To meet an old acquaintance can be simultaneously pleasurable and undesirable. For the Devil, his sudden encounter with an old chum on the beach was certainly a shock but also a relief.

Cecil, hidden behind a wall for what seemed like hours, had decided the time was right to collect the parcel. Without any plan, he had crawled to the edge of the wall and watched intently as the package moved ever closer. His concentration was interrupted by a shout: "Stop in the name of the law." He immediately froze. How had they found him? Who had found him and, more interestingly, what had they found him doing? He was not breaking any law. Refocusing, Cecil realised the command was aimed not at him but at his parcel. Hold on, he thought, that's my parcel; and he watched as two policemen attempted to arrest the Devil. Cecil was not having this. These examples of worthless, human scum would not get in the way of his hero-making delivery.

Out he shot from behind the wall. The policemen took no notice as he ran towards the Devil. He looked wildly around for a solution to prevent these two interfering God's pets steal his parcel and found it in the form of a third pet. Simon had heard Cecil approaching and turned around, wondering why this skinny angel, barely a metre away, was creeping towards them. Cecil advanced towards Simon, and as the policemen pounced to make their historic arrest, Cecil gave Simon a nudge. Delicately balanced with his rucksack and two suitcases, a mere gust of wind would have toppled him, so the hefty nudge Cecil produced was perhaps a waste of energy. But it did the trick. Falling helplessly backwards, Simon tumbled like a domino, knocking over both policemen in a chain reaction.

Now at this point, Cecil would have to admit under interrogation that he had no next steps in mind. "Lucifer," he said, with a friendly nod.

"Cecil? Is that you? How the devil are you? What are you doing here? What is going on? I keep expecting to see you down in Hell. I see they haven't kicked you out yet." Perhaps a few too many questions at once under the circumstances.

Cecil grunted and wanted to reply. He did not like the Devil or others thinking badly of him. Cecil wished to rise high in society and craved respect. He couldn't be lumbered with the term 'bad', or have it suggested that he was teetering on the edge of Hell's door. But the Devil was in a rush, so all this could wait until later.

"Take me away from here, Cecil. It appears my cover is blown."

And take him away he did. With the Devil following, Cecil produced a fine burst of speed and ran to the nearest side street. After a few left and right turns, they were soon safely distanced from anyone attempting to follow. Breathing heavily and slowing to a walk, Cecil decided it would be safer to take cover inside, but before he could choose a safe location, the Devil dragged him into a delightful, traditional cafe. He was hungry and had been looking forward to his planned afternoon tea – with or without Simon.

Fifty

A dog that loses his master whimpers, but a butler who loses his, roars.

Simon was not so much roaring — more chastising the policemen over their bungled arrest. He decided that 'attack' was the best strategy to avoid custody. How dare they make assumptions based on the colour of his colleague's skin? Did they not want to debunk the stereotype of racist policemen? How could they not see he was just a large, sunburnt, ex-bodybuilder?

"It must have been a trick of the light," Simon answered, when they pressed him to explain the Devil's superhuman strength. Simon's strategy was so successful that Roger and Guy started apologising for their unprofessional approach and begged for forgiveness, explaining their duty was to investigate all suspicious behaviour. They could clearly see that Lucy (Simon gave this as Lucifer's name) was just an unusual human and not the embodiment of pure evil.

"And now you must both help me find him." This took the officers by surprise, but it was a plan of action that Simon had quickly devised after the Devil disappeared.

"No, we bloody well won't." Guy was still peeved from having to apologise. He had missed the opportunity to tackle the suspect, and now this besuited civilian was giving them orders. He joined the police force to boss, not to be bossed around.

"Just one second," Roger said to Simon and drew Guy aside. "There could be a scandal. Police brutality, racist behaviour and more. We need to keep him sweet," Roger whispered as they huddled together.

Guy uttered a few incoherent noises that were more sounds than words.

"And on the positive side," Roger continued, "we now have a kidnap as well. I've double checked the law book, and it is definitely a criminal offence."

Simon had told them about the angel who'd aggressively pushed him over, and although no one had witnessed the Devil's abduction, the officers concluded that the angel was the culprit. Un-huddling and facing Simon, they agreed to hunt for Lucy and apprehend his captor. "Now let's search the perimeter for clues."

The two officers searched the beach and excitedly discussed ludicrous theories on how everything they found could be related to the case. Simon placed his rucksack by the wall and used it as a pillow. He decided to have a five-minute rest before telling them where the Devil could be found. In his mind he could see no possible way that anyone could overpower the Devil. No, he must have wandered off by himself to order lunch. The Devil would never miss a meal. But how could he lead the policemen there without arousing their suspicion?

Almost drifting off to sleep, Simon was awoken by the sound of Roger chastising Guy for contaminating vital evidence with his DNA. Simon interrupted the officers' argument. "I may have uncovered a clue as to my colleague's whereabouts," he revealed.

Fifty-One

Indeed, the Devil was hungry. At that moment, he was shovelling two scones, smothered in jam, cream and butter, into his light-devouring mouth. Naturally, the Devil and Cecil argued heatedly, unable to agree which should be applied first – the jam or cream.

"Right, after this we need to go," Cecil said, watching the Devil enjoy his food. It looked so appetising, yet it was banned for members of the Brotherhood. Only eat good, wholesome, traditional angel food, the Leader had instructed.

"Going where? I need to find Simon. I can't be returning to Hell without him. Who would warm my slippers before supper?"

"No, we need to leave now," insisted Cecil. "Hold on. Warm your slippers?" Angels still thought of Lucifer as a fallen, evil angel, living an unsophisticated existence in the fires of Hell. Slippers didn't enter this vision.

"Not warming. I meant heating them to boiling point, so I can use them in a torture session," the Devil lied, quickly remembering the image he had to maintain. "Anyway, I need to be getting back before the demons start a civil war."

"You cannot go back yet."

With the fourth scone being dispatched, the Devil briefly pondered Cecil's words. "By what do you mean 'cannot'? I am the ruler of darkness, the bringer of doom, the ….."

"Keep your voice down, Lucifer. And sit back down. I thought you wanted to stay under cover." The Devil, getting slightly carried away with his evil, doom-bringer speech, had risen to his feet for dramatic effect.

"Look, I just want you to meet someone to discuss a proposal."

"No."

"You must!" countered Cecil.

"My diary is full. I have meetings scheduled and meetings about meetings I must attend."

"You will like the proposal. It is in your interest," Cecil responded.

"How?"

"I do not know."

"With who?"

"I cannot say."

"Send me a meeting request, and I'll add it to my diary. I must be off to find Simon."

Cecil put his hand on the Devil's shoulder and pushed him down into his chair. "I command you to come!" Cecil was getting angry.

"You command me, do you? I'll drag you down to Hell if you touch me again!" The Devil too was growing angry. Cecil was not strong enough to prevent the Devil standing. No one is.

While the Devil and Cecil were catching up, Simon had managed to convince Roger and Guy that the 'clues' he had obtained pointed to a location where the Devil was dining. With the policemen each carrying a suitcase, Simon's body was enjoying its first rest in days, with only the rucksack on his back.

As they drew closer to the café, they heard raised voices. Instinctively the officers hunched down, keeping themselves hidden and darting between objects for cover. Their attempts at a stealthy approach would have looked more impressive if it were not for the luggage impairing their movement.

Simon, with far less emphasis on stealth, marched forward as straight as the crow flies.

Using his binoculars, Roger located the fugitive. Surprisingly, he was not bound or gagged but sat eating a scone. Another person, who Roger could not quite make out, sat opposite. An irresponsibly placed lamppost blocked his view.

"Target located. Let's move in. I'll cover the front and you enter from the rear." Roger had read about this tactic and was a veteran, as far as he was concerned, in such arrests. "Hold on, wait. Suspect number one is now standing and appears agitated."

"Let's move in and arrest him. Screw keeping the public calm. We can't afford to let them escape twice!" Guy's urge to arrest was overwhelming.

"Which one?"

"Erm. Well, it doesn't matter. Arrest them both!" With Simon half convincing them that his companion couldn't possibly be the Devil, they were confused who they were arresting and for what.

Simon was nearing the front door to the café. It was at this point the Devil stormed out with Cecil chasing him. Seeing Simon standing there was a welcome relief to the Devil. "Ah, Simon. Where have you been? Take me home."

Before Simon could react, both policemen came charging past, still carrying the cases. With their combined momentum they collided with the Devil and flattened him to the ground.

"Quick, Lucifer. Come with me. These men mean to capture you. We cannot let that happen," urged Cecil. He grasped hold of the Devil's hands and opened his large, slightly off-white, wings. With one graceful flap he lifted the Devil into the air and off they flew. Satan offered no resistance. The idea of being captured did not appeal, and Simon had always reminded him that they must keep a low profile.

Looking from their less than comfy position on the rough, concrete floor, the policemen watched on helplessly as the Devil was kidnapped once again. And this time there was no uncertainty – they knew an angel had done it.

Fifty-Two

Slugart discarded his soup from Hector's stall as he did every day and made his way to his favourite lunchtime venue – a very untraditional (for angels) Chinese buffet. It was, of course, surprising that such a vocal, belligerent advocate for authentic angel cuisine would dine in a restaurant that could only be described as a human import. Slugart chose to eat there for two reasons. The first was his belief that *'to beat the enemy, you must dine with the enemy'*. Knowledge he gathered from watching humans whilst they ate provided invaluable material for his speeches at the Brotherhood meetings. He was inclined not to reveal the second reason so readily – it was because he loved their food. It went beyond love; it was an addiction. He had tried giving up many times, but the smell always lured him back for one more slice of pizza or one last greasy kebab. The food held a power over him, and he hated it for that.

Halfway through his third plate from the *'all you can eat buffet'*, a passing angel dropped something onto Slugart's table. Feeling nervous and excited, Slugart allowed a waiter to pass and ensured no one was watching before opening the screwed-up piece of paper. What he read made him smile. The package was en route.

It had been a long time since he had last spoken to Lucifer.

Fifty-Three

"They came, they saw, they destroyed."

"We must rebuild."

"We must cleanse."

"It is our right and our duty to return Heaven to the angels."

"Heaven is ours, never forget it."

These words were recited each time the cult met; Slugart chanted a phrase at a time with his followers repeating the words in response. He preached that these mantras were the truth, and the Brotherhood believed him as though the words were spoken by God himself. The chants were repeated, and the same simple messages reinforced at each meeting. Like all successful propaganda, the brainwashed Brothers believed and grew to live by these words.

At their initiation ceremony, new members received a book, designed to complement the chants. A book written by Slugart in the style of his speeches. The subject was intense, jumping incoherently from one topic to another with several passages encouraging hatred towards humans. He called it, 'My War', a reference to his campaign. That 'war' was a human concept, was an irony lost on Slugart.

Hector could recall most of the book by heart. Each morning, while eating breakfast, he would read passages and again in bed, before falling asleep. Today, Hector was studying a at work while subconsciously stirring the soup. He held the book close to his eyes in the way so many older, short-sighted people do. Normally a kind and softly spoken angel, today he looked visibly irate as he read. Hector felt angry with the changes that humans had made to Heaven, and with what had become of the angels' traditions. He was furious with life – or with eternal life, at least.

They had a home on Earth, a planet built for their alien way of living. Why did God invite them here?

"Hi, Hector. We've got some spare kebabs if you're feeling peckish?"

Startled, Hector stopped reading and looked up to see a familiar face. It was Jo, the friendly woman who ran the takeaway at the entrance to his side street.

"If they are spare, then, yes, I would love some." He instantly felt ashamed and embarrassed by his earlier thoughts of hatred.

As she went to fetch the kebabs, Hector looked at his book again. His eyes were drawn to the words at the bottom of the page. The words that always worried him. Words he had read over and over again. At each reading, they troubled him more. They confused everything. All his attempts to believe were challenged whenever he saw them.

'Although we are different, we see the same light. Don't believe the hype.'

Perhaps, he pondered, I should share my concerns at the meeting tonight.

Fifty-Four

More and more souls joined the line every day. Sometimes, Peter organised them into rows based on their religious beliefs and on other occasions by nationality. He was always trying to think of new ways to entertain himself.

It wasn't as though he hated them. Unlike Slugart, he only wanted some respect, not just for himself but also for the institution of Heaven. They should be overjoyed, he thought, at being granted the privilege to enter God's kingdom – to be judged worthy of eternal life. Admittedly, the entrance criteria seemed bafflingly low but never-the-less, they should still respect Heaven.

Peter wandered through the throng of arrivals waiting impatiently to pass through his garden gate and listened to their conversations. A few reminisced about loved ones; people hoping to meet lost friends and relatives again in Heaven. But the deafening noise which filled the air came mainly from heated arguments between them.

"Your religion won't be recognised in Heaven."

"Get back, you pushed in!"

Stopping to listen as two men squabbled, Peter's spirits plunged even lower.

"When we are in Heaven, I will hunt you down, your family too, and destroy you all. I will not rest until all your type burn in Hell for eternity."

"It is your tribe that are sinners and will burn, not ours. Our Lord sent plagues of slugs to destroy your crops, droughts so you had no water and hurricanes that turned your homes to rubble."

"Stop shouting, bredrin. You've made it to the Kingdom, just chill and enjoy." Peter didn't plead with them anymore – he just told it how it was.

The feuding men were unconvinced that chilling was a good idea. "We are sworn enemies. We shall wage war here. I'd rather die than share Heaven with his type."

"You're already dead, bro. To die twice is impossible."

Peter had wandered off before they had chance to respond. One thing he knew for certain was that humans are dumb. The vision described by Slugart over dinner was becoming clearer, and the fog of doubt that clouded his mind was gradually blowing away. He needed the power to decide who should enter Heaven. I mean, that's why God put me here. Wasn't it?

Fifty-Five

"Put me down, put me down. For God's sake, Cecil, get back on the ground!"

Once a fully-fledged angel, the Devil had wings and had been able to fly majestically as any other – but that was long ago, before the concept of time had been invented on Earth. Now as Cecil soared effortlessly into the sky, a sense of dread slowly crept up on the Devil. His legs and arms felt floppy, and his stomach threatened to empty. He was feeling scared, an emotion he had never experienced either before or since his exile to Hell.

"Calm down, Lucifer. We are almost there."

"I said now!" and with a strong tug he slipped from Cecil's grip and down he plummeted. His descent was not caused by gravity pulling him down, since Heaven does not experience this force. It was just good old logic that dictates if something is in the sky without wings, it will fall. And fall at a fair rate of knots he most certainly did.

Taken by surprise at the Devil's decision to plunge from the sky, Cecil briefly hesitated to change course and followed him down. By the time he made the turn, the Devil had already landed, but the precise location of his landing was not immediately obvious. They'd been flying over thick forest, and now Cecil could only see trees. If trees were what he was searching for, then he would have struck gold. Devils, on the other hand, were not so readily available.

"Nooooo!" Cecil screamed, and the tree he punched would have screamed too if it had possessed a mouth and vocal cords. "Crap! I can't have lost him. I've already reported that I've collected him!"

Cecil was ignorant of the sound advice that one brave butcher had implored many times before. "Don't panic! don't panic!" Without a clear plan in mind, he started searching for Satan, calling his name and angrily punching anything that got in his way.

True to form, his rage worsened with every painful punch until it eventually overwhelmed him.

If he had acted calmly and thought about his search sensibly, Cecil would have returned to the air and circled above the forest. From there, he would have noticed the large impact zone created by the Devil on landing, or more precisely, crash landing, causing devastation to a good ten or so trees.

Not far from the place where Cecil frantically searched, there could be observed a bustle of activity. A small, lean-to shelter was under construction, large leaves had been crafted into a crude water container and, close by, a plentiful supply of firewood had been gathered.

When the Devil climbed out of the crater created by the impact of his fall, he found himself in what, to his expert eye, instantly recognised as a survival situation. Most courses the Devil endured over the years had merely bored him – 'Become a Better Boss', 'Working in a Modern Office' and so on. But ever since he attended the survival course the Devil had not stopped talking about it or practising its techniques.

Now lost and days from being rescued, with 'danger' lurking everywhere, he sprang into action. His current predicament, he decided, could potentially last for weeks, perhaps even months. Therefore, the first task was to build a shelter. With the readily available trees, felled by his landing, he quickly knocked up a basic lean-to, providing protection from the rain – that Heaven never has. Next was water. It was hammered into the course attendees, that you can sustain yourself for days without food, but death comes swiftly without water. In fact, the Devil could survive forever without water – you can't kill a Devil that easily. For the fire, dry wood was plentiful. He carefully arranged the logs into a pyramid shape then, smashing two large stones together, he attempted to create sparks. Ten minutes later and with no sign of fire, he threw the stones away in a mild rage. Where one would have expected to hear the thud of stones hitting the ground, instead a loud crashing sound reverberated through the trees. Turning around he saw his mistake. The stones had clean-bowled his lean-to with a direct hit on the main support and brought it tumbling down. "For God's sake!" he screamed.

His composure regained, he reminded himself: I'm a survival expert. After all, he had the certificate to prove it. He decided to re-build the shelter later and returned to the fire. Recalling his course, the Devil remembered a top tip – never attempt to light a fire with a stone. Arrogantly, he had ignored the advice as he felt someone of his exceptional skill would succeed where lesser demons failed. He conceded defeat and reverted to the lighting flint that he carried at all times (as recommended). Soon the fire roared, and he had a pile of timber to feed it throughout the night.

Even with the extra support, rebuilding the shelter did not take long. Warming himself by the fire (on this very warm, dry day), protected inside his lean-to, his thoughts turned to food. Yes, he could always forage for mushrooms and berries, but an animal trap sounded a more exciting prospect to the survival expert of experts.

After drawing up a quick design in his head, he started to build. A few failed attempts later, peppered with plenty of shouting, the trap was built. It would certainly seem that he was expecting to catch some rather large prey. First, he had dug a three-metre-deep hole and covered it with weak branches, leaves and mud. Using a second technique learned from the course, he added a spring trap at the bottom. Any unfortunate animal, half dazed by the fall, would stumble into the hidden rope loop and activate the spring-loaded trap, pulling the catch out of the hole and leaving it dangling upside down by its foot. The Devil was in his element.

Knowing that it was essential to keep his fire going, he returned to add more logs and found the lean-to had again collapsed under no influence from anything else apart from its own weight and poor construction. This time he decided to quadruple the supports.

All this work made him hungry. Remember the four c's of survival, he thought, repeating them in his head "Calm, cunning, creative and camouflage." Camouflage! He needed to be camouflaged to stand any chance of snaring a meal. "Simon!" he shouted automatically. "Bugger." Realising he had to camouflage himself, he did his best. Mud and leaves were all he had. Now he would sit near the trap and wait.

Fifty-Six

The wait felt endless. It seemed to Slugart that Hell would freeze over before he could lay his hands on the Devil, the first key to his three-part plan. He still retained faith in Cecil and assumed by now they were on course to reach the safe house before night fall.

For aeons, Slugart had struggled to devise a scheme to attract the Devil into Heaven. In the end, underhand tactics involving espionage were required. There are unspoken ways for Heaven and Hell to communicate – all strictly forbidden and never discussed in public. After calling in some favours and using a hint of blackmail, he secured a mole that was close enough to Satan to leak his future plans. Each day, Slugart received a briefing on the Devil's activities. Most were as boring as mud, but when the spy informed him of Lucifer's planned holiday, Slugart realised this was his opportunity.

Thankful for his foresight to create the Brotherhood, Slugart knew he could entrust the members to carry out elements of his plan. He needed someone to collect the Devil – effectively handling illegal goods. Should anyone catch Satan while en route, there must be no evidence that he was involved. Trusting Cecil allowed him time to concentrate on the second and third elements of the plan. The next key would be unlocked by Peter, but the third only he could collect. He was currently back in the great public Library of Heaven – for a second attempt to obtain the information he so desired.

The miles of dusty shelves within this collection are not filled with books that you or I would recognise. Authors such as Agatha Christie, Roald Dahl, Charles Dickens, Christopher Moore, William Shakespeare and J S Austin are all missing from Heaven's great library. There are instead, scrolls and more scrolls containing ancient records. From records of the names and addresses of all that inhabit Heaven, to the minutes of the biannual meeting of the Heaven's Croquet Committee. Such scrolls occupy over half of the shelves. The remaining space contains literature of quite a different nature. In the early days of Heaven, angels could quite easily be likened to the later Greek philosophers. Debates raged during drink fuelled meetings, when great minds would discuss unresolved issues: the meaning of life, the perfect recipe for a coffee cake, can an angel die. Such topics and others of interest were discussed and argued over with every conclusion recorded. Each document was carefully labelled and filed away by the librarians. Humans were forever searching for their favourite novel or hoping to find a book written by a renowned angel author, only to discover this library contained no fictional works.

Under the flickering light of candles, Slugart searched for the elusive document. It made no sense for the library to be lit by naked flame, but it was a case of style over substance. Each candle was unique. Some were huge and others quite small. All were of a different shade of white, displaying their relative ages, with each one held in a golden candle holder. As they burned, the wax slowly melted, running down the sides in beautiful patterns. The random shapes transformed as they dried into a piece of fine art. Yet it was impossible for the wax to melt and run in a way other than perfection in such a spiritually rich place. Even the shelves knew more than any human or angel ever could. Over millions of years, the knowledge the scrolls contained had leaked into the wooden boards supporting them.

Each time a candle flickered, Slugart would dive out of sight, wary of the passing librarians that stalked the corridors. You can never trust a librarian, he believed, which demonstrated the level of paranoia that Slugart had now reached. He was petrified in case suspicions were raised and had delayed coming here until the last possible moment. The risks were too high to collect the third key in advance.

Years had passed since that chance meeting with the crazy angel who told him about Heaven's forgotten borders. If he had known how long it would take to validate the story, then he would not have resisted the urge to come sooner. Now though, all the key elements of his plan were falling into place, and he just needed to locate the scroll that he prayed contained the proof he required.

After much searching, hampered only by his constant subterfuge, he eventually found the elusive documents. Still hiding, he placed the scroll on the floor. Subconsciously his brain rudely coughed for attention: what if the crazy angel was just that – crazy? Had he really relied on this scroll, yet never checked the contents until now? Slugart breathed deeply and reminded himself that it was not by chance the two had met but by destiny. Carefully he unrolled the scroll and scanned the diagrams drawn so beautifully. For now, he had seen enough. He slipped the plans into his robes and made his way to the exit. As he moved, a big smile gradually spread across his face, and a sense of elation coursed through his body.

Fifty-Seven

Watching from an old oak tree, a red squirrel chatted to his friend the grey and observed Cecil curiously. Unusually, the two squirrels were not quarrelling about the tactically brilliant, overseas invasion of the red squirrels' territory (or genocide as the red squirrel would refer to it).

"He's flying like a drunkard. Even our distant relatives, the flying squirrels, glide better than that," commented the red one as he watched Cecil soar erratically overhead.

"Angels are always pissed," the grey pointed out.

There was a good reason for Cecil's erratic flying. He was in full meltdown. If God himself had appeared, Cecil would have struggled not to throw a punch at Him. How could he have lost Lucifer already!? It was those two pesky humans. The ones that called themselves policemen -whatever that meant. They would be the first of God's pets to be thrown out of His kingdom once this was all over. He'd make sure of it. But if he didn't find the Devil soon, he knew Slugart would see him evicted instead. He flew down to ground level once more in a desperate last attempt to find Lucifer.

The light was slowly seeping out from the woods as daytime ended another shift. Shadows darkened the forest floor, and Cecil, if he had been of a nervous disposition, might have been spooked by the owl hooting. However, he felt no fear. There was no room in his lean body for emotions other than anger. He wanted to punish the owl for taunting him with all that hooting but kicked a fallen branch instead and watched it smash against a tree. Walking on, with hope fading and his hands rammed dejectedly into his pockets, he could not have suspected that his next few paces would turn his world upside down – literally. The first step was ok, and so was the second, but the third step surprised his left foot. It hit the ground and sent confirmation to the brain that it was time to move the right. However, the left foot now wondered why it was still moving downward. Something was wrong. It sent a warning, and the brain responded by flapping the wings. But too late, Cecil had fallen into the Devil's trap.

He landed with a loud thud that echoed around the damp walls of the hole. With the light fading, he failed to see the loop that snapped tight around his leg as he stepped straight into it. His brain, instead of thinking of a cunning plan, simply sent instructions to Cecil's mouth to shout, "Oh crap!", just before he was flung into the air and left dangling upside down.

Out burst the Devil from behind a tree, roaring impressively like a hunter. All Cecil saw, was a huge leaf and mud monster, charging at him threateningly, wielding a large log.

The Devil stopped in his tracks. "Oh, it's you." "Where have you been?" He was slightly disappointed. The lecturer had advised them that catching an animal was the most difficult of all survival skills, yet he had accomplished the feat on his first attempt – or so he had thought. He didn't think angels would count somehow.

"What are you?! Don't hurt me!" pleaded Cecil, the effects of being upside down already disorientating him.

"Calm down, scaredy pants," Satan said, using the jibe he had only heard once in Heaven and assumed it was the worst of all insults "It's just me." And he wiped the mud from his face.

"Oh, it's you. Thank goodness, I've found you." The fear he had felt was far outweighed by the delight of finding Lucifer. "I've been looking everywhere for you."

"Well, you shouldn't have dropped me," the Devil pointed out.

"I didn't drop you. You jumped."

"I did not. You dropped me."

"No, you … can you just get me down from here." Cecil was turning a strange shade of purple from hanging upside down.

After struggling to release him, the two sat under the lean-to by the fire, totally worn out.

"We must get going. I need to take you to our Great Leader."

"Who? Tell me who this Leader is," demanded the Devil. He was not a fan of secrets or surprises.

"I'm sworn to secrecy. I can't tell you."

"So, let me get this straight. You want to take me somewhere, to meet someone, for some reason? And you won't tell me where, who or why?"

"Yes, that's about the gist of it," Cecil conceded.

"And you think I should go without being suspicious? After all, I am still a wanted fugitive in Heaven. How can I trust you?"

"Lucifer, it's me."

"Exactly. That's my point."

"Lucifer!" begged Cecil, who just wanted to deliver his parcel.

It was at this point the lean-to collapsed again. It was too much. The Devil gave a huge sigh. "Just take me to a warm bed!"

Fifty-Eight

Meanwhile, Day ended another long shift and handed his remaining light over to Evening. If Simon knew his master, which he did, then the Devil would be looking for a warm, oversized bed before Night descended.

During the last few hours, Simon had surreptitiously guided Guy and Roger in the direction he wished to go. Along the way, he encouraged them to look for clues and watched the two less than impressive officers interrogate half a dozen bewildered people. Guy might have gathered useful information using the age-old technique of police 'persuasion', if Roger hadn't intervened by referring to the rules and regulations. These always got in the way of everything was Guy's opinion. Even the Devil was now forced to follow certain conventions while torturing his subjects. However, butlers do not follow any written rules (and especially not regulations). They live by their handily named *'Butlers' Code'*. And the first rule was never to lose your master.

When Cecil first lifted the Devil into the sky, Simon managed to stay calm. For the next five minutes he watched carefully to see where Cecil was heading. The flat landscape of Heaven, stripped of a distant horizon, allowed him to follow their direction of travel for some time and fix a bearing. Guided by this, they set off, looking for clues as they walked.

Now Simon was having doubts and wanted to confirm they were still travelling in the right direction. He needed to question possible witnesses himself, rather than rely on the policemen's 'interrogation'. Mentally, he had jotted down a description of the angel who had taken the Devil. It was information he knew would come in handy later. But why had the Devil been abducted? It was true they'd been arguing, yet the Devil had not resisted. He knew that if he had put up a fight, there wasn't a chance anyone or anything could kidnap him. Putting the questions to the back of his mind, he realised they'd arrived at the ideal place to carry out their enquiries. They had arrived in a small cul-de-sac, with around twenty or so houses.

"Excuse me, officers, but we need to find an old lady. I have some questions to ask."

"Why?" demanded Guy warily. He felt Simon was becoming too bossy and failing to acknowledge their authority.

"Just a hunch I have that an old woman might be useful in locating Lucy."

"Listen here. You can't go scaring old women with police questions just on a hunch. We need facts and evidence," Roger pointed out.

"Ah, I see. An excellent point. It's just that while you were bravely rummaging through bins in search of clues, I happened to bump into an elderly gentleman. By remarkable good fortune, he informed me that a woman of some age saw Lucy and his assailant just fifty minutes ago."

This startling news energised both officers. Using their two conflicting approaches, they knocked or banged on every door in the cul-de-sac to hunt for this vital witness.

While the officers searched, Simon made a list of jobs to complete when he arrived back in Hell. He was so engrossed in list making that he almost missed the possible witness being apprehended. Luckily the sound of Guy's head being walloped with a leather handbag and Roger attempting to interrupt a one-way conversation, roused him from his distraction.

Guy had moved to knock at the entrance to the next house, but before his hand reached the door an old woman appeared. Instinctive creatures are old ladies. A frail, ancient woman, clutching a walking stick in one hand and bag in the other, peered out to see who was there. "I don't want any loft insulation." Her voice crackled with fermented with age, not smooth like a fine wine but bitter like a corked bottle.

"Do not fret, we are policemen and want to ask you a few questions. We believe you witnessed an incident earlier involving an angel and a large gentleman." Roger pulled a notepad from his top pocket, while he addressed the old lady.

His mouth opened to start his questioning, but the woman jumped in. "Mrs. Radmore, not two days ago, saw a girl stealing a bike. Mr. Radmore had to chase the girl and would have scolded her if it were not that, after the girl explained everything, it turned out to be her bike after all."

"Yes, but the angel…"

"And Mrs. Ravignani is always saying her apples go missing from her tree…"

Roger kept trying to interrupt but in vain. He heard all about Mrs. Robinson and Mr. Hedges. Not forgetting the suspected affair between Mr. Roland and Mrs. Taylor. You see, old women such as this, know everything that occurs on their street. From truth to rumour, they live to tell others about the goings on. Sky divers get their thrills by jumping from a plane at ten thousand feet, inquisitive, old ladies get the same enjoyment from boring others.

Roger felt that politeness and patience, were traits the public respected in a police officer. Guy differed in this opinion.

"Madam, you will be quiet and answer our questions."

Quite shocked that someone would be so rude, the woman fell silent.

"Right, that's better. If you do not answer these questions truthfully, we will be forced to escort you down to the station and charge you with providing false evidence."

Swapping his notepad for the rule book, Roger quickly thumbed through the volume, but before he could tell Guy there was no legal basis to charge her, a handbag striking Guy's head attracted his attention.

Smack went the bag. "Ow!" exclaimed Guy. *Bang* went the bag. "Arrest her, Roger!" *Clunk* round his head once more.

If Guy were Simon's boss, Simon would have quickly intervened, but as he was not, Simon walked at the speed of an injured sloth towards the scene.

"I see you have found our witness. Very good, gentlemen" And he calmly put his arm around the old lady's shoulder – who was halfway through giving Guy another hiding with her bag. "Would you care for a tea, madam? And perhaps you can tell me about everything happening in the street?"

She gave Guy one more wallop and then allowed Simon to lead her inside.

Sitting Mrs. Kang on a flowery, hideously coloured sofa, he found the kettle and made two teas. The policemen could make their own, he thought. He heard all about the street, how awful it was now, and how it used to be. How the new people were ruining everything, and anything else she could think of.

Feeling the time was right, Simon interjected. "Would you be so kind in assisting me?"

"Certainly, dear."

"Thank you. Earlier today, did you see an angel fly overhead, carrying a large, red man?" A question that in other circumstances could have seemed ridiculous.

"I was just telling Mrs. Beckit about it before you came round. I looked up and, for a moment, thought Heaven had a red shooting star. But when I put my bifocals on, I could see it was an angel carrying, as you say, a large red man. He seemed quite upset and was shouting about being let down."

"You have been most helpful. Just one more thing. Did you observe the direction they travelled in?"

"Yes. I watched them for some time. Not every day you see a red man flying. He must have really caught the sun. It reminded me of when I watched the Red Arrows flying team, back when I was just a young girl."

Simon interrupted with a polite cough.

"Sorry, Mr. Simon, I digress. They travelled straight as an arrow in that direction," she pointed with her walking stick. "I watched for some time and saw another strange thing I had never seen before."

"And what was that?"

"A red man being dropped from some height and landing in the forest."

"You have been of great assistance." Clearing away the teacups, Simon ushered the police out of her house while thanking the ancient one for her considerable help.

So, he knew where the Devil was heading. It was slightly surprising that he'd been dropped but nothing to worry about as his boss was pretty much indestructible. Now he needed to persuade Guy and Roger that they knew what to do and where to go. He definitely couldn't rely on them getting anything right.

"Splendid work, gentlemen. You will find Lucy in no time at all, I'm sure."

"Yes, well, we were just doing our job," Roger spluttered, not really knowing what had just happened. "Remind me again, which way did the crow – I mean the old woman – see them fly."

"This way." Guy confidently pointed – in the wrong direction.

Flabbergasted by their stupidity, Simon jumped in to help. "I see all your hard work has fatigued you. It was in fact this direction she pointed." And he led them away at a brisk pace.

"She just kept hitting me, Roger. Can't we arrest her?"

"Just leave it, Guy."

Fifty-Nine

Jealousy is a dangerous ingredient. At first glance it can be overlooked as a harmless, undesirable emotion, yet in the right conditions, it can be mixed and baked into a fatal dish. The result can take two forms: the instant snap reaction or the simmering brew of resentful rage. The first – the snap reaction – generally results in an 'Oh, I didn't mean to kill him' moment. The second – the slow, simmering type – can be much worse. When jealous thoughts are gradually brought to the boil in one's brain, it is prudent not to add other ingredients to the dish. Mix a pinch of anger with envy, and it creates a reaction so potent and so explosive that the effect is almost nuclear. You might think nothing could be worse, but you're wrong. Now, instead of adding a tablespoon of spite in one large dose, try regularly adding half a teaspoon every few days. This is insufficient to cause an eruption but enough to slowly increase the tension, until one day, the pressure is twice that of an atomic explosion. A psychotic maniac is created. One such fanatic was Slugart.

Slugart's metamorphosis from your run-of-the-mill angel to a deranged and anger-fuelled psychopath was long and complex but began with one emotion – jealousy.

Angels were created for greatness. Chosen by God to lead, admired by all, worshipped by some. Or at least that's how Slugart felt it should have been. When Gabriel was chosen to visit Earth he thought, 'why not me?'. When Raguel was asked to deliver punishment to fallen angels and take vengeance on the luminaries, he asked 'surely it was my turn?' but later, on reflection, whispered, 'thank the Lord it wasn't'.

Then his negative thoughts turned to humans. A spoonful of jealousy was added with each new arrival, and anger stirred in with each welcoming comment he heard other angels utter. It was rumoured that God preferred these mortals. He became aware of the changes in Heaven's culture, and his bitterness grew, mixed with ample measures of hate. Even a few well-respected groups of angels began to act like humans. At first, he did not notice that angels admired their earthly traits, but slowly they were absorbed into celestial life. Angels eating human food, making friends with the pets, adopting their slang words or worrying about the weather, were not sufficient triggers on their own to excite Slugart's attention. However, the sight of an angel acquaintance dining at a curry house with a mortal, discussing the weather as though they were best of friends, made him aware that these new arrivals were changing traditional culture forever. Observing their gradual encroachment into angel areas of Heaven regularly added a half teaspoon of resentment. He saw how they walked around, acting as though they owned the place. Settlements such as Human Town, built exclusively for the pets, appeared over-night. And they seemed to breed, or more accurately die, at an uncontrollable rate. No wonder Peter's gate was always so busy.

A psychotic angel does not flip; it doesn't go on a killing spree. It patiently waits and plans. Slugart planned. He set up his secret society, but he knew recruiting members could be problematic. The favoured option of posting flyers to advertise clandestine meetings was unavailable. So, instead he anonymously invited close friends while ensuring they were unaware of his role as organiser and leader.

The early gatherings were simple and brief. He wore a mask to cover his face and stood on a wooden box to address the few who attended. The majority felt awkward and disagreed with the hatred flowing from Slugart's mouth. They never returned. But others that empathised with his views found covert ways of inviting their own acquaintances.

As the attendees grew in number, things began to change. Slugart's costumes evolved to become more elaborate. He hired larger rooms and lit them with candles for effect. Then one evening, by chance, he found himself in an 'angels only' bar, with a human entertaining the crowd. This added anger to the brew. Bloody humans being allowed in, what next? Humans performing instead of angels! The act appeared on stage, wearing a tall black hat. Not paying much attention to the performance, he glanced at the crowd who gasped in amazement, as a rabbit was pulled from the hat. He asked an angel how had the rabbit got into the hat, but before she could reply, the show continued: doves seemed to appear from every part of the magician's body, and playing cards were correctly guessed. And so it continued until eventually the performance was brought to a premature end when the magician appeared to chop a colleague in half. Intrigued by what he had seen, Slugart, against his better judgement, engaged the performer in conversation and discovered that the act was all an illusion – a simple trick, he clarified.

Always quick to identify an opportunity, he studied the art of magic, and with several basic tricks mastered, incorporated them into his increasingly popular meetings. Slugart moved the small gatherings to a larger, more atmospheric building with the intention of creating mystery and suspense. The rooms were decorated for dramatic effect, bringing his rhetoric to life. He added music, enough artificial smoke to put any asthmatic's life at risk, and to top it all, he dressed in the most exquisitely tailored outfits. His robe was woven with a golden thread that made the light dance as it reflected back into the crowd's eyes. (Unfortunately, to Slugart's regret, he was forced to replace the robe with a dull grey version after receiving complaints that it conflicted with his own teachings on the importance of traditional dress.)

A natural at sleight of hand, Slugart became a talented magician. He invented tricks to manipulate the minds of those attending the meetings. Without warning, he would clap his hands to 'control' the candles in the room, leaving his followers aghast. Throwing doves into the air from seemingly empty hands added to their amazement, and the Brothers grew to respect their Leader as wise and powerful.

Evening still clung onto the remaining light before Night snatched the baton in their never-ending relay. Tonight's performance was planned to enhance his reputation further. The room for this pivotal meeting 'reeked' of all things gothic. The interior designer seemed to have cleared the 'everything must go' gothic sale and then bought extra gargoyles just in case. Intricately carved, dark wooden furniture was positioned around the room. Some pieces were finished in deep red velvet and others in smooth black leather. All were imposingly large and lit by an enormous candle chandelier, hung from the ceiling by large, black chains. A central stone stage was surrounded by fold-up, plastic chairs – which did rather ruin the look.

As the followers entered, they removed their sandals (a recent ritual added to the many that had accumulated over the years) and felt the cold of the smooth flag stones. Some muttered quietly that even humans had under floor heating.

They took their seats around the stage, avoiding eye contact with one another. Although interaction was discouraged, general chat was not. A casual observer would struggle to tell the sex or age of the Brothers as everyone dressed uniformly from head to toe. Obsessed with hiding their identity, many spoke using disguised voices. High pitch or deep, gruff accents were most common, which did tend to detract from the seriousness of any conversation. Many wondered what the leader would announce as they waited for him to appear. 'Would this be the day that the final solution was revealed.' All were hopeful.

Candles burned brightly everywhere, not only in the chandelier but dotted around on every piece of furniture and windowsill.

Suddenly, an angel appeared at the centre of the stage, and the room fell silent. It was their Leader. Slugart slowly turned, scrutinizing the audience and eyeing all his followers intensely. As he passed through the final degree of his rotation, he spoke. "Let there be light!"

The room exploded in a blaze of white light. Light, not of candles, nor daylight but far more intense. The followers shielded their eyes; it burnt so brightly it hurt. Despite the pain, all fought to keep their eyes open, not wanting to miss a moment on this day of reckoning. Slowly their pain subsided as they became accustomed to the glare, and their gaze became fixed on the Leader. A contrast of colours framed him. In pure night-black silhouette, he stood at the centre, striking a heroic pose – despite not possessing the stature normally associated with heroes. His arms thrust forward, with the palms open, as though the beam was radiating from his hands. It seemed that the energy had been sucked from him, but even though completely black, his presence radiated far into the room, illuminating all there.

Slugart raised his hands and brought them together with a loud clap. The lights went out. (This was his favourite way to start or end any trick.) Only the candles were left burning, filling the space with just enough energy to retain the atmosphere.

"Brothers. We have at last acquired the missing key."

A cheer erupted. Waving his arms around, he appealed for silence.

"I spoke of the great plague these humans are bringing."

Booing replaced the cheers.

"Well, we now have the means to save Heaven from the invading parasites."

"How, oh Great Leader? How can we save Heaven from the human infestation?" There is always a keen member of the audience who sits at the front, ready to join in. The question was delivered in such a strange, deep voice, it could only have been from a female attempting to hide her gender.

"Tomorrow, I will reveal all. We will meet and you will see. I cannot tell you the details until then, in case there is treachery within our ranks."

Everyone looked at each other suspiciously, each certain in their own minds they knew this treacherous spy.

"Together we will achieve the impossible. Dark will become light. No longer will you be subjected to the humiliation that these 'things' impose on us. We seek the truth." This was the first line of the cult's chant. All repeated the words with each line getting louder. They felt an unsettling sensation, like a wind growing stronger, after each word.

"We seek the truth."

"We seek to cleanse."

"We are one."

"We are not a cult."

The wind stopped as the last word was spoken. Most assumed, believed, or even thought that the wind was yet another manifestation of their Leader's growing power.

With the customary cult chanting over, a more relaxed leader continued: "Now let us begin tonight's agenda."

The meeting continued with nothing else of importance or excitement discussed. Hector watched quietly. Thoughtful quietness. He held his book close throughout. Fingering the page that encapsulated his doubts, he struggled with his timidness to question the Great Leader about the words.

A moment of calm filled the room as the Leader consulted the agenda. After an intense debate on what brand of tea they should drink at their meetings, he'd forgotten the next item. At this moment, a surge of energy jolted Hector into action, overriding his previous decision (made only a minute before) to raise his question at the next meeting, and found himself shouting out: "Excuse me, excuse me." The calm turned to deadly silence. It was not customary to directly address the Leader unless spoken to by him. Eyes all turned towards Hector. "Er, excuse me, Great Leader. I have a question about the book."

Slugart kept calm, not taken aback by the sudden interruption. He held up his arm to bring further silence to the room. "You shall not..."

Hector, against his better judgement, carried on. "It's just this line on page forty-nine. The bit that says 'Although we are different, we see the same light. Don't believe the hype.' Is that about the humans? As it does not specifically mention angels or humans like other chapters but uses the inclusive word 'all'."

The silence stayed silent. Slugart stumbled for an answer but delayed too long.

"Yeah, what does that mean?" an eager angel shouted from the back, suddenly deciding that Hector had a point.

Having mulled it over in her brain, twisting the sentence this way and that, another angel shouted. "Hold on, doesn't that make humans ok?"

Slugart felt a bead of sweat forming as his brain fought for a quick answer. Why would his book say this? He wrote the damn book! Then an angel in the crowd came to his rescue.

"What page was that, matey? Can't find it anywhere," enquired the saviour.

"Forty-nine. I've wondered about it for a while," replied Hector with more confidence.

"That's what I thought you'd said. It don't say that in mine, fella."

Other angels decided to check their books.

"Nor mine." "Not in this one." And so on.

Slugart demanded to see a copy. Satisfied, he walked to the gold-plated book at the back of the stage. It was said that this version was infallible and created by God's own hands. "They are right!" he pronounced triumphantly. He smiled. "Bring that book up here, brother, and we shall burn the blasphemous page.

Hector's emotions had gone from scared, to brave, to shocked. He did not resist as a Brother snatched the beloved book from his powerless hand. The words that bothered him so much were not even meant to be there! Watching in shock and horror, his book was set alight from the flame of a nearby candle, and as it burnt, Hector felt a pain deep within. It wasn't the humiliation that bothered him. It felt more personal than that as though the words were attached to him – even being a part of him. Hector stared in horror as his treasured book fell into a pile of ash.

Slugart ensured the book was fully destroyed – while instructing someone to remove the battery from the fire alarm they'd set off. He found a new copy, checked the page and handed it to Hector.

"They say we are a cult. We are not a cult," preached Slugart, hoping to move on quickly from the embarrassing interruption.

"We are not a cult," all repeated without thinking – very much in the manner of a cult.

All left the meeting, anticipating the next day with heightened excitement. Except Hector, who went home deflated. He checked his new book in vain – the words were indeed no longer there. Inside he felt empty, inside he felt hurt.

Sixty

Wood has been used to construct buildings for thousands of years. Even now, wooden framed buildings are commonplace – despite the well-known 'threat' from wolves. But thanks to the warnings issued in bedtime stories, there is little evidence that humans or pigs ever constructed a home made from straw. It is with some amazement that people still use alternatives to wolf-proof bricks to construct their homes.

Looking through the deep dark forest, a pack of rather delightful, friendly wolves watched Guy attempt to rebuild the shelter that the Devil and Cecil had recently abandoned.

"If we first lay the logs out in order of size, we could plan how to use them optimally." Roger was an avid list maker, with an inner urge to organise and plan. Guy, however, favoured intuition when approaching a task and always began by discarding any instructions. This is perhaps why the lean-to had collapsed three times already.

There had been some success elsewhere. While the two officers argued over the details of shelter construction, Simon busied himself lighting a fire. It now roared, heating the chilly night air. He sat on a moss-covered log and pondered as he gazed up into Heaven's starless sky. His first concern was for his master, but with no obvious explanation for his plight, he next wondered how to make a cup of tea. There were two options to explain the Devil's disappearance. He might have been kidnapped – but this was unlikely. His superior strength would have enabled him to defeat any would-be kidnapper. The only other plausible reason was that he had left of his own free-will with an old acquaintance. But why would an angel want to talk to the Devil? They surely detested him; he was the anti-Christ, a polar opposite. They should be throwing him out, not having lunch with him. Hard though it was to accept this second scenario, he came to the conclusion that it must be correct – this angel knew his master was in Heaven and needed something from him.

The night sky was doing its best to remain dull and uninteresting, so Simon amused himself watching Roger organise and categorise each item of wood, while Guy grew increasingly frustrated. Simon was happy to pass the night by the fire. He'd experienced worse places on Earth.

The pack of wolves watched over these three 'little piggies', resisting their natural urge to huff and puff and blow the lean-to down.

Sixty-One

Satan reigned as the undisputed king of his realm and was unaccustomed to sleeping on forest floors. Which is why he chose to sleep in a comfy bed instead.

Cecil had lifted the Devil and flown from the forest to their prepared safe house. As they flew, the Devil felt a tinge of jealousy. He recalled the freedom of flying when he was still an angel. Regret featured rarely in the Devil's vocabulary. Words like pain, suffering and stand-up-meetings were used more frequently. But at this moment, he certainly felt a degree of remorse over his attempt to seize power all that time ago when he risked oblivion by seeking to overthrow God. In truth he felt no guilt, only a sense of loss. His wings, friends and the excitement of watching angels' sport were amongst things he missed most.

After asking Cecil three times to disclose where they were going and why, he gave up. The Devil had no fear of who he would meet, or even what they wanted — he was the Devil and angels were no match for him. But he was intrigued. So, he'd decided to humour Cecil for a while. Once the reason for his mysterious abduction had been divulged, he could head back to Hell as planned. Simon would catch up sooner or later.

He rolled over in his warm bed only to find Cecil lying next to him, eyes wide open, watching him intently. "Go to sleep, Cecil. Stop acting weird."

Cecil planned to do the opposite. He refused to lose the Devil again and would stay awake the whole night if need be.

Sixty-Two

Dejected, humiliated and exhausted, Hector removed his brown robes and washed his face before climbing into bed. He switched on the bedside lamp and thumbed through his book until he found the page that caused so much confusion. Looking up to the heavens – or wherever is up from Heaven – he gave a slight sigh and placed the book under his pillow. Hector hadn't the energy to read it now; he knew the words were no longer there. The Leader was right – mortals had caused too much unforgivable damage and must be dealt with. Laying down, he turned off the light.

Unable to sleep, Hector rolled on to his side, wrapping the warm covers around his body. The problem remained that, deep down, he liked the humans and enjoyed their company. If they were no longer here, he'd miss them. But the Leader said they did not belong in Heaven and evicting them would be in their own interest. They would find a better life elsewhere. It must be true, for he was the Great Leader after all. The power and authority demonstrated during the meeting made Hector shudder, but he felt deflated now and hoped a good night's sleep would bring clarity to his thoughts in the morning.

Sleep came eventually, although the room was far from silent. It was filled with the sound of snoring, registering a high number of decibels on each exhalation. The noise was sufficient to attract the attention of wandering dreams. Dreams, you see, are creatures of the night. They roam through every bedroom, invisible to humans and angels and look for a brain to supply the energy they require to function. In sleep, you become a target. Hector's snoring attracted their attention and soon one infiltrated his mind. It drifted unnoticed past his brain's resting guards and floated into the area where dreams are played out, ready to reveal their vision to Hector's unconscious.

His new book lay closed in a void of blackness. Nothing stirred for some time. Then in a sudden commotion, the book sprung open to page forty-nine, and slowly, letter by letter, the rejected words carved themselves back onto the paper. With the message glaring at Hector through the dream, the book slammed shut. It woke him with a jolt as though he had fallen from a great height. Sweat ran down his back. Hector looked round for reassurance and realised it was only a dream, and he was not in any danger. Laying back down in the safety of his bed, he closed his eyes once more. Subconsciously he reached his hand under the pillow and felt for his book. It was still there.

He tried to settle and closed his eyes once more. Five long minutes passed, and no matter how many sheep were counted, he could not relax. The dream had disturbed him, and now he was wide awake. He needed a familiar story to lull him to sleep, so he took his new copy of 'My War' from under the pillow. It was a suitable choice – the text was far from thrilling. But the page he'd randomly selected made his eyes open wide. Hector snapped the book shut, blinked a few times and re-opened it. It was page forty-nine. They were still there, the words had reappeared. But how? It was impossible! He closed and opened the book several times to make sure. What was happening? Everyone had checked, and none had found these words. The Leader insisted they should not be there. Breathing slowly to calm himself, he fought to think logically. If the Leader was convinced the words should not be there, then they shouldn't. They were blasphemous! In a panic he ripped the page from his copy, crushed it in his hands and threw it to the floor. He stared horrified at the screwed-up page and could not comprehend what had happened. Hector's brain scrambled for answers but there was no fuel left to power his understanding. His eyelids struggled to stay open, and after blinking in a last ditch stand against sleep, they finally closed. The room was silent. He was too exhausted to snore.

Sixty-Three

A magician relies on a controlled environment to perform his trickery. Within four walls, illusions are viewed from a managed perspective, using hidden props and technology, but outside, these things are much harder to control. That is why, in the depth of night, Slugart was carefully arranging the set ready for the next day's meeting at the entrance to Heaven. He'd tripped over many a sleeping human and cursed more times than angels should, but nothing was to be left to chance. Tired and full of excited anticipation, he made his way home, for tomorrow was the day of enlightenment.

Sixty-Four

Light flooded into Cecil's eyes as morning found a gap between the curtains. He'd been awake. Right? Made sure Lucifer stayed put; guarded him all night. Right? Then why was he laying down? He had been standing all night, hadn't he? His head flashed sideways to where the Devil had slept. The light poured in, but no red light reflected back onto his retinas. Cecil sprung upright and turned in all possible directions, searching for the red of the Devil. Nothing. His lower body decided to join in. He sprang to his feet and dashed around the room, checking under the bed, in the wardrobe, in the bedside tables. (In no known dimension of the universe could the bedside table possibly accommodate the great mass of Satan.) Still nothing. This was disastrous – a catastrophe. He sank to his knees, clenched the bed sheets and screamed in anger. He tore the sheets off as he got to his feet, and a lamp minding its own business, found itself hurtling through the air. Cecil swore as though he were going for a gold medal in the bi-centennial, foul mouth championship of Heaven. It was a disaster. Surely lightning had not struck twice, and he had lost the Devil again. It was the day of the foretold enlightenment, and Cecil – the so-called heroic, parcel deliverer – had lost the blessed parcel. He tore a painting from the wall and smashed it against the nearest object he could find. Surprisingly, the object spoke.

"Cecil. What the hell are you doing?" Standing in just his underwear and filling most of the bedroom doorway, was the Devil. The painting had not hurt, but it took him a little by surprise.

"I came to ask if you wanted tea with your fried breakfast. I hope you don't mind, but I found all the ingredients in the fridge and was feeling peckish. And I arrive here to find you having a tantrum over something. I could recommend a few anger-management courses I've been … I mean, I've sent people on. But don't go using the one in Heaven. It's run by a con man. Anyway, it was a tea you wanted? Right, I'll just be a minute." The Devil left

Cecil with his mouth hanging open and whose breathing suggested a heart attack was imminent.

After pausing for a minute or two, Cecil's brain acknowledged the mess caused by his brief rampage. He was still cleaning up when Lucifer returned with tea and breakfast. (Not to be mistaken for two meals that should be taken at opposite ends of the day but simply a drink with a morning meal.) They ate together and chatted of old times. The Devil had decided not to probe Cecil any further but to wait and see how events unfolded.

"I just wish Simon was here with my clothes. I don't understand why you didn't take him too."

"The human that was with you?" enquired Cecil.

"Yes. He's my butler."

"Your what?"

"Do I have to explain everything to you? Butler, man servant. You know, lays out my clothes, makes tea, gets me things before I realise I need them. Everyone should have one."

"A Slave?" That was more like it thought Cecil. Making God's pets do what you told them.

"Don't be such a fool, Cecil. Butlers are not slaves. Anyhow, today is a big day you say?"

This brought a smile to Cecil's face, "Yes, the most special day."

"And I have to wear these dirty clothes?" The Devil looked down at his stained, knee-length, off-white shorts. According to Style Magazine, they were an ideal choice for the sophisticated gentleman when visiting a beach but certainly not what he'd choose for a potentially important meeting. "I could be dressed in one of my many bespoke suits, matched with a suitably suave pair of shoes but no, you had to leave Simon behind."

"Well sorry, Lucifer. It's just you know – he's a human."

This sentence confused the Devil, but he let it pass and dressed himself for the first time in a long while.

Sixty-Five

"So, Lucy was just sunburnt yesterday?"

"Yes, his skin is particularly pale."

"And he often gets sunburnt in Heaven?"

"Yes, he is very prone to burning."

"Even though there is no sun...?" Roger let the question hang in the air.

"Like I said, he burns easily" Simon answered as casually as possible.

"I see. And he goes to the gym?"

"No, he is naturally a strong gentleman."

"Strong in the 'oh my god, he must be a super-hero' type of strong?"

"Just averagely strong, by all accounts. Whatever you saw to suggest he has abnormal strength must have been an illusion." Simon didn't particularly care if these idiots wanted to think that Lucy was the Devil, but he wanted to keep control over them by making sure they retained their doubts for now. It was not their powers of deduction that Simon required but their knowledge of Heaven.

"Interesting. So why do you believe this angel has kidnapped your friend, Lucy?"

"Almost certainly over a disagreement between them. I'm sure we met this angel in the pub the other day."

All three were eating cereal, uncomfortably seated around a table designed for two. Guy listened to Roger's subtle questioning, but he was not in the mood for subtle. He'd shared a single bed with Roger and lacked sleep, and now Simon's knees were in his way. "Look, Simon, is he the bleeding Devil?!" Unintentionally he knocked over the milk for added effect.

Roger jumped to his feet and pulled Guy away, leaving Simon to clear up the milk.

"We just need to be careful, Guy. Our reputations could be ruined if it became known we mistook a sunburnt man called Lucy for the Devil taking a vacation in Heaven," Roger whispered pointedly.

"Ok, ok. It just frustrates me, all this tip toeing around." And he received a pat on his back for being so understanding.

With the table now clean, Simon brought a piping hot pot of tea to complete their breakfast. "Are you gentlemen ok? Did I hear you mention the Devil?" asked Simon, pouring three cups as he spoke.

"No, no, no. Of course not. Rest assured, we will find your friend."

"Perhaps I could answer a few questions about Lucy. Build up a profile to help you deduce his whereabouts? Merely a thought of course. I'd feel terrible offering suggestions you feel are too obvious." Simon delivered the line with a look of innocence.

"We were this very moment about to do that exact thing of..," Roger struggled for the word he had just heard.

"Interrogation?" Guy jumped in with his version.

"No, you idiot."

Still unable to remember, Simon helped Roger out.

"Perhaps you meant 'profiling' the captured Lucy."

"Yes. Thank you. I'd have said just that if you'd given me a few more seconds."

"Of course, officer."

"I would, you know."

"I do not hesitate to believe you."

"Honestly. It was in my very next breath."

"He would, you know." Guy backed him up, giving some moral support to his partner "There's no fibbing allowed in the police. It's in the rule book."

"Thank you, Guy. That's enough now," said Roger, feeling the heat rising on his cheeks as they turned red.

"The one we swore that oath on. Where we repeated about never telling a lie. You know that bit with fancy words," Guy persevered.

Roger was remembering the oath. He took it very seriously, and now he had just told a lie while on duty. "That's enough now, Guy. Can you fetch some paper and take notes, while we build up this...bugger what's that word again?"

"Profile," both Guy and Simon replied this time.

"Yes prrr ..." Roger's guilt attack had the effect of preventing him from delivering the word. "Yes, that word. Right, let's get started."

To say Roger was grossly under qualified to conduct a profiling session, was an understatement akin to stating a whale lacks the qualities to perform exquisite ballet. The first two minutes consisted of silence, broken by a few coughs. The next few produced an in-depth profile of the Devil's name. How knowing this could help locate him, remained a mystery.

Simon grew impatient and helped by answering questions before they were asked.

"Lucy will be looking for a tailor. He has left without his suitcase so will not have had a change of clothes since his abduction. Therefore, a tailor and shoe shop will be high on his list of priorities."

"I'm really building up a good picture of him now. Guy, are you taking all this down?"

"Yes, Roger. Just one question. Why would the kidnapper allow their victim a visit to a tailor?"

Damn. Why hadn't I considered that, thought Roger. "Yes, as my colleague said – why?"

"Lucy has amazing powers of persuasion. I am certain even a hardened criminal would be convinced by him."

"Hmmm."

"And it would have to be the best tailor in the area," Simon hinted. He had pretty much told them where the Devil could be found and could do no more for now. Roger and Guy huddled together in deep, whispered conversation. Simon could tell it would be a while before they took action so, to relax, he started tidying.

Sixty-Six

The function of sleep is a little understood yet much researched human trait. Many of the various theories have significant flaws.

Being as we are in Heaven (so we accept God did create humans) we can park any heated debates between the Pope and atheists on the matter. This makes it a fact that Darwin was mad, and the 'all mighty', bearded one did indeed create people with His own hands. But something so complex cannot just be made on the fly, without designs drafted and prototypes tested. At some point, perhaps while working on one of the early versions – chimpanzees for example – He realised these creatures always ran out of energy at the end of the day. They inevitably failed to restart the next morning unless He gave them a good kick up the backside. This was not a permanent, working solution for the number of humans God planned to create. There would be no time to do all this kicking, so he developed the charger – not a modern, plugin device but a bed. In later models, He dispensed with the bed and designed a recharge function – aka sleep – which could be activated anywhere. A genius solution by a genius, God. Genius!

There's nothing more comforting after a long hard day than to cosy up under the covers and fall into a deep sleep. Humans should rejoice in the gift of sleep. And they would have celebrated if God had bothered to watch what happens in the morning. The trauma experienced when waking from a sound slumber is one of God's great oversights.

Argghhh," went Hector. "Urghhhhh," he replied. His eyes attempted to open from their eventful dream but instead shut tighter, disobeying any orders from his brain. He rolled over and cocooned himself tightly inside the quilt. Every morning, humans and angels get a brief reminder of Hell while they try to escape their nightly recharge.

Brrrrrrrrring, brrrrrrrring, sounded the bedside alarm.

"Gargggggg," replied Hector. His arm responded with a swift right hook, knocking the clock from the table and onto the carpeted floor.

Brrrrrrrring. The clock continued, now slightly muffled by the deep pile. This time it was out of reach, and Hector's body accepted defeat. Up, his brain commanded, but the body made one last stand. He rolled over to the edge of his bed, eyes still clenched shut, and stretched as far as he could, probing the floor for the clock. Bingo, he had it, but it was too soon to celebrate. Just when his finger found the off switch, his body tipped past the delicate balance point and landed with a thump. Luckily for Hector the carpet was new and still soft, otherwise the landing would have occurred on the stone floor hidden beneath. At least the fall had finally freed him from the hellish, waking struggle.

Even with only a hint of light creeping in through the blinds, his eyes instantly recognised the crumpled page laying on the floor as the one he'd torn out during the night. Powerless to resist the overwhelming urge, he straightened the page to reveal its blasphemous message. His brain recalled the text instinctively, but his eyes failed to see any words. He stood up and opened the blinds. The bright light made Hector squint as he tried to read, but the words had vanished, and they were still missing after he had washed and poured a coffee. Hector struggled to rationalise their absence, but there was no logical explanation. He could only assume fatigue had caused him to imagine their presence last night.

Hugely relieved he wasn't going mad, but secretly disappointed that the text had not magically reappeared, Hector went about his morning ritual – wash, teeth, dress and breakfast – a bog standard, average angel sort of routine. As always, he limited his choice of breakfast to the traditional porridge, (which is similar to the human version, except it doesn't require sweetening). Routines are performed on autopilot, and so it was, at the end of his breakfast, Hector automatically reached for the book and randomly turned to a page. He felt that reading a line would motivate him for the day ahead.

Although we are different, we see the same light. Don't believe the hype.

Instantly, he recognised the words as he scanned them in horror. They couldn't be there. He had torn the page out last night! Or was it his over eager imagination playing tricks? What was happening? Panic tried to take control, but Hector was too old and wise for that and a sense of calm quickly returned. Of course, he had obviously ripped out the wrong page, he concluded. But how they got there in the first place still remained a mystery. Now he was awake, there would be no mistake this time. He did not want to damage the book more than necessary so crossed through the line using a black marker pen instead. He could request a replacement book later.

Before leaving his house, Hector tried to read another line of text to prepare him for the day ahead. Flipping the book open randomly once more, it didn't take more than two words to realise it was the same damned line again, the one he'd already pulled out. The one he found just now and scored through was still there without any black ink to obscure it. He opened the book to a different page and again, the same line appeared. What in Heaven's name was going on?

Sixty-Seven

Why could he not stick to the bloody script? Cecil had tried all the distraction techniques he knew and concluded that a change to his original plan was inevitable. Slugart wanted Lucifer delivered once darkness had fallen, so Cecil intended to remain in the safe house until evening. What he had failed to remember from his past acquaintance with Lucifer was that the Devil never kept still. He craved activity, whether it be a spot of tennis or a war against God – anything to stay busy.

For the past hour, the Devil had been pestering Cecil about their schedule for the day. Cecil kept him at bay for a while by promising a mystery tour later, but the delay made Lucifer bored and restless. He knew something must be done.

"If you do not take me to the finest tailor in Heaven to replace these battered clothes, I'll forcibly remove your wings. There must be enough time before we go to wherever it is we are going." There wasn't a chance the Devil would attend a potentially important business meeting wearing anything other than the finest suit. "And I want to see more tourist sights on our journey. I came here on a holiday and I want to see them." In truth, he and Simon had already seen everything they had intended but plenty more attractions were mentioned in his guide.

"Alright, alright." Cecil's anger was rising, and he realised this would end in a fight if they didn't get out of the house soon. "Where do you want to go? The great maze of Heaven? Or maybe the bowling green in the Old Heaven village?"

Looking at Cecil in a *'you blithering idiot'* sort of way, he replied, "Why would I want to see that load of crap. I can't believe it's still there. I want to see the zoos, the water parks, cinemas. Modern stuff."

Cecil returned a stare which clearly said, *'are you serious?'* "But that's all human stuff. Surely, we should visit good old angel places," he whined.

"Angel fun is for grandads," the Devil retorted.

Cecil didn't know whether to reply with either *'but angels don't have grandads'* or *'humans are worse than the dirt on the mud on the sole of my sandal'*, but in the end he kept shtum.

"I have read about all the new attractions. They sound exciting, and I wish to visit as many as possible. I'd planned to have returned home by now, but as you have inconvenienced me, I command you take me today." Adopting his *'ruler of Hell, bringer of doom'* persona, he loomed over the cowering Cecil. "And then we shall visit the tailor," the Devil concluded, more calmly.

"But humans are scum. They have destroyed Heaven by bringing their evil ways."

"Admittedly, they can be annoying, especially their obsession with pointless rules and regulations," (the introduction of mandatory rest between torture sessions had infuriated the Devil), "but they do seem to know how to enjoy themselves."

"But..."

"Cecil, I am going. Whether you join me or not is up you." And he turned and walked towards the front door.

"Ok, ok. Where do you want to go first?"

"That's better Cecil. You'll be my tour guide. First, we shall bungee jump."

Sixty-Eight

It was already late morning, normally a busy time for Peter. The backlog of new arrivals was cleared yesterday, before retiring to bed, but he was faced with more each day who had inconsiderately died overnight. Peter found these fresh newbies especially annoying; they were overly worried, continually asked questions and persistently demanded answers. A busy man like him did not have time for this. All they had done was die.

Fed up with the morning rush, Peter posted a list of FAQs at the gate, yet they'd still repeat the question when he arrived. None showed him any respect. Well, today they could wait. Heaven was closed until further notice – or at least until the evening.

During one of their discussions, Slugart had suggested drawing up a contract that humans must sign when they arrived. Peter liked that idea and agreed to draft a few thoughts for Slugart to see when they next met. So, after an extremely late breakfast, a long, hot shower and a lengthy search for his rarely used reading glasses, Peter was ready. Pen poised above the paper, he tried to extract the key words floating around in his mind as 'ingredients' to bake a coherent sentence. But what came out of the 'oven' were not coherent phrases but simply childish doodles of humans in unfortunate situations. He wasn't a student of advanced hieroglyphics but a hapless angel with nothing of substance to record. There was not a dicky bird of a suggestion from his brain to re-tweet. It dawned on him that he had no idea what factors should determine the entry rules. In all the time he had guided souls through the gate, he'd never actually thought about the operational details. His mind focussed solely on how to wind them up.

He tried to concentrate once more, and the rusty cogs in his brain gradually started to turn. Religion. *Man should dig religion*, he wrote. Hold on, he thought, God had never actually said anything to him about religion. Those meddling angels blew that trumpet. Crossing 'religion' out, he tried again.

He was on a roll now. *No murdering your bredrin*. But God would have already vetted the murderers before they reached the gate. 'Murderers' was scribbled out too. This was going to be harder than he first thought.

Helpfully, an idea flashed into his mind. What better way to be inspired than to mingle amongst the subject of his problem He dressed quickly and opened his front door to be met by the sound of the impatient human throng. No, he couldn't face answering their questions today, so he quickly retreated inside where something caught his eye that would enable him to join the crowd without them ever suspecting his identity. A quick change of clothes later, and he ventured outside once more to brave the horde.

The French are credited with inventing modern camouflage, stealth was a German idea and Inspector Jacques Clouseau was an expert at surveillance. Sadly, Peter's choice of disguise provided none of these benefits. The old fancy dress costume he now wore (discarded after the human carnival) had at the time seemed ideal, but his brain had concentrated solely on disguise and had skipped any thought of appearance.

Ignoring the strange glances he received from the disorderly line, Peter joined their throng and observed them as he waited. *No queue jumpers* was quickly jotted down. They made him angry; he always gave them the hardest time when they reached his gate.

He was quite obsessed about queuing. Some days he would demand they form a large snaking line, whereas others he would arrange them by nationality. His favourite option was to organise them by height, creating the impression of the mystical stairway to Heaven.

Rule one ticked off then. Rudeness was another easy contender. Mind your p's and q's, or no entry. Two possible candidates, but after standing in the queue for ten minutes, he struggled to add any more.

"Funny way to die, there mate. How'd it happen?" enquired the smartly dressed, bespectacled guy in front of Peter.

This interrupted Peter's concentration. "What you say there, bro? I ain't dead."

"What do you think all this is then?" the bloke gestured around them. He felt it was Peter who perhaps required glasses.

Snapping his brain into action, Peter remembered that he was meant to be dead. "Yeah, dead. Forgot all about it."

"How'd the Grim Reaper get you then?"

Peter was taken by surprise. He had no cover story prepared, but he recalled talk of wars recently and opted for that. "Was tragic, bro. Got gunned down on the field of battle."

"I'm sorry, did you say war? You were actually on a battlefield?" A look of bemusement scanned Peter up and down.

"Yes, bro. Was shooting bad guys like no tomorrow and then pow. Some sneaky sniper clocked me and that was it. Woke up in this ghetto." Peter was pretty pleased with his ad-hoc story telling.

"So, you were in an actual battle? At war?"

It was the constant questions from humans that could really grind Peter down. "Yes. That's what I've just told you twice. Three times now, geez!"

The man paused just to check with himself that he wasn't missing anything obvious. "Just that you're wearing a banana costume."

Oh crap, I am, Peter thought. "And?" he replied assertively.

A bit taken back by the confident reply, the man protested, "You can't wear a banana costume in battle."

"You bloody well can, bro. Special forces gear, this. First rule of combat is to surprise your enemy."

"Well yes, I can see it'd surprise them alright but.."

"Enough of this crap," Peter retaliated, admitting defeat. "I'm off to see who's in charge." And Peter walked away with as much swagger as a banana could muster.

Sixty-Nine

For the first time in God knows how long (and He did), Hector arrived at work late. In vain, he had paced back and forth at home for too long, trying to rid his book of the words. With little time to prepare the soup before his first customer arrived, everything had been rushed. The stall looked a mess, in stark contrast to its orderly appearance on a normal day.

The words. Why were they following him? Why did no one else see them?

Although we are different, we see the same light. Don't believe the hype.

Over and over they echoed in his head. Even though Hector had left the book at home, he could think of little else.

Although we are different, we see the same light. Don't believe the hype.

A polite cough interrupted his thoughts. A second made him realise he was reciting the words aloud. Staring at him inquisitively, stood a member of the Brotherhood as she waited to be served. Hector rushed to fill the cup containing the hidden message. The soup overflowed and ran down the sides as he passed it to the angel. She took it without the usual pleasantries and muttered something under her breath about poor service.

He cleaned the spillage, but the words returned.

Although we are different, we see the same light. Don't believe the hype.

Desperate to blank the words from his mind, he focussed so intently that he failed to hear the next customer approach.

"Good morning, Hector."

"Arghh", screamed a startled Hector causing him to jump in the air together with the soup, which landed on the equally startled customer.

"Arghhh," echoed the customer.

"Please forgive me. I don't know what happened. I apologise a million times." Hector found a towel to wipe the angel's robes as best he could.

"Yes, yes. That's enough. Just give me the message. Oh crap, I meant soup and let me get on." Pushing Hector away, he grabbed the cup and left without even saying goodbye.

Hector collapsed onto on his stool to recover. I need to concentrate, he told himself. Today the Leader will enlighten us all. I must forget about the words. Hector unconsciously patted his pocket where the book would normally be. He knew that it should be at home. But something was not right. He touched the pocket again and wondered what was inside so obviously disguised as a book. Nervously, he pulled the object from his robe and entered a brief staring contest with the book. But how did it get there? He was certain it had been left at home. Perhaps he had picked it up subconsciously as part of his routine. Hands trembling, he opened the copy. And there on every page were the blasphemous lines. No other words remained. On every page they stared back at him, some in bold, imposing fonts, others in ancient, coloured script. But all said the same.

In sheer panic, he hurled the book high into the air.

Plop – it nosedived into the pot of soup.

"Glorious day, don't you think, brother?" greeted the third customer of the day.

"What? Oh yes. It is a glorious start to the glorious day." While he spoke, Hector kept a close eye on the soup pot, wondering where the book had landed.

"My soup, please, Hector."

"Oh. Yes, of course."

As he poured the liquid from a large ladle, he watched in horror as the book dropped into the cup. Quickly he attached the lid and put it to one side.

"Pass it over, please. I'm in an awful rush today. Lots to do."

"Oh, that one? You don't want that one. It's, er, cold."

"Cold?"

"Yes, cold. Let me get you another."

"Another from the same pot? Surely that would be cold too?"

"Er, potentially, maybe. But you know, definitely worth a try." Hector was panicking.

"I can see what's going on. That's a special one for someone else. Well, I want it. Now give it here."

"But it's cold. Honestly."

"Give it." The angel held out his stretched arm, demanding the soup.

Hector admitted defeat and reluctantly handed over the book-contaminated soup. "Enjoy," he said.

He watched with relief as the blasted book disappeared around the corner. Perhaps he could concentrate on his work again now.

Hector tidied the stall and prepared the soup and message for the next 'customer'. If he had thought more deeply, he would have realised he was the only angel entrusted to recognise all members of the Brotherhood and secretly pass them covert messages every day. No one else knew their identities except him.

Because he was not a deep thinker, the unrelenting words found his brain open and 'well-greased', allowing them to slide in unchallenged. Slowly and quietly, they regrouped and repeated themselves in an endless chant. In a whisper at first, the rhythm and noise grew faster and louder until Hector started to take notice. Finally, he could stand it no longer, stuck his fingers into his ears and countered with the chant of the sect.

"We do believe, we will succeed."

"The Leader is the truth."

"He will guide us to the promised land."

But the words battled for attention, growing louder and louder. Hector sank into his chair, grasped the sides of his head and squeezed it tightly between his knees.

"Arghhhhh, leave me alone. Leave me. Please, leave me alone."

Silence. The words stopped as though obeying a command. He raised his head slowly and removed one hand. A deep sigh of relief exhaled from his body. Then he noticed something. One hand felt different to the other. After a momentary pause, the brain deduced the hand was holding something. No, it couldn't be. But when he looked down it was there.

"Can I have my soup, Hector?"

"Arghh." Hector's heart jumped and he screamed again.

"Is this your book? Why have you just thrown it at me?"

"Yes. Sorry. Here's your soup."

"And this is yours, I believe. You know, it's not nice throwing books at innocent angels. It could have taken my eye out." The customer handed over the unwanted volume. "Well, aren't you going to take it?"

"Erm. You can keep it if you'd like?"

"No, no. You keep it just in case you feel the urge to hurl it at someone else."

Hector reluctantly grasped the book. The angel departed, and Hector ducked behind the stall. Hidden from view, he turned to a random page. The words were still there. He held on to the cart for support, momentarily feeling faint. There were only two beings who had the power to do this. The Leader – and God!

Seventy

Weighed down with a suitcase each, the two policemen trailed some distance behind. Simon drew on his training during a spell in the army, shortly after leaving school, to maintain a fast pace and fell into the brisk marching rhythm he deployed whenever he was rushed. Occasionally, he would stop to hasten the trailing officers along, emphasising the importance of finding any kidnap victim within the first forty-eight hours. Unfortunately, this observation slowed proceedings further, while Roger explained it would be more accurate to say fifty-four hours as there were twenty-seven hours each day in Heaven. Simon agreed and suggested they should, therefore, not waste these extra hours God had bestowed upon them. Which Roger concurred with, only to be interrupted by Guy, who couldn't understand why the rule was now fifty-four hours, when his education (extensive reading of detective novels) clearly indicated the correct answer was forty-eight. Eventually, he grasped the concept – or at least, said he did.

The speed of an angel flying through the skies of Heaven compared to the pace of a human trekking through the undulating terrain beneath is reminiscent of the fabled race between the hare and tortoise. Except there is no happy ending for the tortoise. Instead, the tortoise will always lose and be ridiculed for even suggesting the race in the first place. So, understandably, the chasing 'tortoises' were still some distance away from the Devil. Fed up with carrying the burden of Simon's suitcase, Roger used his last reserve of energy to catch up with Simon. "Could we not leave your cases at the next shop or pub until we find Lucy?" Roger protested.

"I'm afraid it contains many valuable items that I cannot risk being snatched by an opportunistic thief," replied Simon

"Let me assure you, we are in Heaven. Things like that do not happen," countered Roger.

"I see."

"You do?" enquired Roger, suspicious that Simon was seeing something he didn't.

"If there is no possibility of thieving in Heaven, suggesting that you are confident no criminal activities take place, then why, may I ask, am I standing with two fine officers of the law?"

"Well..."

Butting in, Simon continued, "Are you suggesting that your roles are pointless? Perhaps your positions could be made redundant?" Simon had a way of making people feel rebuked without overtly doing so. Even his masters had occasionally experienced the feeling.

"No. Of course. You are quite right. Guy, you can carry both suitcases, while I read through the case notes." Guy had just drawn level, hoping for a rest, and looked in dismay at the two cases. Roger cantered off with his notepad poised, leaving Guy staring at the bags.

"I do hope you don't mind. Only I have the rucksack and cannot carry anything else."

"Yes sure. Hold on though, you were carrying all three bags when we first met."

"Ah, yes, but if I only carry one suitcase, then I will be unbalanced. And I'm sure you wouldn't want me carrying all three again, would you?" And he too set off at a canter. Certain that the Devil would head for the finest tailor, Simon was keen to 'stake the joint' before the Devil arrived. Guy suspected he was being screwed over, but not one to overanalyse situations, he heaved both cases off the ground and followed at a slow trot.

Simon was in a hurry, concerned that the Devil would be unable to cope without his assistance. Reverting to his rhythmic march, he recalled the time one extremely dependent master – although considerably less evil than the Devil – became separated from him while catching a train. Simon was collecting the luggage when the carriage and master unexpectedly left the station without him. Normally reliant on his butler from morning until night, Simon worried about his employer's fate. It later transpired he was thrown off the train at the next station for travelling without a ticket, where Simon later found him shivering on the floor with his expensive coat stolen. This is how dependent the upper class had become on their butlers. Simon continued to worry how the Devil would manage without him: no morning pint of espresso, no clothes laid out at the bottom of his bed and no one to refill his bowl of cereal.

"Are you worried about Lucy?" A breathless Roger had caught up with Simon again and attempted to make conversation after regaining his composure, "We will find him, you know."

"I have great confidence in you. I can see you are exemplary police officers. I do not worry but only fear we will miss him if your colleague does not pick up the pace."

"Do not fret. I shall chivvy him along in two ticks. But first, I'd like to know more about Lucy, so we can ascertain who kidnapped him and why. Have you known him long?"

"Ever since my death."

"I see. So, you met him here, in Heaven?"

"Yes. He was meticulously inspecting some wheel clamps, and I enquired as to what he was doing."

"And you're certain it was Heaven not anywhere else?"

"Where else but Heaven is there?"

"There are other places, but for now I shall not go into details. What relationship do you have with Lucy?"

This was a good question Simon thought. For in Heaven no one would have a butler. "A close friendship and a work colleague."

Simon had increased the pace and Roger struggled to control his breathing and questioning at the same time. "A friend. Hmmmm. So, you wouldn't say that you were employed by Lucy as his assistant?"

"Certainly not," Simon expressed surprise as best he could.

Roger's breathing was becoming more laboured. "His strength. How…. Wait there. Hold up…" He couldn't keep up any longer. "I'll just hang back and get Guy to hurry up," he shouted as Simon sped off.

Roger was still recovering as Guy reached him. Not the sharpest tool in the shed, Guy's brain reacted with unusual lightning speed. Seeing his partner in a state of exhaustion, he didn't stop. Instead, he muttered the words, "your turn", dropped both bags alongside Roger and kept walking.

Roger regained his breath and, seeing no alternative, lifted both cases with a great deal of effort. As Simon had said, he knew they must reach the tailor before Lucy but while carrying two cases this was never going to happen.

Seventy-One

The baboon smiled at the feeble strength of humankind. Four suitcases, maybe even five, would present no problem for her. She would carry one in each hand and the others with her feet – and still be able to swing gracefully through the treetops. By chance, she had stumbled across Simon and his gang while on the search for the elusive banana tree. Her instinct would normally be to help, but instead she decided to observe them as subjects in her scientific research and not interfere with nature. A rumbling belly confirmed this decision and reinforced her view that there really ought to be more banana trees in Heaven.

As she watched their puzzling behaviour, a strange realisation gradually dawned. The longer she looked, the more she felt something was wrong. It took a while to understand, but at last, she concluded that the source of her disquiet was Simon. It was as though he should not exist or was out of place. He was an anomaly.

This was a phenomenon to study further. Perhaps the baboons back home would respect her research – red bum or not. The struggling luggage carriers deserved further observation, always, of course, keeping one eye on the lookout for bananas.

Seventy-Two

Fear can be a wonderful thing and, if conquered, can be a powerful driver towards success. But first you must harness its power and energy. In times of danger, fear is your friend. It guides you through life-threatening situations. Not many appreciate its role or thank fear for its insight when perhaps they should. Without fear what would prevent you swimming with sharks or failing to run when a volcano is heard to erupt. Of course, fear is the enemy if not held in check. It can be a destroyer of confidence through anxiety of rejection, or paralyse your brain when under conditions of stress.

As Cecil stood high (and I mean high) above Heaven, on what claimed to be the highest bungee jump in all of Heaven, he was not feeling stressed or afraid. Unlike Lucifer, he avoided the two gazillion steps leading to the jumping platform and, instead, flew to the top. There was not a drop of anxiety running through his body as he peered over the edge of the mighty drop.

A bungee jump consists of being harnessed up and attached to a stretchy bit of rope. You then you throw yourself from a high ledge, only to be slowed down by the stretchy rope just before (if all goes to plan), your brain becomes a pancake shaped blood-stained mess. The adrenaline rush feeds the brain with an endorphin rich high, as it falls, praying not to die. This is, of course, the human experience which Cecil had no plans to replicate. He intended simply to jump and slowly glide to the ground using his scruffy yet fully working wings. He didn't want to be here, but it was the only way to keep Lucifer under his control.

Earlier they had agreed on the day's activities and identified a tailor for the Devil to visit before the meeting tonight. It was the best plan Cecil could think of to entertain Lucifer, and he was certain the Leader would reward him for his efforts. After all, bungee jumping was a small sacrifice to pay in order to rid Heaven of the mortal scourge. He tried to avoid people as much as possible, but even now, while the harness was being attached, they insisted on talking to him. They were really starting to get on his nerves. While the humans remained here in Heaven, they should at least have separate queues and not be allowed to use the angels' fast track lanes, he mused to himself. What gave these pets the right to address an angel, a being so much mightier in every way? It should be banned, but he kept his thoughts to himself. The Leader often made it clear that only after the day of enlightenment should they talk openly of their contempt for the inferior race.

Cecil, however, as we know, had problems controlling his anger, and the unruly group waiting behind him, was really winding him up.

"You look petrified, grandad," they called out.

"Be quiet. I have no need to be scared, human. Unlike you."

"Ooh. Looks like we touched a nerve, grandad," the group of friends taunted.

"Angels have no nerves, you imbecile."

"Don't blow a blood vessel, grandad."

"Shut up, will you!"

"Grandad, grandad, grandad," they chanted at him.

"Why are you calling me grandad?! Angels can't have children like you disgusting humans."

"True, you're too old to be a grandad. We'll just call you, Old Man Jo."

"I'm not a man! How dare you call me a man."

"Ooooh, a lady then. You don't look much like a lady."

"I'm an angel, you dysfunctional drain-piped goats."

"Time to go, grandad," the bungee operator said, joining in the fun. "Bungee rope attached."

"How dare you call me grandad. I have a good mind to give you a kick…." And at that point the operator gave Cecil a gentle nudge and over the edge he went.

This is when fear usually kicks in – and it did temporarily. But Cecil's brain kicked it out and sent the calming reminder for the wings to open and flap. Nothing happened. It was sent again. Still nothing. Alarms sounded, and a continuous command was issued that demanded flapping – but to no avail. For while Cecil had been arguing, he'd failed to realise that the harness not only secured his body but also his wings. There was no way he could fly.

Fear rushed back. "Arggghhhhh, crrraaapppp!" was Cecil's response. Instead of keeping his eyes closed he made the mistake of checking the target his head was plummeting towards, at close to terminal velocity. "Craaaaappppp, bugggerrr!" The ground grew closer as the screams grew louder. "Helppppppppp!" he pleaded, as the concrete below drew worryingly close. And on the last 'p', his lips touched the ground and he fell silent. The descent was judged to perfection. Before he could thank God, he was catapulted back into the air, uttering expletives as he oscillated up and down until he was slowly lowered to the ground.

Unable to hide his excitement, the Devil rushed to greet the trembling Cecil. "That was amazing. Let's do it again." He gave Cecil an encouraging slap on the back and dragged him towards the steps.

Seventy-Three

That was it. Peter had given them one last chance, but all he received in return was abuse, aggression, rudeness and hatred. Now, he wasn't going to say that he knew exactly why God had created them, but Peter was pretty damn sure it wasn't for any of that.

There exist many schools of thought on why God created man. And even more theories on why humans are referred to as 'man', when they consist of both men and woman. The most vocal point to misogynist communities, where men have always dictated how things should be. However, the more probable suggestion is that people are inherently lazy and using the shortened form 'man', requires less effort. In fact, historians have discovered early experimental versions where the word was originally shortened to 'hum', but this was soon replaced by the favoured word, 'man'. 'Hum', it is proposed, sounded too much like the speaker pondering an idea.

Anyhow, returning to the topic of creation and God's love of humans, boredom is an alternative theory often thrown into the debate. The proponents argue that God became bored with the unending universe and so decided to try His hand at planetary arts and crafts. Using bits and pieces laying idle in space, God crafted the world in seven days – analogous to a child using toilet rolls and detergent bottles to complete a school project.

God was pleased with His rock world, but after admiring His work for a while, He concluded something was missing – it was time to decorate. Plants and water were added to produce the greens and blues of Earth. The colour scheme was widely acclaimed by all, but it needed movement – it felt too static. Dinosaurs provided the solution and were hailed a great success. For millions of years, they satisfied God until the unfortunate accident with the comet. God wished to add an extension, so He repeated the method employed previously and smashed a few rocks together. This technique worked well when the world was formed but was a disaster when He slammed a gigantic comet into the Earth at enormous speed. The comet brought the end of the dinosaurs. God was most upset and ignored the Earth project for a while to allow the dust to settle (literally). He still loved His creation but wanted future developments to be self-supporting. Always on call to make adjustments, was an annoyance He didn't want to repeat.

With the planet fully recovered, post comet, God started work on new ideas, bringing life to insects, animals and birds. Errors of judgement were occasionally made – the daddy long legs, for instance, remains unexplained even now. Finally, He created man, a primitive animal but with one bonus feature – a brain. A brain that could learn and enable the species to slowly evolve to what it is today. God pictured the human as His house sitter, a trusted janitor, who would keep the animals in order (mainly by killing them) and control the growth of plants (again, by killing them). They also kept each other in order by killing themselves. Far too much killing, but God had granted them a brain with self-will to make their own decisions.

Peter never understood why God created the humans, but he would swear on his gate's life that they should be thankful and polite to him once in Heaven. There must be conditions for entry, and tonight, Slugart and he would set these in stone. Heaven was to become an exclusive club, and no one was getting in without shoes.

Seventy-Four

It is often said that all angels have a unique role they are destined to perform. Every angel will deliver an act of spiritual importance at some point – the unknown is when. History records Archangel Gabriel as the most famous messenger of all. He was the chosen one, selected by the *Big Man* to tell Mary she was pregnant with His child. (It is often overlooked that he mistakenly told at least five other surprised Marys they were pregnant, before he found the correct one. This, and the ensuing uproar when Joseph was informed, is conveniently omitted from history books.) There are other angels, not so well remembered, who did equally sterling deeds. Angel Fredrico, for example, now actively campaigns for his part in Maradona's *'hand of God'* goal to be deleted. Initially, he boasted of his involvement until the English football fans arrived in Heaven, to make his 'life' unbearable.

Meanwhile, Hector had barely managed to survive the morning at his stall. Unable to concentrate, he rushed serving the soup, spilling much of the contents as he poured. Yet he ensured everyone received their message. The remainder of his time had been spent pacing up and down, sitting in despair or attempting to destroy the book. No matter what he did, the book and words returned. And the chant remained in his head, deafening and constantly repeating itself over and over. He was certain the words meant something fundamentally different to the views delivered by the Leader – they expressed opposing values, and it was beginning to make sense. Before he had misinterpreted them, but now he could see that the Leader was wrong about the humans. If the Leader could be ruled out as the perpetrator of the words, that left only one other option. God. And if God was doing it, then this was his 'Gabriel' moment.

Unambitious and contented with his lot, Hector never really imagined he'd play a starring role one day. He thought it was only the loud, brash types that performed God's work. But from where he was sitting (against the food cart, one bum cheek sitting in spilt soup) it seemed glaringly obvious: God wanted something. And the 'something' centred around the Brotherhood.

The way the Leader articulated his arguments made the hatred sound acceptable. It seemed reasonable when he listed the negative impacts mortals had inflicted. Yet the contradictory words in his book also made sense.

Since the influx of humans, his business had declined at an alarming rate. Why was it fair that he, an angel that had existed in Heaven from the very beginning, should be driven almost out of business by these migrants? Angels should look after their own kind first. That's what the Leader preached, and he had agreed. But the Leader also wanted to rid Heaven of humankind, to keep them segregated from angels and reject their friendship. Hector had met many humans – some pleasant, others very annoying – but he thought much the same of the angels he had known. The Leader claimed they ruined Heaven, destroying everything he loved. Yet Hector enjoyed the modern facilities: the waterpark, golf courses, gyms and was looking forward to the grand opening of the ski resort. He had to admit, building all these features caused disruption but this was far outweighed by the pleasure they brought.

He finally understood the importance of the words he read every day and night. They had meaning at last. God was asking him to do something. But what? Then the realisation slowly dawned. Tonight, at the great meeting, he would be called upon to act. Perhaps make a heroic gesture or deliver an inspirational speech – well, something. He was no hero, he knew. Hector despaired and panic set in. Yes, panic was what he would do – until tonight.

Seventy-Five

Slugart's worn-out carpet was experiencing extra wear today. Pacing up and down, he wished time would hurry up. Every hour spent before tonight's meeting was wasted as far as he was concerned. All the preparations for this historic moment had been meticulously planned: the sermon had been practised to death, and he'd laid out his costume, ready to dress that evening. Slugart had expected to be either excited or nervous – perhaps even both – about the forthcoming event, but instead, panic was taking control. To add to his sense of unease, he was growing increasingly annoyed that there was no word from Cecil. Since he had confirmed his contact with the Devil, little had been heard. All morning, he had sent messages to the safe house, but replies were not forthcoming.

Slugart attempted to distract his mind by imagining the terrible acts he would inflict on Cecil if Lucifer was not delivered on time. He waited anxiously, pondering Cecil's fate, and glanced at the morning's paper. Disgusted by the contents, he discarded it into the bin with an angry grunt. All the articles featured human stories with hardly any news relating to angels. Heaven's newspapers should focus on the home race, he thought.

A walk in the fresh air was the diversion he needed to clear his head. Slugart stepped out of the house, trying to forget his worries, while he ambled through the front garden towards the gate. But even this journey could trigger resentful emotions.

"Good morning," beamed his neighbour, enjoying the wonders of Heaven and happily pruning her wisteria.

Slugart snorted in response. He detested his neighbours with their passion for earthly flowers. When they first arrived, he had protested and demanded they be forced to live elsewhere, but no one would listen. 'Why don't you move, if you're not happy', was the most common response? Him! Move?! Why should he? He was there first.

"I hope you're not going to eat my seedlings. What with your name having slug in it." The neighbour repeated the same humourless joke whenever they crossed paths.

"Pah!" Slugart returned. He found it unbearable that they mocked his traditional name. Soon they would meet the same fate as a slug, he smiled.

Seventy-Six

"So, Cecil, you're telling me you are scared of heights?"

"No, of course not, just..."

"But you were screaming in fear?" The Devil was obviously enjoying this.

"Yes, that was because I couldn't fly, not because of the height."

"Of course you couldn't. Have you less brains than a demon? Your wings were tied up. It wouldn't be a bungee jump if you just floated down."

"I wasn't expecting them to be tied, and then they just pushed me." Cecil whined in protest.

"What is it you don't understand about a bungee jump? Are you sure you weren't scared?" the Devil persisted.

"I wasn't scared! Just shut up about the whole thing." Cecil was losing his temper.

"Look, just because you were scared of heights doesn't mean you have to get angry with me." The Devil didn't intend to wind Cecil up, but he was doing a good job.

"I AM NOT SCARED OF HEIGHTS," Cecil replied through gritted teeth as he fought to control his emotions.

"Ok, ok. But if you ever take a trip to my kingdom, I can recommend a hypnotherapist to help with your fear of heights," said the Devil and then quickly added, "which of course you have no fear of." He held up his hand to stop Cecil protesting. "I know a fabulous anger therapist as well, if for any reason you'd want to see her."

"I am not... Hold on one second." Cecil disappeared around the corner of the building, and the sound of a fist making impact with a wall could be heard. "As I was saying, I am not angry," Cecil continued, now nursing a rather bruised hand. "So, where is it you wish to go before visiting the tailor?"

"Ah yes. Simon has often mentioned that, as a youth, he enjoyed flying a kite."

This was met by a blank look from Cecil.

"You know, kite flying."

"I have no idea what you are on about, Lucifer. I thought humans couldn't fly."

"Not humans. Kites. From what he told me, you fly this kite thing in the wind on the end of a string."

Cecil quickly spotted a way to avoid this unnecessary activity: "Oh dear, what a shame."

"Hmmm. What do you mean a shame?" The Devil's eyes narrowed in suspicion.

"Well, there is no wind in Heaven, so unfortunately we cannot fly these kite things."

"We can," the Devil countered.

"We can? How? I think you'll find we can't." Cecil was pretty sure on this.

"We will run."

"What, why will we run?" And now Cecil was not so sure.

"Simon alluded to this problem. He warned me that many a kite flying expedition is almost thwarted at the first hurdle, with the wind not playing ball. Admittedly I have no idea how the wind playing with a ball is of any relevance, but Simon seemed sure. Anyhow, if there is no wind, then you run as fast as you can with the kite behind you instead. Hours of guaranteed fun, he claims."

"Are you certain the human used the word fun? Only it sounds more like the opposite of fun."

"I said, it sounds like fun!" And when the Devil is so adamant, you tend to accept he's correct.

"Alright, but where do we find these kites?" asked Cecil, resigned to yet another human activity.

"Luckily, while he planned our holiday, Simon spotted a kite club in this very vicinity. I'd say a ten-minute brisk walk, and we'll be there."

Cecil gave the Devil a look of disgust which quickly morphed into a smile. Little did the Devil realise the look had nothing to do with kites. It was the use of the word 'minutes', a human concept that angels were starting to adopt when telling the time. "Destroying our cultural values," the Leader would say. And here was an ex-angel – a fallen one but still an angel none-the-less – using the term minutes as if it were normal. He could not wait for tonight when the humans would finally be evicted – or at least the great cleansing of Heaven would begin.

"Come on, Cecil. The kites aren't going to fly themselves."

"I wish they bloody could," Cecil mumbled under his breath.

Seventy-Seven

Every morning, Hector would arrive punctually for work and make his way home at the same time each evening. Today though, was an exception – he was already sat by his fire, deep in thought. The panic that had taken hold of him earlier had subsided, but he had much to consider.

The ever-repeating words were here to stay. He had to accept they must be from God. That he had concluded, not through choice but due to a lack of alternatives. Acknowledging this resolved one issue at least and allowed him to focus on other concerns.

So, God it was. But why?

The words had always troubled him. They contradicted so much of the great Leader's teachings. Confused, he started to list some of the key points where their views coincided.

Heaven losing its values and identity.

Traditional business in decline.

Too many humans given access without proper vetting.

Hector agreed with or could at least empathise with these statements. But others had troubled him, and he often chose to turn a blind eye towards them. On a second sheet of paper, he wrote:

Moving all humans into a separate area and building a Great Wall to contain them.

Banning them from communicating or making eye contact with angels.

Cleansing Heaven eventually of all human inhabitants.

Humans are inherently evil.

Taking a separate sheet, he carefully copied the words from his book — not because he needed to be reminded of them but because doing so dulled the continual noise reverberating in his head. Without doubt, his words contradicted everything listed on the second sheet and even some on the first. This was not the conclusion Hector desired. The facts were clear. God's words were contrary to the Leader's teachings, and in a game of *'who to trust'*, God trumps everyone.

For some time, Hector had attended the Brotherhood meetings where slowly his views were moulded by the Leader's rhetoric. Only the day before, he had been excited that the long-awaited announcement was imminent, but now he was overwhelmed by a feeling of disgust. How could he have trusted and admired this angel, an angel that preached hate, against God's will. Hector understood clearly now the mist had cleared. At first, the Leader had not demanded the humans be expelled but, instead, had cunningly raised issues and concerns that many angels agreed with. It was like a teenager dabbling with seemingly innocuous weed before working their way up through the classes of drugs until, finally, they are hooked on heroin.

This realisation made Hector uncharacteristically angry. He felt disdain creep up on him, fighting its way through the noise of the words. His emotions were running high; he was scared but at the same time excited and elated. He could not believe that he and all the others had been so blindingly stupid. Tonight, he would make sure all the Brothers were told the truth. Like him, they would open their eyes again without the Leader blinding their vision with his lies. He'd show them. It was his calling — God had now spoken.

Seventy-Eight

Simon and the two policemen continued their quest to free the kidnapped Lucy, now following a winding path through the surrounding suburbs. As he looked skywards, Simon observed a flock of crows and cursed them for their annoying ability to navigate – very much *'as the crow flies'*. The pace set by the three men was well below the brisk hike that Simon had hoped for. For some time now he'd refrained from encouraging the others to increase their speed, accepting it was pointless as one of them would inevitably fall behind. No longer worried about the Devil's safety, his only concern was to reach the tailor (where he was certain the Devil would go), before his master. If they arrived too late, he knew that locating the Devil would become far trickier.

Simon's determination to reunite with the Devil was astonishing when you consider his options. Only a trained butler of the highest calibre would expend so much effort finding their evil master. In essence, Simon had 'lost' his enslaver and 'lost' him in Heaven. One might suppose that Simon would be elated by his new-found freedom and focus on remaining in Heaven indefinitely. He was potentially now a free man, living in God's paradise. Instead, he chose to march across rough terrain in search of the Devil, only to eventually return willingly to Hell's land of fire. But dedicated butlers are passionate about their profession. They are loyal and unwavering in support of their masters. And that is why Simon's mind focused on one thing only – ensuring that Satan did not have to make his own hot chocolate at bedtime tonight.

At least they now knew where they were heading. Simon had earlier steered the conversation to the identity of the finest tailor, and Roger, for once, had shown his worth in the investigation. Guy had shrugged when prompted to recommend a name since the world of suits was a mystery to him both on Earth and in Heaven. Guy was more your *'rough jeans and t-shirt'* type. Roger, on the other hand, habitually dressed in smart clothes, even on dress down days at the office and was able to quickly list all the tailors in the area before selecting the most likely establishment Lucy would aim towards.

"Which way should we head?" asked Simon.

Roger pointed. "As the crow flies, that way. Not far."

"Excellent".

"Not far for the crows maybe, but we will have to take a longer route to avoid several impassable obstacles," added Roger, with a faint smile on his lips.

Simon cursed those damn crows again.

Seventy-Nine

"Look at those kites, Daddy." A simple statement designed to instil fear and dread into many a loving guardian. But the words hold no apprehension for well organised fathers who always carry a professional-looking kite in the car, ready to fly. Normal parents hate them, knowing their children will expect a kite to be mustered up as well.

"Daddy, can we get a kite? Please." A request the father knew was coming. Even with the full knowledge that "no" will not be a viable reply, he still makes a valiant stand.

"I'm sorry, dear, but they don't sell kites here." As he speaks, the child follows the parent's gaze to witness a boy exit a store with kite in hand. "Oh, Daddy, look! They sell kites in there. Please Daddy, please."

With options limited, the parents concede and return to the field with the cheapest version available. This of course is a big mistake. After unwrapping the kite from its packaging, they find one made from the flimsiest of materials, which looks prone to breaking in the lightest of wind. Undeterred, the father assumes the alpha male role, ready to show-off his flying skills. His wife stands nervously, holding the kite at a distance and, on command, throws it into the air. Any professional kiteist (for that is what we shall call them) would hail the launch as perfect. Up goes the kite as the wind catches it, pulling the string taut as Dad makes adjustments to keep it aloft. For some two seconds it's airborne, but then the inevitable disaster occurs as it performs a barrel role and spirals into the ground.

"You didn't throw the kite correctly, darling." A local kiteist overhears this lame excuse and tut tuts the father.

"My turn, now Daddy," the eager girl begs.

"Hold on, dear. Let your mother try one more time, so I can show you what to do."

On average it will take ten attempts before the father finally allows his child a turn. Of course, he still hasn't demonstrated how to fly the kite, and it will be all Mum's fault.

At about this point, the wind will go on strike, ceasing to co-operate any further. (Kites employ the power of the wind and demand its service for free. But the wind can't blow forever and occasionally it downs tools. The Union demands more leaves on the breeze and trees to sway to its will, before powering up once more.)

The child bursts into tears. "It's ok, dear, we can still fly it."

"How, Daddy?" the girl stutters through her tears.

"Mummy will throw the kite again." Dad throws a *'you best do it right this time'* look at her, "And as soon as it's in the air, you run."

"Run?" says the confused child.

"Yes run – as fast as you can. Right, ready. Throw."

Up goes the kite, attracting a nod of approval from the watching kiteist before it starts falling to Earth.

"Run!"

The girl runs, the string pulls tight and up flies the kite, laughing as it outwits gravity. Round and round she gallops. The father cheers and beams with pride at the perfect flight. He gives a nod to a fellow parent that says, *it was all down to my teaching.*

The girl darts to her Mum and passes the kite string to her. But disaster – she's, not prepared and doesn't move. Dad sees the kite falling. "Run! Run!"

The mother obeys, but too late. Down falls the kite for one last time, crashing into the ground, leaving broken pieces strewn all around. Dad exchanges glances with his wife to say, *this is all your fault – again.*

Currently the Devil was giving Cecil a remarkably similar look. "What do you mean, you don't know what to do? Every guidebook I've read says this is a great activity enjoyed by all in Heaven."

"Yes, but it's a human activity."

"So?" Cecil winced slightly from the glare.

"It's un-angel like."

"I repeat. So?"

"God would not want us taking part in these un-angelic activities." Cecil felt on solid ground with God's opinions.

"Oh, always God with you lot isn't it. When was God ever right?"

Cecil's mouth opened, ready to respond to this ridiculous assertion, but his brain failed to answer quickly enough before the Devil continued, "He's still running this place in the past. I doubt he even outsources any of the everyday, *'anyone can do it'* sort of stuff. Take a look at Hell, and you'd see how a finely tuned organisation operates these days. In Hell, I'd have staff trained to throw the damn kite in the air for me. Not relying on you. Now watch that human there and copy him. And it best be good."

Muttering to himself that fallen angels shouldn't be allowed to talk to him like that, he watched as a super dad launched a kite gracefully, allowing enough time, and with sufficient height, for his partner to start running.

"You got it? Now throw the bloody kite."

Cecil's irritation was growing. He was meant to be the Devil's captor – not the reverse. Summoning all his strength he threw the kite, but like a paper airplane when thrown too hard, it became unstable, stalled and fell to the ground. The Devil hadn't even moved.

"Not like that, you dawdling muppet. Do it again. Do it better!"

Cecil tried again and threw it with even more force – and it fell to the ground with proportionate speed.

"Again!" shrieked the Devil

The indignity. Being spoken to in this degrading manner. If he had not been slightly afraid of Lucifer, he would have stormed away. But his anger failed to walk. Anger can boil and expand, but the mind it expands into does not. The mind has nowhere to go; it is caged within the skull. Pressure can diffuse through the ears, but if the anger expands quicker than the escape valve can release it, an explosion is on the cards.

Every time Cecil threw the kite, the result was predictably disappointing. The uneasy peace could not last much longer. For the final time, Cecil gripped the kite tightly, piercing the material with his fingernails, before hurling it skywards. It landed on his head. The Devil stood motionless in amazement as he watched Cecil grab the kite by its tail and smash it into the ground. Then, to make sure the instrument of torture would not tease him anymore, he jumped up and down on it until the frame was destroyed and his pent-up rage fully discharged.

"Listen here, Cecil," said the Devil having walked over and placing a caring arm around the hyperventilating angel. "We can sort your problems." Slipping him a business card, Satan explained, "Just contact this guru. She will teach you self-control." Cecil took the card and placed it in his pocket without comment.

"Now back to flying," the Devil said chirpily, "and don't worry, you can take a rest. I shall join this pair. I'm sure they will not mind."

The Devil trotted off and politely asked a couple of kiteists if he could fly with them. Any onlooker would never believe they were witnessing the Prince of Darkness playing happily with a kite, talking merrily to others, and all without evil intent. But of course, the Devil was wearing his disguise – no one would recognise him wearing his cap and sporting a moustache.

A short distance away, the baboon sat peeling a banana and watched Lucy flying his kite. She was more confused than ever. It was certain that, like the man she'd observed earlier, this kite flyer did not belong in Heaven. Only her work on the theory of black holes had taxed her investigative powers to this extent before. Having written equations to prove their existence (some so long and complex that it would take a plague of Leonardo Dr. Vincis to decipher) she needed to call upon the same skills to demonstrate that this 'man' was unwelcome in Heaven. Who was he and where did he come from? It was her destiny to solve this mystery once and for all – this baboon would have her day.

Eighty

"And that is why we are certain to find your friend Lucy at the tailor's. A highly professional investigation, I'm sure you'd agree. Guy and I feel proud of the role we have played." Roger concluded his debriefing while Simon listened patiently, even though he already knew everything.

"A remarkable job. I am forever grateful," Simon replied.

For ten minutes, Simon and Roger had waited for Guy to catch up, and just as Roger finished his de-brief, Guy came bounding up behind the two, now struggling with the bags again. His sudden burst of speed had been triggered by the tailor's shop coming into view. "Stop, stop!" he called. He seemed unusually anxious and excited. "This is now a covert operation," he shouted loudly (and certainly not covertly), before tripping over an inconsiderately placed rock and sending Simon, Roger and the cases flying with all three landing in a heap.

"Thank you, Guy. We are certainly inconspicuous now," Roger continued sarcastically. "I agree though. We must move into a covert phase now."

"Then I shall take charge," said Guy firmly. "We agreed on this. You promised," he declared. "I've read the books. I'm fully trained."

After giving it some thought, Roger reluctantly admitted he had promised that if they were on a mission, considered to be covert, then Guy would assume command.

"Right. First we need surveillance to assess if the target has arrived."

Blessed with a stronger physique than either Simon or Roger, he'd drawn them both into an awkward huddle and began to issue orders dramatically in a low voice, "I need you, Roger, to perform a perimeter scan. Check all the points of entry or escape. I shall clear the area of any guards and you, Simon, will be our eyes and ears in the shop. You shall enter incognito but remain in plain view."

"Now hold on, Guy."

Roger was ignored.

"Enter the shop and confirm if the target has been there already," resumed Guy.

"But he's a civilian." Roger was not happy, but Guy continued to ignore him.

"We shall rendezvous back here." Guy was in his element. He felt they should synchronise watches at this point, but glancing down at his bare wrist, he carried on unabated. "This is a high-risk operation. Let's do it once and let's do it right. Who's with me?!"

"Guy, I have to protest at the use of a civilian in a police operation. The rule book states…"

"Damn the rule book. We are working in a special operations mode, and sometimes the book must be ignored. Simon, being a civilian is precisely why we need him to reconnoitre the shop. Either of us would stink of being a copper. They will never suspect Simon."

"Well, I suppose, but the rule book…" Roger drifted off in thought, worrying about his beloved rule book and the precedent being set.

Guy was enacting a drill he had rehearsed many times in his head and now, for the first time, had the opportunity to practise. He checked for concealed enemies (very few), covered the area with his gun (pointing his fingers to mimic his weapon) and used army rolls to move forward (during which he became stuck halfway, having forgotten to take off the large rucksack). But as he completed his moves, he was on a high. Roger never let him do 'proper' policing. It was for the occasions like these that he'd set up the Heaven Police Force, but then Roger arrived and introduced rules and regulations which controlled his enthusiasm. Once Roger joined its ranks, the excitement disappeared. Yes, they actually had rules and regulations now, and the operation did run smoothly, but the fun side of being an officer had dwindled away.

From his vantage point, Guy watched Roger make a sweep of the perimeter. Army crawls, short dashes, hiding behind bushes were the techniques Guy had taught Roger to deploy. Why then, was he witnessing his partner on all fours, crawling more like a baby than a Royal Marine? Whenever anyone approached, he stood looking awkward and embarrassed until they passed. Roger had the demeanour of an office clerk not a special ops agent. He didn't look the part, feel the part or want to be the part. But he had promised that Guy could lead this covert operation – a mistake he wouldn't make twice.

Simon had fared considerably better. He walked calmly into the shop with a suitcase in each hand. He looked not like an officer of the law but the tourist he was – demonstrating the old adage that the best disguise is to be yourself. Roger had returned to the agreed meeting point, waiting for Guy, as Simon exited the premises with news.

"Officers," Simon shouted from the entrance. "No need to proceed with the plan any longer." And he stepped back into the shop and out of sight.

Shock and extreme annoyance pulsed around Guy's veins. The one time he was in charge of a dangerous, covert operation, and some reckless civilian puts the lives of everyone at risk by disobeying orders, he fumed. He was angry, not just with Simon but also because Roger was correct. They should never have allowed a civilian to take part in police operations. He would throw the book at Simon and make an example of him. His cheeks assumed a deep shade of plum, and his ears let off steam.

"Guy. Wait," said Roger, as he made his way over.

"What is it?!" Guy's cheeks puffed out – beating a puffer fish for the most puffed cheeks. "Why are you not behind cover, out of sight? This whole mission is a disaster."

"Let's just go in, Guy. I promise you can organise a training session on how to perform these kinds of operations." Roger sensed how upset he was.

"A weekly training session?" Guy asked, brightening a little.

"Perhaps monthly to start with. Now let's go in."

Inside, they were met with tea and biscuits, courtesy of Simon. "While you enjoy some refreshments, officers, I shall give my summary of the situation – or a debrief as you professionals refer to it."

Impressed by the lingo, Guy was buoyed once more. "Proceed, civilian Simon."

"Once I entered the shop, I glanced around and confirmed my friend was not here. On your suggestion, that of a qualified policeman, I asked the owner of the establishment if anyone of Lucy's description had been in today. He confirmed, after some thought, that no eight-foot-tall, sunburnt, moustachioed gentleman had entered that day. He did say that the previous week an eight-foot-tall sunburnt gentleman had visited, but that gentleman had no moustache, so unless the gentleman has grown said moustache, within a week, then the gentleman, of which we are discussing, has never been in the shop. I further pressed him on this familiar sounding gentleman and concluded that the previously stated suspect was only lightly burnt – not fully reddened such as the aforementioned gentleman by the name of Lucy."

Guy's brain struggled to keep up. "So, are you saying that Lucy was or wasn't here at any point?"

"Negative."

The cogs in Guy's brain turned again, trying to understand.

"Negative in a *he wasn't here ever* sort of way, or negative in a *he was here* way?"

"I can confirm, for clarity, that although the shop assistant suspected he may have been here last week, he has not entered the premises today."

Guy gave up. "Roger, you proceed from here."

A far less physically imposing presence than Guy, Roger had perfected other attributes in order to succeed. (Or at least attempt to succeed.) Rules and regulations were his forte, and he knew that a restraining order to place the shop in temporary control of the officers, until the case was solved, was essential. Roger explained to the confused owner that they were empowered to commandeer the premises, and he must leave immediately. Unsurprisingly, this was met with disbelief and anger. It fell upon Simon to step in and prevent the argument turning into fisty-cuffs. Simon drew the now perplexed and exasperated man to one side and explained, in a calm and reassuring manner, that these two gentlemen were complete fools, but if he let them play their little game, they would soon leave without incident. Comforted by Simon's promises that no stock would be touched, he reluctantly agreed.

Roger was particularly happy once Simon confirmed that the owner now understood, and that all rules and regulations had been followed correctly. Guy, however, was annoyed that Roger did not have the necessary warrant to allow a full search of the property.

"Now, that's settled I need to ask you some questions," stated Roger, returning to the tailor and reaching inside his chest pocket for his notepad. He flicked it open in one seamless movement, almost as if he had spent hours alone at home in front of a mirror perfecting the move. A pen clicked ready to take notes. Years of practice back on Earth had honed his skills in official note taking. If any notes were needed, Roger was your man. The difference in Heaven was that he also got to do the interrogating. His earthly police career had never taken him far enough to be trusted with actual interrogation of suspects.

"You are aware, are you not, that we have commandeered these premises for official police activities?"

"Yes, yes, you've gone through that already. Jeez, can I just get on with my job. I've got some important clients coming in today, and I do not want to be hampered by so-called police." The tailor was a flamboyant personality, who when agitated, emphasised his words with a lot of hand waving and hair swishing.

"What do you mean, 'so-called' police?" Guy jumped in, recognising an insult that was blatant enough even for his limited brain to decode.

"Guy. Go and set up an observation post at the back of the shop," Roger commanded, moving quickly to diffuse any confrontation. He knew rumours of over-bearing police aggression could ruin his force's reputation.

"That is exactly what we want you to do," Roger continued, addressing the owner. "Just carry on as normal. We have reason to believe a wanted fugitive will be entering this building sometime today. If they do, we will apprehend the said fugitive." Roger put away his book without making any notes.

"A fugitive? Is he dangerous? I can't act normal if there's a dangerous fugitive on their way," exclaimed the tailor, embracing Roger with both hands. Roger was slightly taken aback.

"Don't panic. We have the cream of the force located here for your protection. You are in no danger, my friend." The tailor appeared satisfied and hurried off flamboyantly, returning to his tailoring duties.

"We shall get this kidnapper, Guy. You and I will be heroes."

"Heroes?"

"Yes. Heroes." And they both puffed out their chests in a display of heroic pride.

Eighty-One

Following their kite flying expedition, Cecil and the Devil were indeed on their way. Still annoyed that Simon had been left behind and unavailable to discuss his requirements with the tailor, the Devil mentally made a note of the outfits he needed. Normally, Simon would take care of everything. He, Lucifer, would only become involved during the fitting, occasionally raising his arms and warning the tailor about where his hands were wandering, before relaxing on a sofa. Looking at Cecil, he knew there would be little help offered in choosing a suit or advice on the latest trends. Living in the dark ages of fashion, is how the Devil described Cecil. Sporting the traditional, angel brown (with a subtle hint of more boring brown) woollen cloak, a style the Devil last wore some ten millennia ago. A glance at his own dirty and worn outfit horrified him. *Wear it once, then bin it*, was the Devil's policy.

Approaching their destination, the Devil became agitated, worried that he had relied upon Cecil's recommendation. "This is the finest tailor in Heaven, you say? You had better not fail me on this, Cecil!" the Devil threatened. And he knew many impressive tailors in Hell for comparison.

"It's frequented by all the highest-ranking angels, Lucifer. No need to worry about the quality. It is the pinnacle of tailoring."

"Humph," the Devil grunted a response. In Hell there were many tailors who'd worked for evil dictators, film stars and royalty, all offering a wide range of styles and looks. With such an abundance of choice, he had no problem keeping on trend in the underworld.

"You'd better be right," he repeated.

As they reached the shop entrance, they both stopped instinctively. There was an eerie silence in the street which both Cecil and the Devil sensed. Something felt amiss. They were unaware that they might have bumped into Simon as he made his way along the very same street if playing with the kites hadn't delayed them.

Cecil cautiously pushed the door open – more cautiously than could ever be justified when entering a store – and peered nervously inside. As the door opened, a loud bell rang to alert the owner that customers were there.

"Ahhhhh!" screamed the Devil.

"Eeeek!" shrieked Cecil.

Looking at each other, they silently agreed that neither had really been startled at the sound of the bell and entered the poorly lit shop. While their eyes adjusted to the darkness, their brains sent direct orders for the ears to be on high alert. The ears laughed at the eyes for being too reliant on light waves, but any smugness was interrupted when sound waves hammered against their inner drums.

"Eeek!" shrieked the Devil.

"Ahhhhh! screamed Cecil.

An almighty bang made them both dive to the floor.

"What in God's name are you two doing on my floor?" the owner of the establishment demanded, making her appearance from the rear of the shop. She was a stern looking angel who wore similar robes to Cecil. "Don't say the door slamming caused you both to dive to the ground in fright?"

"Of course not," snapped Cecil as he stood up.

Inspecting the strangely paired customers, suspicious they might be potential thieves, she enquired, "How can I help, now that you've stopped inspecting my carpet?"

"I have brought my friend, umm …"

"Lucy," the Devil jumped in to finish the sentence.

"Yes, Lucy needs to be fitted for an important meeting tonight. We need the clothes urgently."

"I'm sorry, did you say Lucy?" Not only did they look unusual, but the customer with an ultra-masculine appearance was using a girl's name.

"Yes," replied the Devil. "Why?"

"No reason, no reason. Just an unusual name for a gentleman that's all." Inexplicably, he looked familiar, and the partial recognition unnerved her. "My name is Gevine. What precisely are you looking for?"

A silence followed. "I asked what are you looking for? What style, colours? Is it for a formal occasion?"

Cecil gave the Devil a nudge. "Oh, you're talking to me. I'm accustomed to my butler, sorry I meant friend, dealing with these matters." After giving his response some thought, all he could say was, "Something on trend this month."

Compared to their human counterparts, angels work at tremendous speed. It's hardly a surprise considering angels have practised their craft forever. Within the hour, the Devil's garments were wrapped and ready to be worn when he dressed later for the meeting.

To pass the time, the Devil and Cecil had played Frenzo, a game requiring great skill and tactical prowess. Frenzo is similar to chess, but with a circular board and pieces styled on mystical beasts, the game looked noticeably different. However, the main contrast is apparent in the level of violence exhibited by its players. Most of the pieces used by Cecil and the Devil had become damaged from outbursts of rage (mainly Cecil's) during their game. A set of Frenzo pieces often need replacing every five games on average, with the board lasting perhaps ten, at a push. The rules of the game gave no indication of the ferociousness displayed, but the short fuse of these two competitors was the source of the aggression they deployed to win.

Collecting the garments, the Devil showed his gratitude by warmly thanking the tailor. Now he had some new clothes, and although not Prada, at least he could attend this business meeting dressed as a professional. At Cecil's suggestion, he decided to delay wearing them until nearer the time of the meeting, to avoid any further accidents. The Devil thanked the tailor again as they left the shop, loaded with bags and headed in the direction of Peter's great gates (to Cecil's huge relief). Still wary of the Leader's wrath should he arrive late, Cecil tried his best to increase their speed. He was feeling excited and set a brisk pace knowing the reawakening of the angels was fast approaching.

Browsing unseen inside the same shop was the baboon. Elated that her equations had at last revealed an alarming conclusion concerning the identity of the red, horned gentleman. But at this moment, her excitement was focussed on the embarrassing problem of her red, non-horned bum. The fact that baboons can't make clothes is as true as the sun is hot. Their lack of co-ordination between hands and feet inevitably leads to failure. If they used just their very capable hands, then all baboons would have been fully clothed long before humans. However, now in a tailor's premises for the very first time, she had met someone to make clothes, designed for her figure. She had never encountered such skills before.

Even the incomprehensible lack of bananas could not dampen her spirits.

Eighty-Two

Guy, closely followed by Simon and Roger, who struggled to keep up, came storming through the same door that the Devil and Cecil had exited from only forty minutes before.

Earlier, while they waited for Lucy and his kidnapper to arrive, all three took advantage of the hospitality on offer in the store and enjoyed a strong cup of tea and biscuits. Roger continued his investigation, but the ensuing 'interrogation' of the tailor only established many pointless facts (including the name of his cat, favourite car and a detailed account of his stamp collection). He politely answered all Roger's questions, unaware of the impact the following exchange was about to make.

"Tell me, is Lucy an angel?" the tailor enquired pleasantly. "It might help me identify him if he returns later."

Simon quickly replied that he was undoubtedly human – without question – and was accompanied by an angel. It was then, the tailor casually dropped the mother of all bombshells.

"I'm surprised," he said, "that the angel didn't take Lucy to Wings & Sheppard's, the outfitter situated on Mavile Row. It's the angels' favourite tailor."

Jaws dropped and biscuits hovered in front of mouths. The policemen had failed to take into account from the start that there were other tailors, frequented only by angels. A smell of surprised shock and panic wafted through the air, which left Roger too overwhelmed to utter any words. Simon felt he should take charge and quickly confirmed the second establishment was merely fifty yards along the road. There was no time to lose. Roger ran from the shop, pausing only for a puff on his inhaler. Guy sprinted the wrong way until he checked over his shoulder for backup and realised his error. Simon walked calmly at the speed of a butler. The result – they all arrived at the same time.

"Red, huh, red, huh, man. Big, huhh." Guy struggled to speak and breathe at the same time.

"What are you saying? Breath and speak clearly," insisted the tailor. She was unhappy having a person drooling saliva around her freshly cleaned premises.

"He means to say, madam, has a large, sunburnt man, accompanied by an angel, recently visited here?" Simon always spoke coherently and clearly, no matter what situation. Ask him to run a marathon while in the heat of a ferocious battle and his message would be delivered as crisply as a crisp crisp.

"Indeed, there has. But why do you ask? Is he ok?"

The latter question was directed at Roger who had just arrived on the scene sounding acutely asthmatic.

"He is merely exhausted after his daily run. We are meant to meet these two gentlemen – our old friends – later today but have forgotten where. They mentioned a plan to purchase new clothing from you, so we aimed to catch up with them here."

"Oh, if that's all you're after I can tell you where they will be."

"You can?" Roger's notebook was extracted so quickly it might have caused a mini-sonic boom.

"I can. I'm invited in fact." The angel seemed the type who would be attracted to the cult's views. "That is, of course, assuming it is the same place you intended to meet."

"Excellent. Then we will enjoy getting to know you better when we all cross paths later. Where is it exactly?"

"Oh, just outside old Peter's gates. Bit of a strange place I thought, but maybe he's done it up recently."

"Peter?" Simon enquired of Roger. Simon of course, being a resident of Hell, had neither experienced Peter's welcome nor seen his gate.

"You know. Saint Peter. Head up his own arse. I'd hoped never to meet him again. Do you know when I got to his gate, he accused me of being Hitler!" Roger looked incredulous at the thought.

"Yes, he does that a lot," commented the shop owner.

"Ah, he sounds a hilarious gentleman. I shall enjoy making his acquaintance. I trust you know the way?" asked Simon.

"Yes. Should be an hour's walk from here," Roger confirmed.

"We thank you, madam, for your help and shall continue our conversation later on this fine evening. Good day."

"Goodbye." Watching them leave, she mused to herself, "A bit strange these humans were invited." She could have sworn it was an angels-only event.

Eighty-Three

Dusk crept its way through Heaven, slithering in from the shadows where it hid during the day. The light was slowly consumed as Dusk adjusted the dimmer switch to create a more romantic spectrum. It considered itself the matchmaker or perhaps Cupid, the romancer, providing a key ingredient for love.

Slugart flicked on his light. Dusk hated lights yet had no power to dim their intense, artificial glare. These devices were not of God's making. In his dressing room stood a magnificent, silver, floral-etched mirror, which dominated the room. His clothes, ranging in colour from brown to very brown, were hung neatly along a golden rail, suspended within a grand, oak wardrobe. Unfortunately, Slugart had ruined the sense of grandeur by using garish, blue plastic hangers to arrange his robes.

With eyes closed, he ran his hands along the line of clothes. He chose a robe that felt 'right', one that radiated a warm feeling in anticipation of tonight's climactic event. His size eight feet slipped comfortably into a clean pair of sandals as he stood admiring himself in front of the mirror. Using scissors to make final adjustments, he trimmed his beard and swept back his fringe. He was ready – well, almost. Annoyed that he could no longer wear his favourite, flamboyant clothes, Slugart had decided that at least he should accessorise his outfit and slipped a red band over his left arm, fastening it tightly above his elbow. A gold emblem, which he had designed as the Brotherhood's badge, shone out from its red background. Striking the pose of leader, he admired himself once more. (If he had known of the Snow White fairy-tale, Slugart might have been inclined to ask: 'mirror, mirror on the wall, am I the most heroic angel of them all?' And it may have replied: 'the lines in your face reflect wisdom gained from battles of old, your eyes shine with knowledge and power, your feet walk the path that legends have followed. You are the most magnificent of them all.' Or there is the possibility it would have said, 'Not a chance, you power crazed old twerp.')

Now fully prepared but still anxious, Slugart sat quietly, attempting to relax, while he mentally reviewed everything for one last time. Roused from this contemplation, his gaze rested on a painting that could perhaps have been of his father (although angels do not have parents, and this was no ancestral home). Seeing it, shot a bolt through his calm meditation and unleashed his suppressed nerves as he dashed over to the wall. There was no reason for them not to be there, he thought, but their importance was so immense he had to check yet again. (It was an unease, much as people experience at airports when they check constantly for their passports but are never reassured.) Running his right hand down the side of the frame, his fingers found a catch and clicked it open. Slugart swung the painting aside to reveal a hidden safe. The scroll, collected earlier from the library, lay stored within. It was a vital key, not to the safe, but to the future – one without humans. He carefully removed the document and placed it into a leather satchel.

Events were unfolding quickly. Tonight was going to be epic.

Eighty-Four

For the last twenty-seven hours, no new souls had passed through Peter's gates. They were locked, with no immediate plans to reopen. The number of souls massing at 'heaven's_door' had quadrupled in that time, and the sound of arguing and pointless questioning was getting on his nerves. The previous evening, Slugart had seemed keen to meet before the main event, but with time ticking by, Peter was losing hope that he would arrive. As he peered over his newly creosoted gate, he could see a lone figure in the distance running towards him. This must be Slugart, at last. Over the many drinks consumed the previous night, the idea of creating a checklist for vetting the new arrivals had appealed to Peter. With the discarded versions filling his bin, he now had a proposed draft to share with Slugart.

Skilfully ignoring the rants from exasperated humans attempting to catch his attention, Peter saw that it was not Slugart running towards him. Instead, a breathless messenger arrived to inform him that Slugart sent his apologies for being unable to meet as planned. Another emergency had arisen unexpectedly, and he would be very grateful if Peter completed the preparations alone, ready for his arrival that evening.

This news displeased Peter greatly, and he made sure the messenger had a response to that effect. However, there was little point in getting worked up, and so he might as well carry on as Slugart asked. It would at least distract him from the irksome humans.

During the previous night, a team of builders had constructed a wooden stage. The simple design allowed an audience to gather round and still be able view the platform from wherever they stood. Raised about the height of one and half angels from the ground, a beautifully detailed, golden lectern and a simple, small table had been positioned centrally, with two chairs arranged nearby.

Peter scanned through the list of unfinished tasks – passed to him by the messenger – and decided his first undertaking was to cordon off an area around the stage. This was so the audience could be kept apart from the waiting humans. Decorative red rope (the type used at airports and post office queues) had been supplied earlier to construct the barrier. Slugart was very precise about the size of the expected crowd, so Peter started arranging the rope to accommodate them. With about three quarters of the perimeter sectioned off, it became clear that he had underestimated the length required.

Fearing everyone would think him a fool for miscalculating the quantity, he demanded his brain hatch a plan. And quickly. (The brain is, of course, a colossal processor, which can devise wondrous solutions. But unlike a computer, it panics. A machine will not blabber unrelated, panicky answers if you ask it to perform quickly. A brain, however, will.)

"Belts," it blabbered to the brain's frontal lobe, past the parietal lobe onto the temporal lobe and out through the cerebellum.

Belts, Peter thought. Of course, it was obvious. He could assemble all the belts he owned and link them to form a long rope.

Having ransacked his house, he returned shortly with a surprisingly large number of belts. Linked together, they formed a good length 'rope', but still not long enough to stretch the distance required.

Peter ordered his brain to provide an alternative solution. The brain wanted backup this time, as it could sense Peter was not satisfied with its original belt suggestion. It needed a scapegoat so turned to the eyes. "Eyes", it said, "Provide a solution based on your observations". The eyes instantly panicked, not expecting to be involved in any of this. "Humans," they shouted back, as they blinked in shock and caught sight of the growing queue.

"Humans," the brain relayed to Peter.

"Humans?" Peter said in an unconvincing manner.

Damn the eyes, thought the brain. It privately acknowledged that it should have vetted their response before forwarding it to Peter. But it thought fast and came back with a solution. "Get all the humans to take off their belts."

Of course! It seems so obvious, thought Peter and asked – or more accurately told – the first belted human to hand it over. "Bro, you'd best give me this belt and make it snappy. Man ain't got all day."

"Why?" the man quite rightly enquired. He'd been warned to be wary of scams and fraudsters, and this unusually obscure request raised his suspicions – especially as it was the first thing anyone had said to him since his death.

"What you mean, why?" This of course was a *'fighting for time'* response, as Peter lacked any adequate reason to give in reply. His brain had best be giving him one soon, he thought.

"This is my belt. I don't see why, just because I'm dead, I should give it to you. Look, that woman over there has a belt. How come she gets to keep hers?"

"She don't."

The lady overheard this and did not like Peter's tone of voice. "What do you mean I don't? This was a present from my late husband. The last gift he gave me before his death. I will never give up this belt."

"Don't matter then now, does it love, if he's already dead." The lady gave Peter a deathly stare. "You know. 'Cos you're both dead now, so you can go see him anytime. No need to have that belt to remind you of him anymore." She carried on staring, a stare with a hint of *don't you even try it mate*. "And anyway, everyone has to give up their belts before entering Heaven."

More people were paying attention now.

"Why?" a few shouted.

Yes, why brain? Peter needed help. " Because… Because they're banned. Isn't it in one of them bible things you lot read?"

A few shouted, no, others replied that they had never read the bible.

"Health and safety." A recent crop of humans had introduced the concept of health and safety regulations and Peter's area had been inspected recently. "Things like them belts can cause serious whipping injuries and pose a risk of strangulation."

"Health and safety gone mad," said an easily convinced soul, as she dropped her belt at Peter's feet.

"That's it. Come on the rest of you lot. Hand them over." More were surrendered, accompanied by rumblings of annoyance.

"I'm still not giving you mine," the first man Peter had asked, interjected.

"Then you ain't going nowhere. In fact, you'll be going to Hell."

The mention of Hell increased the flow of belts, and soon Peter had plenty to complete the cordon.

Eyeballing the stubborn man, Peter made downwards gestures and waved goodbye.

With Slugart's list completed, it was time to take a break – so Peter walked home to rest before the evening's events unfolded.

Eighty-Five

Dressed in traditional robes, with the hood covering his face and sandals neatly tied, Hector might possibly be mistaken for a ninja squirrel ready to perform a nimble summersault, spinning through three hundred and sixty degrees, before effortlessly grasping his book and jumping through an open door. History often paints a hero in this sort of way, to be more heroic than perhaps they ever were. And if Hector was to become a hero that night, historians may have described his exit with such words. But if the truth were to be chronicled, it would read more like this: Hector tripped, clutched at thin air trying to reach for the book and tumbled through the door. Hector certainly did not leave his home as he hoped to return – a hero. He wasn't feeling heroic now either. Or at least it is rarely mentioned, if ever, of heroes having a gut churning feeling of sickness before performing their heroic deed. No, he felt more akin to a fainting goat than Herculean.

Chosen by God, he had confidence that He would lead him through the evening's events (although he was still worried enough to pray there were toilets nearby). Why God had selected him, an unassuming angel with a bad back whose special powers included making soup, seemed to have no logical explanation. Was it a mistake? Did God pick his heroes by a form of lucky dip or was there a hidden destiny that he was programmed to follow? There was no obvious reason for Hector being *the chosen one*.

He walked slowly towards his fate. Along the dark side street that led from his house, he felt each cobble of the pavement as it pressed into the soles of his sandals, urging him forward towards an unknown destiny. Altering his speed to ease the discomfort, and with a hand supporting his aching back, he crossed the inn's large courtyard. Hector's path avoided the slightly merry humans who tended to congregate outside at this time of night and passed through the main entrance. In the distance, Hector could make out the fabled gates of Saint Peter. Humans made their entry into

Heaven along this route, and now Hector retraced that journey in reverse. He could not repress a slight feeling of jealousy, or even of anger, towards humans who were blessed with their own gate. Angels had never arrived in Heaven; they had always been there. We angels always get the worse deal, he thought.

Hector reminisced as he followed the cobbled road which led onto the red carpet. It had been rolled out in times gone by to greet the humans with gaudy neon lights added later to celebrate their arrival. Hector recalled this was once a park where angels played Frenzo or went for walks and discussed weighty matters. Now it was only used by humans. He might have reservations about the Leader's teachings, but he certainly sympathised with some of his views. While these thoughts passed through his mind, the flashing neon sign continued to emit its annoying electrical buzz, welcoming all into Heaven. Everything was garish and untraditional. This was not how it should be.

The scene tonight along the tattered red carpet was unusual. Hooded angels strolled out through Heaven's gate, instead of the dead who normally passed in the opposite direction. A trickle of angels had started to appear not long before Hector arrived, but this had grown to a steady stream by the time he reached the 'pearly' gates. None of the angels spoke; all were hooded and most kept their eyes directed towards the ground.

Hector always felt uncomfortable that they were made to wear hoods. If they were proud to attend, then why hide their faces? But now he understood; there was no good. They were covering their faces to hide the evil before them. He'd find the strength to stop this unholy plan tonight though – somehow.

Eighty-Six

Roger had succeeded in getting the three of them lost, or 'temporarily off-course' as he preferred to call it.

Never at his best under pressure, once, while still a young and eager cadet, he performed the crucial task that falls upon trainees in all professions – the tea and coffee round. Even back then his love of lists made him ideally suited for the task ahead. By writing down everyone's requirements, he'd cleared the first hurdle where many had stumbled. Roger carefully prepared the drinks and placed them onto a tray. Then the inevitable happened. An attractive officer approached, just as he went to leave the kitchen, and exchanged a friendly, innocuous, "Hi". Roger, overtaken by surprise, knew his facial warning light had flashed to red and barely managed an inaudible, "Hi" in return before dashing out. But the embarrassment, although a set-back, had not affected his execution of the drinks mission. So far so good. It was on delivering the first coffee that panic attacked. He remembered the person's request and knew that he'd made it perfectly, but the position of the correct cup on the tray was a mystery. So, Roger guessed. And continued to guess the recipients of the five remaining cups. Thirty seconds later, and the sound of an unwanted tea being spat out by a senior officer confirmed disaster.

Meanwhile, Simon had disturbed Roger's concentration, much to his displeasure, by firmly insisting they quicken their pace to reach this meeting without further delay. Impatiently, Simon thrust the cases into Guy's hands, further antagonising the officers, but realised he didn't have the foggiest idea which direction to take. With little option, he sat back and calmly demanded that Roger and Guy lead the way – and fast. Never particularly confident with directions at the best of times, Roger buckled under the pressure and started to confuse his left and right, back to front and inside with outside, delaying their journey by some fifteen minutes.

Eventually stopping to breathe slowly, he recovered the situation and, with his anxiety finally under control, unpicked the incorrect turns and headed in the right direction at last.

Eighty-Seven

The assembled crowd of angels numbered some two hundred. At previous meetings only half that amount would normally attend, but tonight a 'full house' stood securely within the roped off (or, as some had noted, belted) area. The increasingly agitated souls, waiting to enter Heaven, occasionally watched the activity but paid little attention, being more worried about their delayed entry into paradise.

Peter felt awkward. Normally the master of his domain, tonight he was met by a horde of angels, all with covered heads. This unnerved him. He thought he recognised many, but without seeing their faces, he could not be sure. They stood with heads bowed, silently waiting, hardly speaking or even looking at one other. Peter had watched his fair share of films since humans had introduced cinema to Heaven, and the view before him felt like a scene straight from a horror movie.

Time marched on; light was tightly tucked up in bed, and darkness rained down. The wooden stage, illuminated by candles, had been completed, while Peter was at home changing into his best jeans and a comfy hoody. Impressed by the number of candles, and the ambiance their glow provided, Peter wandered onto this well-lit podium. He felt he should at least say something, as this was his land they were assembled on. It needed someone to break the silence.

"Hi," Peter shouted and repeated even louder, to make sure they took notice. All the angels fell 'deathly' silent – not the reaction that Peter had hoped for. Only the constant background noise from the disgruntled souls could be heard.

"Man's name is Peter," he said, unable to think of a better introduction.

"Get on with it. We know who you are, you pleb," an unidentified hood shouted in an exceedingly high pitch voice.

"Yeah, well, man don't know which brethrens you lot are with your hoods on. Bunch of delights." (This was a derogative term that humans used for angels. It was assumed to be an ironic word play on the dessert, 'angels delight', suggesting that although the pudding may claim to be a delight it is very much the opposite.)

"Language! That is an unclean term. Keep to the angels' dialect." This devout follower was quick to chastise Peter for his use of human slang, something the Leader was keen to ban.

"You shut your damn mouth, mate. Here mans speaks how I decide."

"Not after tonight," came the response and quite a few others murmured in agreement.

"Dunno what you on about, mate?"

"Change is coming tonight. The Great Leader has promised."

"Yeah, well, if he don't get his shit together and turn up soon, I'll be kicking all you lot out of my garden."

Things were getting out of control. An argument erupted between Peter and the crowd, but just as Peter was about to execute his threat to evict the angels, it happened. Thunder roared. Lightning struck. Or at least the rumbling sound and the flashing light gave that impression. (Quite surprising, as Heaven doesn't experience either phenomenon.) The air around them seemed to chill, and everyone felt a spine-tingling moment of excitement and fear. Suddenly, Slugart's voice was heard, booming from the sky above.

"Tonight, I bring freedom. Tonight, I reveal our destiny."

The crowd looked around, bewildered, for the Leader was nowhere to be seen. A loud series of explosions engulfed the stage in a terrifying wall of sound. Out went the candles, plunging everything into darkness. Even the humans fell silent, distracted momentarily from their grumbling.

"Anyone got a match?" Peter asked casually. Unlike the others, he was not in awe of the unexpected pyrotechnics.

Another deafening explosion, and the candles burst into flame again.

"Is that light enough for you to see, my friend?" Slugart asked, magically appearing, holding a lighted match. Although hooded, he did not disguise his voice, which Peter instantly recognised.

"How you do that, bredrin?"

"That is none of your concern for now," Slugart curtly replied and turned to address the expectant audience. "Standing before you, brothers, is the first key to our destiny." He raised Peter's hand in the air, and a cheer erupted from the crowd. Peter looked totally bemused.

"What you on about, bro?" Slugart flashed him a smile before turning his attention towards his loyal following.

"Today, we are victorious."

The crowd let out another triumphant cheer.

"Aktone." Slugart spoke the word majestically as he began the cult's chant. The crowd echoed each line, hypnotically following Slugart's lead. As their voices merged, the chant became alive and intoxicating. The sound reverberated in the air, giving the members a heightened feeling of combined purpose.

"I promised you all from the start that I would lead you to enlightenment. To empower us all. To return what is rightly ours. Today I fulfil my promise." A jubilant cheer rang out in response.

"Mate, what's going on?" Peter shouted, tapping Slugart on the shoulder as he tried to be heard over the noise. Slugart, in full flow now, turned towards him, irritated by the interruption.

"You will hear. Just listen and wait until all has been explained." Slugart tried to continue but Peter sought reassurance.

"This ain't going take like more than an hour, is it? I'm starving."

Slugart looked at him, without answering, then swiped his arm in an arc across his body, and one by one, all the candles were extinguished, each emitting a small popping sound as it died. But the darkness did not last for long. Five seconds later, each one crackled into life with a short burst of bright light before resuming its gentle glow – and Slugart was gone. Peter was now totally confused. He scanned the stage and the surrounding area but there was no sign of him. To his amazement, Slugart reappeared in the centre with his arms raised to the sky, looking as masterful and inspirational as only a small, strangely bearded guy in a brown dressing gown could.

"Feel the power we have. They cannot stop the tide of change."

Tapping Slugart on the shoulder again, Peter enquired, "Bro, I don't know how you did that stuff with the candles but what's going on? I thought we were going to discuss rules on who can enter Heaven. And anyway, what we going to do with the bredrins we don't let in?"

Slugart's first instinct was to ignore the question but decided to go with the flow and answer by addressing the crowd once more "Our friend, Peter, has been in close discussions with me recently. He has a growing problem that we will fix right here, tonight. We know that all must pass through Peter's great gates to enter Heaven."

"Garden gates more like," someone shouted.

"Be quiet!" demanded Peter.

"Thank you, Peter. For millennia, I have observed Peter's heroic attempts to keep Heaven safe from the parasites," Slugart continued, spitting out the word 'parasites' with theatrical distaste. "Yet for all his efforts, there can be only one outcome – the human must enter. There are many he wants to turn away but how can he? Keep them here, behind his gate, perhaps for eternity? Look around you. This is a finite area, not like Heaven's ever-expanding spaces, so the available land would soon be filled. What is there to be done, you may ask?" Slugart walked slowly around the edge of his stage with one hand stroking his square beard. The audience waited, totally silent, desperate to know how. "A question I have mulled over, agonised over, all in the hope of returning Heaven back to its former glory."

The crowd leaned forward in anticipation, with everyone longing to hear their Leader's plan.

"There seemed to be no solution, but I knew there must be. God could not want Peter to let in such vile creatures. So, I concluded it was not a question of how to stop them. Peter has the experience and expertise to do this already. It was instead a question of what to do with those who were refused entry."

Peter stood in the centre of the stage, trying hard to keep up. He decided now was the time to join in. This must be about the list he had prepared for judging their suitability.

"Exactly, bredrin. I'd cut the crap from coming in all day long. This here is the list I've drawn up to decide who can enter. Just a first draft." Pulling out the screwed-up note, he thrust it towards Slugart, who tried his best to ignore it. Undeterred by Slugart's lack of interest, Peter started reading the criteria aloud. Slugart twiddled his fingers and tried to remain calm, but inwardly he was anxious and irritated by Peter's uncalled for interruptions.

"An excellent first draft, Peter," Slugart continued, as Peter drew breath. "We would of course tighten these rules until the final solution is achieved."

Regaining control, Slugart pointed at the candles in an exaggerated manner, causing the flame to burn brighter. It appeared as though oxygen was being magically injected from his hand as he aimed his finger towards each candle in turn.

Again, he initiated a chant:

"The final solution."

"The angels' re-birth."

"Forever we shall be."

And the Brothers chanted with him.

These dudes are mental, thought Peter.

The flames' short burst of energy dulled as Slugart continued. "How do you solve a puzzle like this? My mind whizzed into action reviewing the alternatives. Construct multi-storey containers was an initial thought. Or perhaps put them to work, building, cleaning – any general jobs we don't care to do ourselves. But, as we all know, they are lazy and useless at such things. I'd been thinking so hard and for so long that I started having doubts. There is no solution, I thought. But every time I addressed you, I was inspired. There had to be one."

"For the angels. For the rightful owners," he chanted, and waited for the response.

Slugart could sing, "death to all angels" and they would happily chant with him. For such an uncharismatic looking angel, Slugart was able to manipulate an audience. He could whip them into a state of fury or send them spellbound into a trance. Something about the way he delivered his message and animated his body was a power in itself. Much like the magician's sleight of hand diverts your gaze, Slugart possessed a similar ability to convince you that his teachings were the truth; a process strengthened by his cunning techniques and carefully chosen words – Slugart was a master of deceit.

He paused dramatically, catching his breath before continuing. "It was a during, what I assumed was a chance meeting, that things changed. Now of course I realise it was not by chance but God's way of holding my hand and leading me."

Amongst the crowd there was one hooded angel who also believed God was guiding him with a helping hand. But with Slugart's mesmerising performance, Hector had forgotten about his mission for now. He was entranced, listening to the Leader and hypnotically reciting the chants along with the other angels.

"At this fateful meeting, I discovered vital information about the land we stand on today. The ground beneath our feet led me to a document, one of the essential keys, the final piece in the jigsaw. Or at least I thought it would. First, I needed to verify its authenticity, and by the will of God, I found it was true. Tonight, is the first time that I can share the secret unearthed on that momentous day. Now, I bring you the proof." The Brothers gasped as a fireball rocketed skywards from the stage, with an explosion of red and gold sparks lighting its path. Slugart waited until all was quiet then held his arm aloft to reveal an ancient scroll. "This, friends, is the second key. With Peter and this document, we hold two of the three keys needed to free us from the scourge forever." He unrolled the scroll and again held it high. The writing was too small for anyone in the crowd to read, but they believed unconditionally it was indeed as Slugart claimed.

"What I bear here, in my hand, are the deeds to this land. Land that stretches out from Heaven's great gate to the place where the human souls first materialise. There are two, particularly important features to comprehend. First, it is incredible that this area has deeds at all. Such documents do not exist for any other part of Heaven. They are not owned – they are all within God's domain. Yet this area, Peter's area, does. And I say 'Peter's area' deliberately, as this manuscript confirms he owns this land. A contract drawn up for Peter to stand forever as guardian of Heaven's gates."

Peter's brain whirred into life. He'd forgotten all about this contract, but Slugart was right, he'd signed the paperwork in what felt like a lifetime ago.

"Yes, I remember signing that contract. Swear God got some lawyers to screw me over."

"Today you will be doing the screwing, Peter," smiled Slugart.

The crowd stood listening uncomfortably. They were embarrassed, not knowing how to respond to an ancient scroll, which was far from the grand announcement they had been promised.

"I can see you're all confused. Not everyone possesses my great intellect. Let me explain. These deeds transfer to Peter the unchallengeable right to control his land. God bequeathed this power to him. If he wants a hotel, Peter can build it, a lake – let him dig."

Peter's ears pricked up. Swimming pool, casino, nightclub. What should he build first?

"Fortunately, Peter is a devout purist like us so would not scar his land with such filth. Imagine such evils as a casino, nightclub or swimming pool." The audience muttered in condemnation, and Peter laughed nervously.

"Instead, we shall build an exit. For all that do not deserve God's love and protection, there shall be a path for Peter to march them along, out of Heaven and never to return!"

An enthusiastic cheer erupted. This was more like it they thought. Peter smiled, as he pictured the hideous humans he could turn away. A smile that quickly disappeared when he thought through the logistics.

"Hold on, hold on. It's all ok saying you're going to build an exit, but where is this exit going to lead?"

"I can see why God entrusted you with such an important task. Your brain is inquisitive and quick. The answer to that question is about to arrive. It is the third and final key – the special parcel." And with a sharp clap of his hands, the candles went out. Instantly, others that lined the path from the gate, burst into life.

There, walking towards the entrance, dressed in his new 'suit', was the Devil, followed closely by Cecil (who quickly covered his face with a hood). Just before making his entrance, the Devil had changed into his tailored clothes. They were not quite the on trend designs he had expected. When he opened the package, he stared in total disbelief at what lay before him and had only just recovered from the shock. The anticipated well-fitted, high fashion suit was in fact a grey, woollen robe. A traditional angel garment was not the look the Devil had envisaged. How could he be asked to attend a business meeting dressed in a woollen cloak? Cecil, recovering from the full fury of the Devil's anger – as it was clearly his fault for taking him to such an inept tailor – was relieved they had arrived. At last, he could hand over this devilish parcel and receive his rightful acclaim and due reward.

Standing taller (and far redder) than anyone else, Satan looked every inch an imposing character. He strode confidently through the assembled angels who, like the Red Sea in the scripts of old, parted as readily as magnetic north poles spring apart. Raising himself onto the stage, he confronted Slugart.

"What the hell is this all about? I've been rudely kidnapped by this deranged lunatic, taken to a tailor that doesn't sell suits and now forced to come here to see you."

"Lucifer, forgive me. All the discomfort was necessary, I assure you. In just a few minutes you will be enlightened, and joy will replace your anger."

"Are you trying to tell me I should be happy to see you again? You always were a mad angel. You haven't changed." Even with his face hidden, the Devil instantly recognised Slugart.

"Just listen for a moment, Lucifer."

The crowd were both shocked and in awe of the size and redness of the Devil, but not one human or angel fled in fear. And there was a good reason for this – they had failed to recognise who he was.

"First, let's thank our brother, Cecil, for heroically delivering the final key." Slugart turned to embrace Cecil as he joined them on the stage. "You shall be richly rewarded for your endeavours." Cecil felt elated, at last receiving the praise he craved from the Leader

What keys? Peter still failed to fully understand what was happening and desperately tried to keep up. His thoughts were muddled, switching between acquiring the authority to turn some humans away and having the power to build on his land.

The crowd were becoming restless, eager for more information. But for once Slugart's confidence wavered, unsure that he could sell the next stage of the plan to his followers. He needed to recompose himself quickly before he dived in to explain further.

"Brothers. This here is someone you all know," he began. "Some of you were friends with him a long time ago. Humans fear him. We too fear that he might attack our homeland, but tonight we shall strike a deal that benefits us all. Lucifer, remove your disguise."

Tempted at first to disobey this impertinent order (like a petulant teenager rejecting the authority of parents) he decided to play along for a while. He gripped the end of his moustache and slowly pulled it off. There was only a muted response until he theatrically flung his cap into the crowd (as a celebrity throws a memento to screaming fans). The reaction was instantaneous. Angels gasped in horror and screams could be heard from the watching humans, worried they were in the wrong place. No longer was there an oversized, sun burnt, poorly dressed angel before them. Now, without his disguise, there stood a horned, blood-red creature, with eyes of black fire penetrating anyone who dared meet his gaze.

Slugart moved quickly to dispel the fear. "Calm yourselves, there is nothing to dread. Despite his amazing disguise which has fooled everyone, I have been aware of his presence for some time. Lucifer knows not why I have brought him here tonight, but he will be delighted when all is revealed."

The sensory shock to Hector's eyes snapped him out of the drug-like trance that Slugart's mesmerising performance had induced. He repeatedly muttered the words from his book and clenched it tightly for comfort. This was the conclusive proof that he had sought. He had been right all the time. God, without doubt, had sent him to stop, not Slugart, but the Devil. What evil the Devil planned he couldn't yet grasp, but he knew it was his destiny to stop it.

When Lucifer had roamed heaven as a law-abiding angel, Hector had never really known him; they moved in different circles with only an occasional greeting exchanged between them. Today though, if God required, he would meet him head on – anything to foil his evil intent. A comforting wave of energy surged through

Hector's body, encouraging him forward towards the stage. But how could he stop him? A question that halted him in his tracks. Yes, he was confident that God would back him, yet an element of doubt still lingered. Perhaps a rough plan of action would be wise before rushing in head-first, he concluded.

Now was the moment for Slugart to explain his plan; this would require his most eloquent, animated performance in order to convince the Brotherhood that his unique solution would work.

"Heaven has a problem, Lucifer. Humans have destroyed much of its culture and tradition. They have driven angels from their rightful land and built hideous things like theme parks."

"Excellent place, that," noted the Devil.

"And... Sorry, what did you say?"

"I visited one the other day. On my holiday. Lots of fun. I shall be ordering demons to build me one on my return to Hell."

"Yes, anyway, as I was saying. God's pets have infected our angel dialect with their_demonic language, driven out our wholesome food merchants and even dig holes in Heaven's historic sands."

"Ah yes, the beach. I did enjoy that as well. These humans know how to have fun."

"Umm, yes. Anyway, they have ruined everything."

Circling around Satan, trying to address him and the whole crowd simultaneously, Slugart continued, "We can change all this. You heard me explain that this land belongs to Peter; he can do whatever he likes with it. He needs and deserves the authority to halt the influx of undeserving souls, and for this he requires help. I want to strike a deal with you."

Hector was in a flap. A deal with the Devil? That was not good.

"I'm listening. But I don't know what you can offer. I am already the ruler of my own domain, where I have all I could ever want."

"Everything? You do not have a permanent entrance to Heaven though, do you?" Slugart responded confidently and waited for the Devil to absorb the idea. "I can offer you that. You would be able to come up here anytime you needed to relax. No more having to worry about God's banishment. If we created a permanent gateway from Hell, here in Peter's land where God cannot interfere, then you could take a vacation anytime you wished. And to make it even more perfect, Peter would open the gate. God granted him the power to control who can and cannot enter Heaven. You'd be free to roam. I'm not saying you could stay here forever, but regular short trips would be possible, and God wouldn't have a choice." Leaving the Devil to mull the idea in his mind, he turned his attention towards the crowd. They were getting restless, and a range of muttering was audible. 'He's gone mad' and, 'always trust the Leader' were just two examples.

"Listen. I know this is a lot for you all to take in, but you must have faith in me." Then with a voice that that came from deep inside him he declared, "I am the all-knowing and all-powerful Leader. Trust me!"

The words vibrated with unexpected force in everyone's ears and a flash of intense light exploded across the sky.

"I have been given powers by God. He has put His trust in me," Slugart roared, above the noise of rolling thunder. Another explosion blasted out, and with it the night sky briefly appeared brighter than day.

Despite the events unfolding, Hector had failed to devise a plan. In despair, he was about to rush towards the stage in the hope that inspiration would strike on the way, but the deafening explosions had left him laying shocked on the ground with his hands covering his head. God really should have equipped him with extra powers if he was to perform this dangerous task, he thought. Super-angel-strength would have been a good start.

Unimpressed by the sideshow, the Devil quietly continued to evaluate Slugart's offer. (Slugart's 'bangs' were mere trifles to him – like dust on a mountain – compared to the fireballs that roared from Hell's seas.) He'd really enjoyed his vacation and to be able to return was appealing. God was always interfering and getting in his way. He was such a bore. Forgiveness was something that God raved on about yet he, the Devil, never seemed to receive any. (God, of course, was not always a big fan of clemency. It was only after He made the mistake of killing the dinosaurs that He coined the phrases, 'everyone deserves a second chance, forgive and forget'.)

How long can someone stay angry? It was just a misunderstanding, after all. He had never been shown any mercy so perhaps this was an opportunity to revisit his old haunts.

"A permanent entrance to Heaven, you say. And it's all above board?"

"Completely. We will insist, of course, on a *'no demons'* clause, so that only you can use the passage from Hell."

"Of course, can't have demons here. They are enough of an annoyance in Hell. I wouldn't want them ruining my holidays." Slugart could see Lucifer was warming to the idea.

Also recovering and warming up was Hector. He sprang from the floor with the look of heroic determination etched across his face. It was time to do battle. Attempting to 'muscle' his way through the crowd, he was quickly reminded that he had no muscles to speak of. Instead, he edged his way awkwardly past the massed throng of angels – albeit a little more slowly than intended.

"How would we proceed with this arrangement if I were to agree?" Satan was a businessman, and he knew that a verbal contract was hard to uphold in court.

Before Slugart could answer, Peter cut in. "Hold on one second, bredrins. Who said I'd agree to a door from Lucifer's manor into my backyard? Why'd I agree to that, bro? God trusted me to protect his land, not open it to this guy." Peter finally understood the situation and eyed the Devil cautiously as he delivered his undeniably valid arguments against the proposed arrangement. Peter had known Lucifer from way back and suspected that the Devil also remembered their wild parties together; memories that he'd prefer not to share with others. But their past friendship or even potential blackmail was not a sufficient reason to allow him an entrance into Heaven.

"Peter, dear friend," Slugart resumed, "The door will not be just an entrance for Lucifer, it will double as an exit door as well. It is the solution to all your problems. After you rigorously scrutinise each new candidate, you will, for once, have the power to do what God asked of you. You will protect Heaven from the unworthy. If they fail your test, you simply open the door to Hell. Send them down, banish them from our great land. Once you have started the process, we can collaborate on tightening the rules." Peter, not known for his long attention span, had tuned out of Slugart's frequency already. He was focussed on the joy of sending some of the most annoying and disrespectful humans to Hell.

Continuing with his sales pitch, Slugart was unaware that Peter had stopped listening. "Once the flood of humans is under control, we will be able to take it further. We'll round up those already in Heaven and rate them against the same criteria we applied to the new pets. Any that fail will be put on a donkey train for you to banish."

"Yes bruv, the power... What did you say?" Peter had not registered that current residents would also be subject to the new rules.

Hector too had failed to hear. If he had heard the Leader's rhetoric on cultural cleansing, he'd have been furious. God had opened Heaven to all who embrace His love. No one, not even a powerful angel like the Leader, should have the right to evict them. But for now, he was embroiled in his own battle and was becoming angry trying to push past the last few rows of angels. It was a nightmare. These angels were diehard fans, similar to concert goers who are unwilling to relinquish their space to anyone, especially a soup seller trying to push his way through.

Slugart was now in full flow. "Tonight angels, we witness the rebirth of Heaven. A Heaven where angels will no longer take crap from humans, where old traditions will flourish once more. Feel the power of this momentous hour. The rebirth has begun." Reaching into his apparently empty pocket, he withdrew a dozen doves and flung them high into the air. He held his arms aloft and more doves, whiter than bleached white, circled around him before flying into the night sky.

"Peter, what do you say?" The Devil, roused from his daydreams, turned to face Peter. "I wouldn't want you getting up to your old party tricks every time I came to visit." A great grin spread across the Devil's face.

"That's history. Anyways, you joined in, remember?" Peter wished Lucifer had not mentioned the old times.

"Yes, well, I'd forgotten about that." Satan decided not to press this issue, having conveniently only recalled the controversies surrounding Peter and not himself. "I'm in, if you are," said the Devil.

"I'm in," agreed Peter. He had some reservations, but overall, it definitely made sense.

Slugart would have tapped out an Irish jig in celebration, were it not a satanic, human dance. "My loyal followers, it has been agreed." The roar from the crowd was deafening. Hector's roar of anger was a few decibels quieter and lost amongst the celebrations. He had to reach the stage to stop this nonsense. Calling upon God's help for one last attempt, he scrambled towards the stage – but simply managed to be pushed backwards.

"I have taken the liberty of drawing up contracts for you both to sign. They are lengthy, so I have highlighted the key points concerning the entrance to Hell from your land, Peter. You are, of course, free to read them, however, they contain a load of mumbo-jumbo, legal terms to cover our arrangement."

Slugart produced two small scrolls from his pocket and led Peter and Lucifer to the table that had been placed on the stage. "Please, sit here while you sign." The crowd hushed again as they absorbed the momentous importance of the events taking place before them. Tonight undoubtedly confirmed the Leader's unquestionable powers. They were witnessing the almost magical authority their Leader exerted over everyone – even Lucifer – and he was now delivering on the promise he made to return Heaven to the angels once more.

Hector, however, hadn't quite given up. God could rely on him. He needed to reach the stage, but he had underestimated the task. This was all the Devil's work – his trickery – not their so-called leader's. In desperation, he resorted to screaming and pleading for attention, certain that someone would react and see this charade for what it really was. No one listened. They were too focused on the stage.

"Here is the contract with a copy for you both to sign," Slugart said as he produced two golden pens from thin air. The crowd remained silent. The Devil and Peter pretended to read the contract, both too embarrassed to admit they understood nothing of the detail contained in the small print. Only the increasing noise from the humans, bored of the ceremony and complaining about the delays, disturbed the hushed atmosphere.

Peter picked up his pen. What's the worst that could happen, he thought hearing the irritating voices of the whining humans. If Lucifer tried any funny business while up here, God was certain to sort it out. And now, at last, he would be able turn away the ungrateful good-for-nothings. Slugart was right, that is what a God had entrusted him to do. He scribbled his name on the dotted line.

Lucifer finished pretending to read the contract. "Yes, all seems in order. I once went on a law course, you know." And he signed his copy.

Slugart smiled contentedly. "Thank you. Now exchange contracts and sign again. Then you will each have your own signed copy, and we can all celebrate."

I'm too late, thought Hector. I've failed God. This cannot be. From deep within, he drew on his last ounce of fight and aimed to charge the stage. (In an action movie Hector would have sprung onto the stage, dodged the explosions around him and, at the last possible moment, rugby tackled the table, hurling the contracts into one of the candles, to explode in flames.) But instead, he was knocked over by a suitcase.

"Out of my way. Official police business. Make way, make way!" Roger shouted commands that no one had time to listen to. Before anyone could obey, Guy shoved them out of their way with the assistance of the two flying suitcases. There was no escape; unsuspecting angels were scattered either side of Guy, flattened by one case or the other. The luggage easily cleared a path, allowing Simon to follow calmly in its wake. Roger and Guy scrambled onto the platform, but Simon waited to be lifted – butlers do not scramble.

Cecil, who still lingered on the stage, attempted to intervene. "Listen here, you lot. Get back down. How dare you barge onto this stage. Humans have no right to be near our Leader." His next sentence included the words 'arghhhhh' and 'oh crap' as he was unceremoniously thrown off the stage by an exuberant Guy.

The officers slowed their advance once they saw the scene at the centre of the stage. Simon, though, motored on, not energetically but with the effortless, gliding motion of a butler.

The Devil's head was stooped, deep in concentration with his pen poised above the contract. Without looking up, he stopped as Simon approached. "Ah, Simon. About time. Take a brief look over this would you."

"Of course, sir." And Simon took the contract and started to read.

Peter finished signing his papers and looked up. "Who's your bredrin, Lucifer?"

"He's my butler. Can't live without him now. I always wonder how I ever coped before." Leaning back in his chair, arms behind his head, the Devil felt fully relaxed. Simon had returned.

"An expert in contracts, is he?" Peter had no concept of what a butler was.

"It never ceases to amaze me that he is actually an expert in everything."

"What is the meaning of this interruption? Get this disgusting creature off my stage!" Slugart fumed. He called for Cecil to remove the unwanted guests but couldn't see him anywhere.

"Cecil! Cecil, get here now and remove this pet!" Unfortunately, Cecil was still embedded within the crowd, facing the same issues as Hector and unable to help.

Not one to tolerate anyone calling his personal butler 'disgusting', the Devil rose from his chair. "Who are you calling disgusting?"

"This ...," Slugart pointed in horror at Simon who continued to study the contract, "this thing. All humans are scum."

"For real? That's a bit extreme, mate. Yeah, some are annoying, but others are dope," Peter said, defending the human race despite his eternal annoyance with them.

"He is my butler. And he will be treated with respect, while he is in my employment. Do I make myself clear?"

Regaining his composure, Slugart remembered the Devil still needed to sign the contract. "Whatever you say, Lucifer. Now, please take a seat and sign the contract for your guaranteed time-share in Heaven."

"Simon, please pass me the document. I've given you ample time to read it. Should I sign?"

"Indeed, sir, if you simply want a permanent entrance to Heaven, where you can enter and leave as you please, then this contract is legally correct."

"Excellent. It goes without saying that I knew that. I've been on a legal course myself, but it always pays to get a second opinion." Lucifer grabbed the pen.

"Indeed, sir, and I realise that with your superior knowledge and wisdom you have already considered what I am about to say. But I shall say it again, sir, more for myself than you." The Devil hesitated, recognising that Simon was about to deliver a big 'but'.

"The, what might be called a negative in the contract, is that you will be receiving in exchange an indeterminate number of additional humans into Hell."

"Yes, yes. I've explained all this. That's so Peter can banish the humans," an exasperated Slugart snapped.

An inquisitive eyebrow was raised by the Devil. "How many, Simon?"

"That would depend, sir, on how many humans Peter rejects at his gate. You see, all those Peter deems unworthy of entering Heaven will be sent through the entrance to Hell," Simon continued.

"Ahaha, so just a small percentage. I could live with that."

"To start with, sir, yes."

"What do you mean to start with, Simon? Spit it out." The Devil's suspicions were starting to grow.

"It's just sir, from the way this gentleman. . ."

"Angel!" Slugart angrily corrected.

"Very good. From the way this angel talks of humans, I would deduce he has plans to send more than the few Peter rejects."

"How many more?"

"I would suspect, sir, that eventually all humans that have ever lived and died will be sent to Hell."

"Impossible!" shouted the Devil. "Where would they go? There is no space!"

"A very good question, sir. I know you've set up several committees and sub-committees to look into your overcrowding issues and have yet to find an adequate solution."

"I have! It's only because the slaves' union rejected the idea of 'human soup' as inhumane."

"Precisely, sir. That is why I felt it necessary to bring the issue to your attention."

Slugart was trying to figure out what the issue was. "Hold on, what's the problem? Here in Heaven, space just expands when more is needed. Can't Hell do just the same?"

Satan, talking with a serious, business-like voice, explained. "God, in all his immaturity, thought it would be funny no doubt, to make Hell a defined size that cannot be expanded. It is now reaching capacity. I cannot be the dumping ground for your unwanted humans. And anyway, why can't they stay here? Isn't it said they are God's children?"

The annoyance in Slugart voice was obvious. "They are God's mistake! They have ruined Heaven! They have destroyed our food!"

"Have you tried curries? Or what they call Pot Noodles? I always celebrate with a new menu when a renowned chef is dumped in Hell. Human food is a delight."

"They poison our entertainment with ungodly shows!" Slugart was pulling at his hair and pacing back and forth.

"Most excellent entertainment from what I can tell."

"But the historic games of Heaven – their popularity has ebbed away." His voice cracked with emotion and leaning on the Devil's shoulder for support, he looked a broken angel.

The crowd were listening and eager to join in. "But those games are rather dull compared to the human versions. Angels are not too bothered about Heaven's annual games anymore. The Olympics are much better," someone volunteered from the crowd and many agreed.

"None of them follow the book of God," Slugart pleaded, falling to his knees as Satan pushed him away.

"Book? Do you mean one of those scriptures that we drew up for a laugh? We didn't really expect anyone to follow them. No one knows if God actually contributed, do they?" The Devil remembered the good old days, and the pranks he and his old angel friends used to play.

"Blasphemy!" cried Slugart.

"Yes, that's one of the words we made up for the book. Looking back, that word did cause a lot of unnecessary, violent deaths."

"But you're the Devil. You hate humans," Slugart spluttered in rage and annoyance.

"It is my job to punish the humans who are sent to me. Even that is becoming increasingly hard with the rights of slaves and the rules and regulations that have been introduced over the years. I have nothing against the humans myself. They have improved Hell in many ways by introducing new ideas and customs and, at other times, taken away some traditions that perhaps were getting a bit dated. Sometimes, when wars rage on Earth, and wave after wave of the dead arrive, the rate of change is perhaps too fast. It can seem like they are taking over, not respecting our methods of torture and punishment, but the influx eventually slows, and normality gradually returns. But for you, here in Heaven, this cannot be true. Heaven simply expands, new zones are formed and there's plenty of room for you all to co-exist. Look there's old what's his name, trying to get onto the stage. Hector, isn't it? I bet he still sells that awful soup, even now?"

Slugart nodded without realising, confused by the Devil's defence of the despised pets. "See, even though the humans brought their pizzas, fish and chips and kebabs, Hector still has his business. But where's he gone? I can't see him now."

The crowd were following Hector's progress too. He had reached the stage at last and, without warning, just disappeared. Then, after ten seconds an explosion went off and up popped Hector across the other far side of the stage. No one was more surprised by this than him, but quickly returning to his mission, he ran towards Slugart. Again, disaster struck as he tripped over a rope, causing fifty candles to ignite behind the crowd. This time Hector stopped to see where the rope went. He found another and a short tug sent fireworks up into the sky. As he moved carefully towards Slugart, he inadvertently stamped on a concealed button and once more disappeared. He understood now – it was just a trap door. The Leader possessed no mystical power, it was all just trickery. Hector had accidently stumbled across the evidence – quite literally.

The watching crowd was now totally confused. The soup seller appeared to possess the same powers as their Leader, and the Devil was suggesting humans weren't all that bad, with many tempted to try this recommended Pot Noodle – it sounded so delicious.

Hector reminded himself that he had been chosen by God for a purpose, and the job was not yet complete. He marched forward with pride, for today he was going to be a hero.

As Hector approached, Simon spoke loudly, so all could hear. "If I were to be so bold as to express what my master here is thinking, I'd like to bring to your attention this good angel approaching us. By his timely intervention he has demonstrated to us all how the angel that you call your Leader performs his trickery." The Devil wasted no time. He pulled down the Leader's hood, and the shocked crowd drew an embarrassed breath as Slugart was revealed. Slugart was not an angel they would ever be proud to follow. "He has shown us", Simon continued, "that all your leader's powers were in fact stage tricks, prepared in advance."

"Precisely, Simon. And I shall not be signing this damned contract, Sluggy!" And Satan ripped the scroll in two.

When Simon spoke, the crowd instinctively tuned into the sound of his voice; it captured their attention. The way he clinically and eloquently explained a situation in the rhythm of a butler, gripped the audience much like Slugart could. But instead of Slugart's animated, eccentric delivery, they were hypnotised by the authority of his soothing tone. Simon had exerted a similar unseen but accepted power over all those he had worked for. It was not a form of control that was manic or domineering but more an agreed arrangement to be shared and enjoyed by those around him.

Peter, who was feeling somewhat embarrassed that he had already signed his contract, ripped it up before anyone noticed.

"You're lucky I can't send your arse to Hell, bro." And with that Peter ambled off, still muttering to himself. That was enough excitement for today. Glancing back at the snaking queue, he knew his batteries needed to be fully recharged ready for the morning rush.

Many of the angels had removed their hoods and reflected on the events that had played out. They were embarrassed to have believed all this nonsense and had been deceived by Slugart, masquerading as a charismatic leader. Swept along on a tide of hatred and jealousy, they had always known that humans weren't all bad, but they had been corrupted by the distortions preached by Slugart, which played to their own prejudices. In hindsight, they could see he had fooled them with his convincing arguments, presented as facts. During their meetings he often stretched the truth to make his case and even, at times, told outright lies.

A few angels, however, remained hooded. They were the hardliners that truly believed Slugart's teachings and detested all God's pets. This feeling of hatred was only held by a minority who would never change their views. Stripped of a large crowd to hide behind, they had lost their influence and slowly drifted away into the darkness – for now.

Frustrated and constantly delayed by falling through more hidden trap doors, Hector finally reached the table. He grabbed hold of Slugart who stood motionless, still recovering from the shock.

"This angel," shouted Hector, spitting out the word 'angel', "is a fraud!" There, it had been said. He had done it. God had entrusted him to stop Slugart, and he had fulfilled God's wishes. A surge of energy rushed through his body allowing him to stand tall with a straight back for the first time in years. An inner voice spoke to Hector and demanded 'the words from the book' be heard. Hector instinctively, without hesitation, recited them for all to hear as powerfully as he could manage.

"Although we are different, we see the same light. Don't believe the hype. "

"Calm down, Hector," said the Devil. "We've already been through all this."

"You have?" The energy propelling him along dissipated instantaneously. Hector looked deflated.

"Yes. The magic tricks. How humans are ok and we should get on with everyone. My butler, Simon, has already explained."

"But that was my job," Hector protested firmly. "God sent me," he added more quietly.

"Shouldn't you be getting off to bed? I know you street sellers are always up at the crack of dawn." The Devil ushered him towards the stage exit.

"But the words. He placed those words in my book."

"Yes, yes. Words in your head." The Devil twirled his finger to indicate Hector was a bit loopy. "You run along now and get some rest."

With all his inner determination drained away, Hector was left as an empty shell with no stamina remaining. He made his way home slowly, occasionally moving his lips gently as he chanted the words. But he remained confused. Had he saved the day and fulfilled God's wish, he wondered? Was he a hero? Tomorrow might provide an answer but now, after collapsing into bed, it took only a nanosecond for Hector to enter the land of sleep. Perhaps it was all another dream.

Still on the stage, Slugart stood disconsolate and lonely. His world had collapsed. The plan so cunning, so perfect and yet now so failed. Most of the angels had departed, each trying not to draw attention to themselves. Humans filled the vacated area. They had been too busy arguing, pushing in or arguing about pushing in, to pay any attention to the events that had taken place around them. All Slugart could see were pets; they were everywhere, taunting and laughing at him, he thought. All of them here to ruin Heaven – the vile, disgusting creatures. Growing in intensity, like a migraine's slowly building pressure, the more humans he saw the more painful his feeling of anguish became. A broken angel and no longer able to withstand the strain, he screamed: "Why won't you all just go away and die!" And he ran off with his head in his hands.

A woman stood nearby turned to her friend and commented: "Did you hear what he said? I thought we already had."

Be assured, sir, the moment we arrive in Hell I shall book you into the finest tailor. We shall have you smartly dressed as soon as possible. I regret that I was not able to assist this afternoon, and you had to endure the indignity of wearing these old rags as you so elegantly put it. I apologise and will hand in my notice for my failure, if you so wish.

"Hand your notice in? If you dare ever try, I'll turn you into a suitcase."

"Certainly, sir," Simon replied, as he searched inside the rucksack.

Two others still lingered on the stage – Roger and Guy. They'd watched in amazement whilst whispering a running commentary between each other. With Simon still distracted, fumbling through his bag, they advanced towards the Devil.

"We are arresting you, Lucifer, on a charge of being the Devil," Roger stated as Guy put the Devil in an arm lock.

"That's right, sucker. And if you make any attempts to resist, we'll book you for assaulting an officer too," Guy added.

Simon who'd retrieved the item he was looking for, now stood up. "Ah, I see you have seen through my employer's disguise and no longer consider this gentleman to be Lucy, a kidnap victim."

"We never believed you from the start. There is no such thing as a clamp inspector. I've run a check on that too," replied Roger triumphantly.

"Most clever of you, officer. I commend your powers of deduction and see you are an asset to Heaven's force. But before my master is taken away for questioning, could you do one thing for me?"

Guy looked annoyed; Roger looked worried.

"Can you show me the law that he has broken?"

"Aha," shouted Roger triumphantly. "Indeed, I can. We had it explicitly added to our law book after that unfortunate incident when we arrested a demon on the charge of being a demon. Reluctantly, we had to release him because, at the time, there was no such law to break. But for you, there is no mistake." Roger was ecstatic at finally playing his trump card. They were about to arrest the most notorious, evil criminal in all history, and nothing was going to stop them.

Roger passed the book to Simon, who read the additional legislation and returned it without comment. Unfolding the mysterious device he'd retrieved from his rucksack and placing it on the floor, he addressed Roger.

"I'm afraid you will have to release the suspect."

"Fat chance!" replied Guy.

"Unfortunately, for you, my master has not broken any law."

"Yes, he has. Is he or is he not a demon?"

"He is not."

"Precisely! Hold on, what did you say?" Guy asked.

"He is not a demon," replied Simon calmly.

"Yes, he is." Roger and Guy were united for once on this.

"I'm afraid you are mistaken. My master is not a demon but the Devil, Lucifer. He is a fallen angel. Demons are demons. They have never been, and never will be anything else. You cannot simply turn into a demon. So, unless your book contains an additional law for being the Devil, I suggest you release him before we submit an official complaint of police harassment."

Guy was certainly not intimidated. "Of course, there is. That is the biggest crime of all. Tell them, Roger." Roger just looked at the floor. "Roger, I said tell them."

This time Guy realised why Roger was avoiding eye contact. "Oh, for God's sake!" and he released the Devil in grudging defeat.

"Thank you, gentlemen, and for now, we wish you goodbye."

It was time to return home. Simon aimed one kick at the device placed on the floor, and an eardrum-popping screech of demons filled the air. The ground parted to form a dark swirling mix of pure evil, and a vortex into Hell opened at its centre. The Devil and Simon calmly stepped through, and the hole snapped shut.

"Is there anything in your damn law book, Roger?"

"Oh, shut up, Guy. Let's go home." And the two officers left the stage and walked away dejected.

Eighty-Eight

Unnoticed by all, a fair distance away, stood the baboons They listened intently while an eminent scholar delivered a lecture. It was the same baboon who had stumbled across the Devil during her scientific expedition, and conclusions on how Heaven would react to the impending doom were ready for peer review.

She had reached the climax of her presentation. With her red behind neatly covered by the new robes, for the first time she gained the full attention and respect of her colleagues. They listened enthralled by her theory, applauded her detailed study and would have honoured her with the highest scientific reward if it wasn't for the mention of banana ice cream. It was only intended to be a brief reference just before she wrapped up with a career defining conclusion. She had attempted to illustrate how scientifically monumental her findings were by using an analogy of the discovery of banana ice cream. Then the questions started. Was it tastier than a banana? Did it look like a banana? Where do you get one? Could you write down the directions?

And then they began to leave. The first baboons made apologetic excuses as they departed. Those that followed took longer to think of plausible reasons, and once the obvious ones were taken, they simply told more and more outlandish lies. All were desperate to taste this new banana ice cream. Eventually, only one baboon remained, desperately racking his brain for an excuse to join the others. Unable to do so, he shouted, "Oh my God, what's that over there?" and waited for the lecturer to react. As she turned, he did what all baboons would do in the circumstances – he legged it.

Finding the lecture room empty, she gave a disgruntled huff, whipped off the new clothes that were by now causing serious itching and headed off in the direction of the ice cream vendor.

In fact, she was pleased they had left. Her theory proposed that Heaven could sense when danger was imminent. This it had done without question, but her equations failed to predict how the danger would be neutralised. The modelling suggested a range of scenarios. Heaven might make the floor collapse beneath Lucifer's feet or, in a worst case, summon an army of legendary defenders. Perhaps a heroic angel would be chosen to fight and destroy the invading beast. Yet what happened did not match any of her theories. A man, dressed in a white, high collared shirt and black jacket, looking like a penguin, calmly spoke before both he and the Devil disappeared, presumably into Hell. Had the penguin man saved the day? Had she missed a clue, or did her analysis fail? Who cares, when there's banana ice cream.

Eighty-Nine

The next day Peter awoke, more motivated than he'd felt in a long time. He thought extensively about the events of the night before, and how he'd almost allowed an extremist thug like Slugart to twist his mind, just for selfish gain. It was true, the humans drove him insane on occasions, but that was no reason to label them all as rude, ungrateful pigs. Especially as he quite liked pigs.

Today he needed no reminding that he was now a landowner – this unexpected bonus really pleased him. Already he planned to build a small casino and restaurant. His patch, he decided, would be transformed into a place of enjoyment.

And then there were the humans waiting by the gate. The line of souls waiting by the gate was still humongous, but it didn't daunt him anymore. He had devised new ways to wind up the ungrateful and to fast-track others who were more deserving. In the end, he realised both were here to stay. God had made His judgement and his role was to greet them and remind them of their good fortune. Soon, they would enjoy his casino and restaurant. Perhaps he would even look into replacing the gate.

Ninety

Sleep came easily to Hector, drained by the events of the previous evening. He woke with a sudden realisation that he had overslept for the first time in his life. Rushing to prepare for work, he remembered his regular customers would no longer require messages in their soup. The old way of life was over. Instead, his thoughts returned to the words. Although it seemed God had not intended him to save Heaven after all, he still felt the words were important. They spoke of inclusion, integration and harmony with everyone living together, no matter what their differences.

Over the next few weeks, Hector's business changed. He moved from the side street into a recently vacated stall, more centrally located. A sprinkle of chillies and a dash of herbs had been added to his recipe, and the soup, after a few failed attempts, now tasted different. Opinions on the new version varied, but everyone celebrated the words, God's words, which were printed around the cups in a sparkling Helvetica font. This message became famous. T-shirts emblazoned with their message sold like hot cakes. Angels and humans would quote them in debates and during celebrations or even when alone to provide comfort.

Humans and angels spoke of his bright, modern stall and came to sample the new flavours. It was good, very good, and business boomed. Soon he opened his first café with seating for people to meet and enjoy the atmosphere. It became a hub of like-minded humans and angels, where differences were forgotten but also embraced. Ironically, he had started his own cult, but one that was open and inclusive.

Hector was content. In his own small way, he had made a difference. He had brought humans and angels together, and that was an achievement he was proud of. Sometimes he wondered if God had planned this all along. And all this, he thought, by just adding a few ingredients to my soup.

Ninety-One

Back in Hell and the Devil remained in high spirits following his 'foreign' holiday. Vacations were fun but lounging in his bedroom wearing comfortable blue and red striped trousers with matching cotton pyjama top was heaven. His feet, sore from all that walking, fitted perfectly into a pair of burgundy moccasin slippers, lined with only the finest vicuña wool. No longer limited to a wardrobe choice constrained by the capacity of two suitcases and an oversized rucksack, he once again had access to his walk-in wardrobes, displaying countless items of clothing. He admired the newly delivered Italian suit and brushed the shimmering blue sleeve of its jacket to eliminate any dust particles that might impede the perfection of the tailor's work. He was happy, and to make for even greater contentment, Simon hovered next to him. "A cup of tea, sir".

"Is there any way, Simon, that we could enter into negotiations with Peter about a gateway to Heaven – just for me?"

"I fear not, sir. I believe he would see the risk as too high."

"I thought as much." He paused before adding, "It was a great holiday, wasn't it, Simon?"

"Indeed, sir."

"Yes. We shall do it again soon. But for now, we must meet with the overcrowding committee. I believe they have some new suggestions."

"Very good, sir."

The End

Hector's decision to experiment and improve his soup followed a long tradition that many have tried before. Throughout history, experimenting with food has changed the world. Adam, bored of eating vegetables experimented with fruit. The Romans took the humble grape and turned it into wine. Their descendants took the simple dough and made a masterpiece by adding tomatoes and cheese. The Kentucky Americans, not content with plain chicken, wrapped it in a secret concoction of spices. The English 'up-north' are more than content with adding gravy to anything, while their Scottish cousins would deep-fry caviar if they got the chance. It seems that in life, for food and everything else, change is invariably better than stagnation....

....Well, with one exception. Crumble. Rhubarb crumble!

Four ounces of butter.

Four ounces of sugar.

Eight ounces of flour mixed with oats.

A layer of rhubarb nestling at the bottom.

The resulting pudding is pure heaven. Not even the Devil would dare to mess with perfection like that.

(Alternative recipes are available for baboons with a love of bananas.)

Printed in Great Britain
by Amazon